Hell and High Water

By
John McKay

Copyright © John McKay 2022.

The right of John McKay to be identified as the author of this work has been asserted by him in accordance with the Copyright, Designs and Patents Act, 1988.

First published in 2022 by Sharpe Books.

In memory of Bill Halliwell, Jim Fairhurst and Charlie Erswell

(and all who sailed on the Arctic Convoys 1941-1945)

Table of Contents

Foreword

One

Two

Three

Four

Five

Six

Seven

Eight

Nine

Ten

Eleven

Twelve

Thirteen

Fourteen

Fifteen

Sixteen

Seventeen

Eighteen

Nineteen

Twenty

Twenty-One

Twenty-Two

Twenty-Three

Twenty-Four

Twenty-Five

Twenty-Six

Twenty-Seven

Twenty-Eight

Twenty-Nine

Thirty

Thirty-One

Thirty-Two

Thirty-Three

Thirty-Four

Thirty-Five

Author's Note

Acknowledgements

HELL AND HIGH WATER

Foreword

In October, 2015 my friend and former high school English teacher, Joyce Holden, introduced me to Bill Halliwell.

Bill was about to give a presentation to local schoolchildren at Wigan Museum about his time in the Royal Navy during the Second World War.

Bill had been a telegraphist on *HMS Bazely,* a 'Captain' class frigate that provided escort duties to convoys to Italy and the Atlantic. He also took part in the final convoy to Russia in 1945.

Although I have studied the Second World War in great detail, I did not know much about the naval war and less so about the Arctic convoys.

After speaking to Bill a few times and being given some excellent reference material that belonged to another veteran, Joyce's ex-colleague, Jim Fairhurst, my interest in this theatre of war has grown.

The more I read about the convoys, the more I came to understand the hardships suffered by those sailors, both merchant and military, carrying out those voyages. They not only endured attacks from German aircraft, surface vessels and U-boats, but also had to do this whilst braving the harsh weather of the Arctic Ocean. Savage storms that threw the ships around like toys, waves reaching sixty feet high and more. A war conducted in temperatures as low as minus 30 degrees centigrade. Sailors were often called to go outside in these temperatures to clear ice and snow from decks and superstructures to prevent their ships from becoming top heavy and capsizing.

Considering that a modern houschold freezer operates at around minus 20 degrees, the working conditions must have been horrendous. Ice would form inside the mess decks, it being so cold outside, and anyone falling into the sea had around two minutes to live before they froze to death.

Even on reaching their destinations of Murmansk and Archangel they were still in extreme danger as the Luftwaffe bombed the cities and ports relentlessly until their Norwegian bases had to be evacuated later in the war.

Winston Churchill described the Arctic convoys as 'The worst journey in the world'. He was not wrong.

It was many years later before the Russians acknowledged the contribution made by these young men, without whose heroism and sacrifice in getting vital supplies to the Soviet Union may have resulted in them not being able to sustain their war against the Nazis. It was even later when the British government finally relented and awarded veterans with the Arctic Star.

Bill was possibly one of the nicest and most humble gentlemen I have ever met and he brushed off any praise with a small shrug and a smile.

Having served in the armed forces myself, albeit during peacetime and on dry land, I can appreciate the sacrifice made by those men all those years ago, and I salute all members of the Royal Navy and merchant navies, both past and present.

HELL AND HIGH WATER

This novel is a work of fiction but many of the situations described are based on accounts from men who sailed on the convoys. I hope I have done justice to their stories and their memory.

JOHN McKAY

One

1941

Looking back all these years later, I believe it was the cold that affected me the most. That piercing iciness that stabbed me to my bones like a thousand daggers. For years after I returned home, I could never really get warm again, no matter how hot the sun shone or how many layers of clothing I wore. Despite knowing my body to be warm, something within my brain would not register it. Something in my head did not want me to forget. It was as though it bit through to the core of me, to my soul even; and there was no way I could ever expunge it.

But there are many things I remember just as vividly. The way the waves would rise so high that they seemed to hover over the ship as it rolled along, plodding northwards towards the unforgiving Arctic Circle, across the Barents Sea and on towards the relative safety of the Kola Inlet. The constant threat of attacks from Nazi U-boats and enemy aircraft as they attempted to prevent us from delivering our cargoes to Murmansk and Archangel. Countless attacks that sank so many merchant, Royal Navy and U.S. vessels. How we had to sail helplessly by as our unfortunate comrades struggled in the icy waters, their bodies freezing beneath the waves as their fuel soaked heads burned above them, hoping the rescue ships were not too far behind to pick up survivors. Their screams and

HELL AND HIGH WATER

the smell of burning oil and flesh still fill my dreams even now, all these years later.

I often wake in the middle of the night shivering, a pounding in my head thumping out to the rhythm of those incessant diesel engines from many years ago, until I can stand it no more.

The worst journey in the world, Winston Churchill described it.

He was not wrong. He described it well.

I first met Walter Honeyman on the gangplank to the ship, the bowels of which I would be cooped up in for so many weeks and months to come.

It was early June 1941 and I was newly arrived in Belfast, uniform pressed perfectly and boots shining so brightly it was possible to see the reflection of the grey hulled frigate in the toecaps when I was still a hundred yards from the dockside. The sun was beating down from a cloudless sky and the sound of seagulls could be heard whooping overhead as they swooped down, like dive-bombers, to grab any fish unfortunate to be swimming near the surface in the waters close by.

She was a "V" class frigate, a U.S, ship, given as part of the support from America in our lonely battle against Hitler's Germany. 'Lease - Lend' they called it. We could have them for the war and then give them back when it was over. If any ships were sunk then we would have to pay for them. That was the idea, or at least what I had been told. Whether this was the exact agreement I was never too sure, but all that concerned me was this ship would be my home for the foreseeable future.

The ship looked impressive as I approached it. I was eager to get onboard and to get out to sea. She was the usual battleship grey in colour, designed for anti-submarine warfare. I could see that *"V86"* had recently been painted on its side and so I knew I was in the right place, as this was the pennant number for HMS *Virtuous*. Measuring 290 feet in length and capable of a maximum speed of around 20 knots, she was equipped with three 3 inch heavy guns, two 40 millimetre Bofors and six 20 millimetre Oerlikon anti-aircraft guns. I had become quite proficient with the Oerlikon during my naval and gunnery training. The ship was weighed down with depth charges for its main purpose of hunting enemy U-boats. These could be fired from projectors and tracks secured to the sides and stern. As yet, it had not been fitted with the new Hedgehog anti-submarine mortar which I had seen on other vessels. I had been told this was in the pipeline for the *Virtuous* and, when fitted, would be situated on the foredeck. It was an impressive piece of kit that could fire a dozen missiles into the sea at the same time. I feared for any German submariner feeling the wrath of that particular weapon.

I had turned nineteen only two weeks previously whilst awaiting allocation to a ship at the shore establishment, HMS *Drake,* in Plymouth. I had celebrated the occasion with some mates who were also in the same situation as me, having finished our telegraphy

HELL AND HIGH WATER

training at HMS *Royal Arthur* in Ingoldmells, Lincolnshire. Those incessant days of listening to Morse code until I could dream it, and not think of words without translating them to dots and dashes inside my head, had finally paid off. I had passed the course at the top of my class. I was now Ordinary Seaman George Martin, Royal Navy telegraphist. When I had written to my father telling him, he had quickly responded saying how proud he and the family were of me, which had made me feel ten feet tall.

I had received my call up papers a few months before and was glad it was for the navy. The thought of sailing the seven seas and visiting far off lands was something I had dreamt of since being a small child. Seeing the huge ships come and go from the docks at Liverpool, my home city, had further enhanced this longing for a life at sea. I had been determined to join the merchant navy when I was old enough. However, my mother did not want me to leave home and so instead I took an apprenticeship at a printers' workshop just outside the city. Being a quick learner, I soon become quite adept at the skills of the job, but this yearning for the sea stayed with me.

When I received the call up, Mister Johnson, the owner, had been upset. He had served in the army on the Western Front a few years before and had become deaf in his right ear when a German shell landed close to him near a place called Loos. The explosion had killed two of his mates and I don't think he had ever got over it. He did not want me to go to war, having become somewhat attached to me. He could see no sense in all the killing. He would say the last war should have been the end to all that nonsense. Yet here we were again, a little over twenty years later, embarking on another and against the same nation.

I had been sent to HMS *Raleigh* to do my basic training and while there made friends with a lot of blokes from all over the country, all green in the ways of the world and the military, just like myself. After spending hours on the drill yard, learning basic sailing skills, navy rules and regulations and how to handle the vast array of weaponry the Royal Navy had, I was selected for telegraphy training and shunted off to HMS *Royal Arthur*. Once my training was completed I was again on the move to Plymouth, until my eventual posting to a ship, with orders to go to the Pollock Dock in Belfast to join HMS *Virtuous*.

And so I found myself, only a few days later, walking up the gangplank, my kitbag and hammock slung over my shoulder, being watched by the man who was soon to become my best friend. He was leaning against the gunwale.

'So, what have we got here?' he asked in a northeastern accent, smiling as I stepped onto the ship. He was of average height with brown hair, which seemed little too long for a naval rating. He had dark blue eyes with quite bushy eyebrows and his nose was slightly large and somewhat twisted, as though it may have once been broken. There was also what appeared to be a day's stubble on his chin. I would not exactly call him handsome, but there was something about his eyes I presumed women would find attractive. He was dressed in a boiler suit, which did not give away his rank, and he was puffing away on a cigarette.

HELL AND HIGH WATER

Not sure if I was addressing a superior I said, 'Good morning, Ordinary Seaman George Martin reporting for duty.'

He burst into laughter and flicked the cigarette over the side into the gap between the ship and the dockside.

'Now why would you be telling me that?' he asked between giggles. 'Nothing to do with me, fella. What's your trade? What's going to be your job on this fine vessel?'

'I'm a telegraphist... Morse code and all that,' I replied.

'A bit of a clever clogs then, eh? You'll need to go and find Petty Officer Singer. He's in charge of all that stuff.'

'Where can I find him?' I responded, slightly affronted he was still laughing at me.

'He'll be around somewhere... I tell you what, follow me. He's probably in the galley having his dinner. Elephant's footprints today, George. Don't expect much from the cooks on this ship. The head chef isn't quite to the Savoy Grill standard just yet, I'm afraid. I'm Wally Honeyman, by the way. Pleased to meet you.'

Adjusting the kitbag, which was beginning to get a bit heavy and starting to dig into my shoulder, I followed Wally along the port walkway and into the ship. Passing people coming and going, none of whom took the slightest bit of notice of us, we eventually found ourselves in the ship's galley. A handful of people were eating a simple meal and one or two looked in our direction as we entered. Again, nobody acknowledged our presence.

'That's him, over there,' said Wally, indicating an older man with the insignia of a petty officer sitting with his back to us at a table in the corner. He was eating what looked like spam fritters and reading a newspaper. 'Just go and introduce yourself and he'll sort you out. Got to go. See you later.'

And with that Walter Honeyman, whatever rank he may be, was gone.

I approached the table.

'Petty Officer Singer?' I asked.

Without turning around the man said, in a broad Glaswegian accent, 'Who's asking?'

'Ordinary Seaman Martin, P.O. I've just been drafted in.'

He turned and looked at me. He was around thirty-five years old, clean shaven and had a head of thick black hair, cut very short at the back and sides.

'Ah, the telegraphist,' he said in what I thought was a slightly sarcastic tone. 'You were supposed to be here yesterday, laddie. What have you to say for yourself?'

I was shocked. My papers said to report by the nineteenth, and today *was* the nineteenth. As far as I was concerned I had until midnight to report for duty. So, if anything, technically I was early.

'I… I'm sorry, Petty Officer Singer… I…' I stammered hopelessly.

Seeing the look on my face he started to laugh.

'Look at yourself,' he said. 'I'm joking with you, laddie. You'll need a sense of humour now you're aboard ship if you're going to get on.'

A couple of others in the galley looked over and one or two smiled, no doubt amused at how he had made me feel uncomfortable. I was a bit annoyed with myself for letting it happen so easily.

'Right you are, P.O.' I replied. 'I think you'll find I can give it as much as I can take it.'

'That's the spirit, laddie,' he said, pushing his tray back and standing up. 'Come on. I'll take you to your mess deck where you can put away your gear and find a spot to sling your hammock. Then you can get yourself a bite to eat.'

He stood around five feet five inches in height, but could move remarkably quickly. Laden down with all my gear, I struggled to keep up with him. He talked just as quickly and, with his strong accent, I struggled to understand him.

'As you know, this is a new ship. Very new, in fact. We're all a brand new crew too. Some of us have a lot of experience and some, like yourself, are green as grass. It's actually an American ship, if you didn't know, laddie. An American ship, can you believe that? In my opinion they should be here with us, instead of giving us all this equipment. This war will spread, believe you me, and it'll affect them buggers across the Atlantic just as much as us, trust me. They should give us a hand now, instead of leaving us on our own, like they did in the last war…'

As he droned on, I was only half listening, instead using the time to get my bearings on where everything was, accustoming myself to the set up of the ship. The crew numbered around one hundred and sixty and we all had to live, work and play together. Although I was green, as he had mentioned, I did not want to appear like I had no idea what I was doing.

We eventually came to the mess deck, which was on one of the lower levels, and finding a gap in the already slung hammocks I dumped my kitbag in a corner and started to fit my own above one of the wooden tables.

'You'll be fine here,' smiled Singer. 'You'll do all right, I can tell. Just go about your business professionally, do as you're told, and always speak to the officers with respect. They seem a good bunch. And the captain, Lieutenant Commander Harrison, seems a good fella. Typical naval officer; efficient, sharp and doesn't suffer fools. So make sure you don't cock up in your job. Being a signaller, you'll have a direct connection to the bridge, so don't get it wrong… no pressure then, eh?'

He laughed.

As I watched him walk away, I did not know what to make of him. He seemed a nice fellow but you could never be sure. My father had always told me to take people at face value when first meeting them and then to take your time in forming a more detailed opinion of them afterwards. Never be swayed by what other people told you of them beforehand and keep an open mind. I always thought this was a bit rich coming from a man I had come to realise was quite bigoted in many ways, but I had used this advice to good effect throughout my life and would continue to do so now.

So, of the the two men I had so far been in contact with, they both seemed like typical navy people. They looked like the "work hard, play hard" type and I had a feeling this was going to be a happy ship. I was optimistic about my upcoming service aboard HMS *Virtuous* and I made a promise to myself to enjoy it as much as I possibly could.

Two

The next time I saw Walter Honeyman was the following day at 1155 hours. As I entered the Central Communications Room, (or radio room to use its shortened title), to begin my first duty watch, I found him sitting in the chair next to the telegraphist I was about to relieve. This fellow was leaning back with his hands behind his blond head and I caught them deep in conversation. They did not notice me until I was inside the room and Walter looked up.

'Hello, George,' he said and grinned at me.

The telegraphist turned around and, noticing me for the first time, said, 'Oh, hello, pal. Wally here has been telling me all about you.'

'Has he?' I replied. I was a bit put out to be truthful because, Wally there, did not know the first thing about me. We had met the previous day and our conversation had been limited. In fact, he had slightly irritated me with his manner and the way he had laughed at me.

'Yes,' said Wally, that grin fixed to his face. 'I was telling Harry here that you seemed a nice sort of chap and that we'll all get along fine. It's quite exciting don't you think?'

Harry stood up. He was very tall, at least six feet three inches. I had to look up at him as I shook his hand. He was quite skinny and had a severely pock-marked face, probably due to an acne problem in his youth, which did not look to have been too long ago.

HELL AND HIGH WATER

'I'll be your relief in four hours,' he told me. 'It looks like we'll see a lot of each other in passing, George.'

This was true. I had been informed the previous evening by Petty Officer Singer to report to the radio room at 1200 the following day for the afternoon watch. The ship was about to set sail and he wanted everything in order, everyone knowing what they needed to do and what their action stations were.

'If you're not on duty in the radio room when they sound,' he told me, 'you're to report to the Oerlikon gunner port side, amidships. You'll be his second. Make sure you get your kit from the quartermaster; flash hood, steel helmet and such like.'

This I had done and had even managed to find storage space for all this extra equipment and clothing on the mess deck. Things were slowly coming together and I was starting to feel I had a purpose. Maybe I could be useful to the ship. Maybe I had a contribution to make.

'So who's relieving you?' I asked Wally. 'Who's going to be my decoder?'

'That would be yours truly,' he replied. 'I came here early and let Jack go... Jack Holland, that is.'

'So it's me and you then, is it?' I asked.

'No flies on you, George,' he replied. 'The dream team, that's us.'

With only a few hours between watches Harry wasted no time in leaving us to it and with a cheery 'goodbye' he left the room. I sat down in his place.

I looked at the equipment on the desk before me. A set of headphones, a Morse code key, pens and paper to take down the signals messages, a Siemens receiver and other pieces of electronic communications equipment. All pretty much the same set up I had been trained on at *Royal Arthur*. It was all very familiar and that familiarity meant I felt instantly comfortable in my new surroundings.

In front of Wally was the book containing all the codes he would need in order to decipher the messages I would write down for him. To his side, was a tube and a stack of containers in a wire basket. This pneumatic tubing system would be used to send the messages up to the bridge for the captain or the duty watch officer. It was a simple yet effective system.

I looked at the clock on the wall to my left which displayed Zulu time, the same as Greenwich Meridian Time, and saw it was 1158.

I felt ready.

Suddenly, there was a crackle from the loudspeaker in the walkway just outside the door and a voice I did not recognise, but would soon come to know very well, could be heard clearly.

'Good morning, gentleman. This is Lieutenant Commander Geoffrey Harrison speaking, the captain of this fine vessel. We're about to set sail... in approximately five minutes time... for Gibraltar. We'll be meeting up with other ships en route and then forming a convoy to Malta. As you will be aware, they're having a bit of a torrid time of it at present and we'll be escorting merchant ships to get much needed supplies to them. This is our first voyage together and I trust that I will have your full support. Your dedication to duty, will I trust, reflect well upon the ship,

HELL AND HIGH WATER

myself and the Royal Navy. Good luck, gentlemen, and godspeed.' There was again the sound of static and the speaker went silent.

'Short and sweet,' laughed Wally. 'Looks like we're off then, Mister Martin. Let's hope it's uneventful. At least we're going to somewhere sunny and not the bloody Atlantic. I don't fancy going back there again too soon, I tell you. That's one shift I don't want to repeat just yet.'

I looked at him as I placed the headphones onto my head and turned the volume dial up slightly on the receiver. I did not want to miss anything because of him talking. I could not afford to lose concentration and let anything bypass me. However, I also did not want to appear rude as Wally was doing his best to be friendly and to keep it all light-hearted. We were sailing to war, after all, and I was quite happy with his attempts to keep positive.

'So this isn't your first voyage?' I asked.

'Good God, no,' he replied. 'I've done a few runs, George. Not quite an "old hand", but by no means a virgin, if you know what I mean. I've been in the navy for two years. This is my third ship. I was on the *Belfast* for a while but that was cut short when it hit a magnetic mine off the Firth of Forth in November '39. It's still being repaired, I believe. But I doubt I'll be going back to her. She's a bloody big ship, George, I can tell you. Bloody big with a lot of firepower too. We even indulged in a little privateering on our first voyage. Stopped some German merchantman trying to disguise itself as a South American ship, and hauled it into port. The crew all got a few extra bob in our pay packets too, which made it a bit more fun.'

'So what've you been doing for the past twelve months or so?' I asked. His story was starting to interest me.

'Well, not much to be honest,' he replied. 'With the *Belfast* being out of action they assigned the crew to different duties. I was on a small corvette patrolling the Channel for a while last year after the evacuation of Dunkirk. It was all a bit worrying, if I'm being honest with you. We could see the Luftwaffe passing over every day and saw many dogfights over the Channel too. We even managed to pick up one or two RAF lads who'd been shot down. They were bloody glad to see us, I can tell you.'

'It all sounds very exciting,' I said. 'I can't wait to see some action.'

'What? Stuck down here listening to dahs and dits? Trust me, George, action is what we need to avoid… Look at my tooth here.'

He opened his mouth to reveal one of the incisors on the left side of his mouth was half the size it should be, snapped off near the gum.

'How did you do that?' I asked, my curiosity fully aroused.

'Remember when I said I was on the *Belfast* when it hit that mine? Well I was walking up a ladder at the time and it threw me in the air. I banged my head on the bulkhead and my teeth clamped together. I thought my spine was going to pop out of the top of my head… And you've never heard a sound like it, my friend, never.'

HELL AND HIGH WATER

'Were you afraid?' I asked with all sincerity, but then realised my question may have sounded fatuous.

'Was I afraid?... Of course I was bloody afraid. At first I didn't know what the bloody hell it was and with everyone panicking I thought we'd been torpedoed. But we soon worked out we weren't being attacked and once we realised the ship was safe, everything seemed okay... But not for the poor buggers who were injured. Some were pretty banged up too. Much worse than my little bump to the head and broken tooth. Look, my new friend, out here on the water, there's not a lot we can do if we get hit. Our lives are in the hands of the captain and the gunners. We just have to do our own jobs to the best of our ability, make sure we don't cock anything up and follow orders. If we get hit, we get hit, we'll just have to deal with that if and when it happens. God forbid.'

My opinion of Wally was fast changing. When we had first met, I thought him to be a bit of an idiot, making quirky comments in an attempt at humour, mainly at my expense. However, with the realisation he was an experienced sailor and had seen some action, I understood he was using this outward behaviour to camouflage his real feelings. Or if he was not, if this was his true personality, then fair play to him. He did not let any of this stuff bother him at all.

We could feel the vibration of the ship, its huge diesel engines clanking and grinding as it pulled away from the dockside, the trembling of the huge infrastructure resonating throughout the vessel. Instantly I felt a sudden lurch in my stomach and was not sure whether this was nervous anticipation of what was to come, or whether it was the first signs of seasickness. I hoped to God it was the former. I did not want the next few weeks to be filled with me throwing my guts up over the gunwale. I had once had it as a child on the ferry to Birkenhead from the Pier Head at Liverpool. Although it had only been a short journey, the Mersey had been pretty rough that day and the sense of queasiness and nausea had been quite strong. I remembered taking a few deep breaths and my father telling me to hold it in for a few moments before exhaling. Poor Jimmy, being too young to understand what he meant, had thrown up all over father's new coat. I remember being proud of myself that I had managed to swallow my vomit back. I was seven years old at the time.

'Here we go,' said Wally and, on seeing the nervous look upon my face he added, 'Don't worry about it, George. You'll be fine. You'll soon get into the swing of things. And besides, it's the same for over half the ship's company.'

This was true. Being a new addition to the fleet, over half of the ship's crew were on their maiden voyage. All of them, no doubt, feeling the same apprehension I was at that moment. Suddenly I did not feel quite so alone.

HELL AND HIGH WATER

Three

Just as Wally had suggested would happen, I soon settled into the rhythm of the ship. The seasickness I had feared did not materialise and although the ship would roll from side to side at the slightest of choppy seas, apparently due to the short hull making it sit atop the waves, I did not feel in the slightest bit queasy. The same could not be said for others on the occasions I ventured outside. I would often see ratings leaning over the sides throwing up, their vomit splattering the sides of the ship.

The days on board soon developed into a routine for me. The duty system meant I worked stints of four hours on watch. This was enough to be working at any one time. Our concentration had to be total and I was in fear of missing a message or getting a letter wrong, rendering a signal indecipherable. Although I did not want the rollicking off Petty Officer Singer that would surely come, I also did not want to let the captain or my shipmates down. I wanted to do my bit.

Whenever a message came in I would jot down the letters. These were sent in five letter groups, all of it total gibberish. I would hand this garbled message to Wally who, by using the codes from his "secret" book, decrypted the signal into plain english, popped it into a container and fired it up the tubing system to the bridge. Whenever I asked him what it read he would smile at me, touch the side of his nose with his forefinger and say, 'Need to know basis, Georgie boy, need to know.' He had not once told me the content of any of the messages and after a while I lost interest. This would go on until Harry Benson, and his decoder, Jack Holland, a rather young looking twenty year old from Devon, came to relieve us.

I would spend my stand down time napping, playing cards with my new friends or carrying out other duties that Singer decreed. This was also the time I would eat my meals.

In those initial days I would often find myself on deck taking a look at the water and the wake the ship left as it ploughed southwards down the Irish Sea, towards the English Channel and our rendezvous with the other ships. I found this very relaxing at the time. Nobody to bother me as I smoked my cigarettes, watching the seagulls swooping and flying above our heads.

We never seemed too far from land. I was conscious of us passing the port of Liverpool, and my mind wandered to my family and to Glenda. I imagined what they might be doing at that particular moment. I surmised that father would probably be at work, in his role as a foreman in the Bootle dockyards; Hilary and Dorothy, the twins, would more than likely be at school; Jimmy at work in his new job with the Post Office and Francis, being the youngest, would almost certainly be with mother as she prepared the evening meal for them all. I realised at that moment, that I had not seen them since I had joined the navy. However, I felt only the slightest pang of homesickness.

And Glenda… What Glenda may be doing, I had no idea.

HELL AND HIGH WATER

I would also use this free time to catch up on some sleep.

Getting to sleep was hard to get used to at first. Because of the nature of the shift system, I would only manage a few hours at most at any one time. Ten minutes before change of watch a hooter would sound alerting all those due to go on duty to get their backsides out of their hammocks, grab a quick wash and get themselves on duty. It was therefore necessary to become a heavy sleeper. All around, sailors would be coming and going, some sitting at the tables your swinging hammock hung above, talking and laughing with their pals and ignoring the fact you were only inches above them trying to get some kip. Coupled with this, the constant drone of the engines, the humming of the fans and the clanking of machinery all contributed to make an irksome racket.

However, despite this, I found it easy to sleep. A hammock may not look like the most appealing of beds, but appearances, in this case, are very much deceiving. A hammock is one of the most comfortable things you could wish for in order to gain your beauty sleep. But then finding it easy to sleep was something I had always been good at. As the eldest of five children I was used to sleeping through the din my younger siblings could make.

The food on board was not exactly high class cuisine. The lads in the galley did their best with the ingredients they had. If nothing else it was nutritious and we never went hungry.

For breakfast they would possibly rustle up 'Cackleberrys' which were boiled eggs, or maybe 'Yellow

Peril' which was the slang term for smoked haddock. My particular favourite was 'Tram Smash' which consisted of a mixture of bacon, tomatoes, onion and bubble and squeak. Sometimes, for simplicity, it may be 'Chicken on a Raft', or egg on toast as we called it back home. For dinner we may find on our plates 'Elephants Footprints' or spam fritters to anyone not of a maritime background; 'Schooner on the Rocks' - roast beef and potatoes or possibly 'HITS on a Raft' - herrings in tomato sauce on toast. Following this, for dessert, we could quite easily be consuming 'Figgy Duff and Thickets' which was steamed suet pudding with condensed milk. I was quite partial to the macaroni pudding, also known as 'Pipes' or 'Tubes'. All this wonderful grub could be washed down with copious cups of tea, coffee or 'kye' which was just a naval way of saying 'hot chocolate'.

However, what most of the crew looked forward to each day was the rum ration, which had been a tradition since the time of Lord Nelson. I could not see what all the fuss was about as I much preferred drinking beer when it came to alcohol. I found rum burned my mouth and throat. It did not particularly taste very nice. However, I would drink it anyway as I did not want my shipmates to think I was still a boy. I am sure there were many others onboard who drank it for the same reason. These silly nicknames for the food we ate highlighted the humour I found prevalent throughout my time in the navy. It was a sense that we were all in this together and it brought us closer as people and as a crew.

HELL AND HIGH WATER

The captain would also regularly test the crew's responses by sounding the 'action stations' alarm, to see how quickly we could react to a threat to the ship. If I was on duty in the radio room then I would simply stay where I was and continue with those duties. If, however, I was off duty, then I would rush as fast as I could to the Oerlikon anti-aircraft gun on the port side, amidships, where I would meet Ralph Reid, the gunner, and check it was armed and ready for action. I would assist him by making sure he was strapped in safely and the gun was armed and ready to go. I would then look out for approaching enemy aircraft. After a couple of alerts we considered ourselves extremely proficient and were always ready within a minute of the alarm going off. This could happen at any time, day or night. The first time it sounded, I was asleep in my hammock. Not being totally focused, I nearly fell out and it took me a good few seconds to realise what was happening.

Those first nights in the hammock, despite being only inches away from my shipmates, I did feel a sense of privacy. Cocooned within the canvass, I lay in the darkness waiting for sleep to take me for the relatively few hours I had before change of watch. At first I struggled with such little time between shifts, as I was used to a lot more kip than that but, on the other side of the coin, it meant I was not on duty in the radio room for long periods.

As I lay there, my eyes closed and with the rhythm of the ship swinging me gently like a newborn baby in a crib, my mind wandered back to a year before and to a certain Glenda Bradshaw.

HELL AND HIGH WATER

Four

Liverpool, 1940

I first met Glenda at a dance at the local Catholic church parish hall, where I had been dragged along by Billy Jones, my best friend from the printshop where we both worked. I had no intention of going, as I always found the religious types that attended such functions to be pompous, overbearing and generally self-righteous which ultimately made them very boring. However, Billy was one of those fellows who never took no for an answer.

Looking back at what happened during that time, I really should have insisted on not attending and been more resistant to letting Billy persuade me to go. Being from a Protestant family, with a father who had an odd hatred of all things Catholic, I knew it could not be a good idea. But then Billy had his eye on Iris Shepherd, and who was I to stand in the way of true love? I suppose I went out of a duty to my friend in the end. However, I am not so sure he would have done the same had our roles been reversed. In fact I knew he would not.

I had known Iris since we were children. Her parents lived on Russell Road which was not too far from the terraced house in which I lived with my family on Egerton Street, off Great Homer Street. She was the youngest sister of a boy I knew, Richard Shepherd. My main memory of her was of her sitting on the front step of her house, clutching a doll, while the boys played football on the cobbled street. I remember how my father used to lose his temper at me for playing along their street and mixing with Catholic children (or 'Fenian scum', as I heard him once refer to them), but this did not stop me from spending a lot of my childhood in their company. I remember how my father would tap his right knee with his walking stick and say, 'This is because of them, my lad. Never trust them.'

But I had no real problem with anybody and could not understand his sometimes strange, irrational hatred of them. I could not comprehend it because I saw no difference in any of us. As far as I was concerned, we were all Christians and we were all scousers.

I had never really noticed Iris growing up and had been surprised when Billy asked me if I could introduce him to her. We had walked past her in town a couple of weeks earlier during our lunch break. After I had said a quick hello, he had asked who she was and if I could put in a word for him. I was slightly taken aback because I never saw her as anything other than that small child with the doll. I knew her family was very religious, so when I found out there was to be an event at the church hall, I knew she would probably be going. When Billy got wind of it, he insisted on us both attending.

I spotted Iris as soon as we walked in. She was in the corner with another girl, someone I had never seen her with before. They were sitting on fold-up wooden chairs backed up against the wall, both of them sipping drinks I assumed to be of the non-alcoholic variety.

The room was only half full, with a balanced mix of men and women. There was a mixture of ages, the older ones probably acting as chaperones to the youngsters and to make sure nothing untoward or un-Catholic went on. A small band played slow music quite badly on the large stage at the far end of the room, the singer attempting songs that were quite clearly beyond his vocal range. At a table to the right, soft drinks were being served by two old women I did not recognise, typical of this type of thing. The parish priest, Father Gifford, could be seen mingling with the attendees, trying to ensure they were not having too much of a good time. I hoped he would not spot me as he knew I was not of the same religious persuasion. The last thing I wanted was to be asked to consider converting to the ways of Rome. That was one conversation I could do without.

'There she is,' said Billy, clutching at my arm. 'Come on, you have to introduce me to her.'

'Do I indeed?' I said, brushing off his hand. 'We can't just walk over straight away otherwise it'll look pre-planned.'

'It is pre-planned!' he replied. 'I don't care. I'm not hanging around here all night. Have you heard that bloody singer? He sounds like he's caught his bollocks in one of those machines at work.'

I could not help laughing at his remark. It was funny and it was also very true.

'And he even thinks he sounds good,' continued Billy's insult. 'Look at him. He's singing with his eyes closed.'

I looked over to where the singer, a young man around our own age wearing dark trousers and a cream coloured blazer and hair slicked back with oil, stood screeching out a song I had never heard before. He really was very bad.

When I turned my head away from him, I noticed Iris looking over at us, talking animatedly to the young woman sitting beside her. This was not one of Iris's normal friends I would often see her hanging around with. This new girl wore a red cotton dress with small yellow flowers dotted over it. Her hair was held back from her very pretty face by a red ribbon and the subtle make-up she had applied to her cheeks enhanced her striking features. I suddenly felt that Billy dragging me here may not have been such a bad idea after all.

'Come on,' said Billy. 'They're looking at us. Now's our chance.'

Before I had time to reply, he grabbed my arm and almost frog-marched me over to the corner where the two girls sat.

'Hello, George,' said Iris smiling up at me as we stood in front of them. I noticed her eyes did not stray to Billy, who looked at her expectantly, his own eyes glued to her face. It was as though he had not seen her friend at all which suited me down to the ground.

'Hello, Iris. How are you?'

HELL AND HIGH WATER

'I'm fine. What are you doing here?' she said still smiling. She gave me the impression she was purposely avoiding Billy. 'I wouldn't expect to see you here. You're not even a Catholic. Does your dad know you've come?'

'Billy asked me to come,' I replied, ignoring her question. 'I...'.

'Hello, Iris,' interrupted Billy quickly. 'George has told me all about you.'

I looked at him with disdain. This was beginning to sound like it was I who had the hots for her and not him.

'Has he indeed?' she said laughing, finally looking at him and acknowledging his presence. 'Somehow I don't think he would have brought up the subject of Iris Shepherd had he not been asked.'

Billy started to laugh too and said, 'Oh dear, you've found me out. I tell you what, seeing all this is out in the open, would you like to dance?'

I turned to look at the dance floor and saw that despite the quite terrible music, the floor was beginning to fill with couples. All being watched closely by the older attendees.

'Oh, go on then,' she replied. Before any of us had the chance to respond, she stood up, grabbed Billy's arm and walked him quickly to the dance floor before he had chance to change his mind. I was surprised at how quickly all this had happened.

This left me in a somewhat uncomfortable position, standing in front of the prettiest girl in the room not knowing her name or how she was connected to Iris.

JOHN McKAY

I was about to break the awkwardness by asking her if she wanted to dance too, when she finally spoke.

'You might as well sit down,' she said, tapping the chair Iris had vacated.

Her voice had a strange intonation. One I had never heard before. But then I was only ever used to hearing a Liverpool accent as I had never yet left the city.

I sat next to her and held out my hand.

'George Martin, pleased to meet you.'

She took my hand and shook it exaggeratedly.

'Pleased to meet you, George Martin,' she said with a smile. 'I'm Glenda Bradshaw. I must apologise for my cousin. It was quite rude of her not to introduce us.'

'Yes,' I replied, smiling at her. 'She was a bit keen, wasn't she?'

'What do you mean, "keen"? I'm not sure what you're implying.'

'N…Nothing,' I stammered. 'I didn't mean…'

'You probably have a point,' she said, ignoring my embarrassment. 'She can be rather impulsive at times. Something of a family trait in all honesty. Anyway, enough about them.'

We chatted for a while, my initial discomfort falling away as quickly as it had appeared. She had the ability to do that. Make people feel at ease and comfortable in her company, but at the same time she could say something, maybe only one word, or even a look, that could bring that embarrassment straight back.

'So,' I said, after a while. 'What brings you to Liverpool?'

HELL AND HIGH WATER

'Work,' she replied abruptly. She looked over to the dance floor to where Iris and Billy were making a bad attempt at a foxtrot, which did not look out of place alongside the bad music. 'And I wanted a change from Wales,' she added, not looking at me as she spoke. 'So my Aunt Ida asked me to come and stay with them for a while. There's not much room but at least I get to meet new people and it's a little livelier here than back home.'

'So, where in Wales are you from?' I asked.

'Flint,' she replied. 'It's not really that far from here.'

'Flint?... As in the stone?'

'No. Flint as in the town,' she replied seriously, turning back to me.

I laughed.

'Are you making fun of me?' she replied. I could not be sure if she was being serious or teasing me.

'Not at all,' I replied. By the twinkle in her blue eyes, I could see she was probably pulling my leg.

Eventually we got up to dance and spent the rest of the evening chatting, dancing and laughing together. There was a natural connection between us, as though we were old friends meeting for the thousandth time, not two strangers brought together that very evening. I relaxed in her company, to the point that I gave no attention to those around us or to how quickly time was passing.

I managed to avoid Father Gifford but saw him look over a time or two, no doubt curious to know why a Protestant such as myself would spend his Saturday night here, when the pubs and clubs of the city beckoned my doomed and temptable soul.

We did not see much of Billy and Iris. When it came time to leave we could not find them.

'Maybe he's walked her home already,' I said when we finally gave up looking for them and collected our coats.

'Or maybe they've gone on to somewhere more exciting,' she replied. 'It's a bit ironic isn't it? Both of us have been dragged here pretty much against our will and have now been abandoned by them while they run off to somewhere better. Come on. Put your coat on. You can walk me home.'

It had got quite cold outside. As we walked, she linked her arm through mine and pressed her side against me. I was shocked at this forwardness but at the same time found it exciting. No girl had ever shown me such attention before and, I had to admit, I liked it. Especially with her being so attractive. In fact, I liked it a lot.

It took half an hour to get to Iris's house and when we turned onto Russell Street we could see both Iris and Billy standing at the doorstep, locked in an embrace, their lips stuck together, oblivious to us approaching.

'Hello, hello,' I said as we got near to them. 'What's going on here then?'

They broke apart and turned to us. Iris looked embarrassed but Billy was smiling from ear to ear. He really did look quite stupid.

'Nothing,' said Iris, coyly. 'Nothing to concern you, George Martin.'

HELL AND HIGH WATER

'What will your mother say? Kissing strange boys on the doorstep, indeed,' I laughed.

She scowled at me. Billy laughed, which did not seem to go down too well with her, as she instantly glared at him.

As I started to chuckle, Glenda suddenly grabbed me and spun me towards her. Before I had chance to react, she put her hand behind my head and planted her lips on mine, kissing me almost forcefully.

She pulled away and smiled.

'Come on, Iris,' she said. 'I think it's time we went inside and left these two to talk about the wonderful night they've just had. Goodnight gentlemen.'

And with that she turned away and walked to the front door, unlocking it with a key she took from her handbag, Iris following dutifully behind.

They closed the door without looking back, leaving the pair of us standing on the street gawping at the house like a couple of idiots.

'Well,' said Billy, after a while. 'That was an eventful evening. I never knew that a church do could be so entertaining.'

We turned and walked away. As I took one last look back at the small terraced house that was home to the Shepherds and my new favourite person, Glenda Bradshaw, I thought I saw a curtain hastily moved back into position in an upstairs window. However, it could have been a breeze, as the top window was slightly open.

But then again, it could just as easily have been my imagination.

Five

On the afternoon of the second day we sighted a small flotilla off the south coast of Cornwall. These were the remainder of the group with which we were to rendezvous and form the anti-submarine hunting team. The idea was for us to work collaboratively to find and sink enemy U-boats, to prevent them attacking the merchant vessels we were to protect within convoy.

Each of these ships, which consisted of corvettes and frigates similar to the *Virtuous*, was fitted with ASDIC. I was not sure how this anti-submarine detection equipment operated, but was assured by Wally that it was a fantastic piece of kit and worked "like magic", as he put it. Apparently it could detect submarines under the water without actually seeing them. Wally told me the equipment sent out "pings" and when they "bounced back", it could tell those working in the Electronic Warfare Office where the U-boats were located. It all sounded far-fetched to me, but I suppose I had to believe him.

I stood on the port side with a few other crew members, including Wally, Petty Officer Singer and Midshipman Guthrie, the ship's Communications Officer. We watched as each of the ships joining us blew their horns and flashed messages via the signal lamps at their port and starboard sides. As the various crews waved to each other across the water, something caught my eye. It was a gull hovering just above the surface directly in front of me. My attention was taken completely away from the flotilla and, for some odd reason, placed wholly upon this insignificant bird.

I watched as it swooped down, hitting the waves with a subtleness and grace I did not expect. It vanished beneath the water for the briefest of time before emerging victorious, a fish in its beak thrashing for life, before being swallowed whole as the bird greedily guzzled it down. All the while its wings flapped furiously to keep it above the waves. It was the most majestically evil thing I had ever seen.

We arrived in Gibraltar a couple of days later and anchored just off the harbour. The dockside was filled with merchantmen and more Royal Navy ships, including two huge aircraft carriers, HMS *Ark Royal* and the new HMS *Victorious*. Being mid July, the weather was extremely hot on deck and not much cooler within the ship. We had been issued tropical gear by the quartermaster in Belfast and ordered to be rigged in it when above deck due to the heat. Although the temperature was sometimes unbearable for those of us not used to it, which was pretty much everyone, the breeze off the Mediterranean Sea was refreshing against our bare legs, arms and faces.

I looked at the force gathering off the coast of this British Overseas Territory. It looked spectacular against the backdrop of the huge sloping rock that commanded the skyline. The two huge aircraft carriers dominated the port like grey leviathans, demanding respect from the smaller ships around them. I had never seen anything so magnificent and felt humbled to be a part of it.

We were due to sail in a couple of days. A rumour abounded that, if we were lucky, we may get some shore leave before then. A rumour we all hoped to be true. However, I did not fully believe it as these things had a habit of spreading throughout the ship quite easily. All it took was a flippant comment, or an expression of opinion from a rating, and the next thing you knew you were hearing a more elaborate version of the same story from somebody else. No doubt, the 'Chinese whisper' effect being the cause of the embellishment.

We never felt in danger in Gibraltar. Maybe it was merely a feeling of safety in numbers, but there was something about the place that emanated superiority. A sense of Britishness and Empire. A feeling that nobody could touch us. The sheer size and scale of the ships as they huddled together in the port, preparing to get supplies through to that brave island, was breathtaking. Even in my visits to the dockyards of Liverpool I had never seen such an array of vessels in the same place at the same time. We knew the Germans or Italians would not attack us here. It was too close to Spain and they would not want to upset their friend General Franco should any of their bombs fall astray.

The captain announced we were to be docked for forty eight hours and there would be a draw for the opportunity to go ashore for a few hours. I could not believe my luck when Midshipman Guthrie popped his head around the door of the radio room to tell me I had been picked out.

'You... you can always say no, you know,' he stammered. 'It isn't... isn't compulsory.'

I found him a strange character. Tall and thin with a nose out of proportion to the rest of his face (not in a good way), he did not give the impression of a ship's officer. He stuttered and stammered through every conversation. I was not sure if this was just with the ratings and not with his fellow officers. Wally told me that when he had heard him talking to the senior officers, he sounded fine and gave the appearance he knew what he was doing. This lack of empathy with the rest of us, for the lads who came from normal, unprivileged backgrounds, irritated me a little. The man was pleasant enough and never lost his temper, but his nervousness when speaking to lower ranks got on my nerves. He reminded me of a nose on a stick and I therefore could not take him seriously.

Although Wally had not managed to get a "ticket" off the ship, he was somehow able to persuade another rating to give up his. What he promised, threatened or paid him, I have no idea, but a few hours later, twenty five of us sat aboard a launch heading towards the port, including my friends Wally Honeyman and Ralph Reid. Earlier we had been gathered on the foredeck and addressed by the captain. We were told to behave ourselves when ashore and that we were representatives of both HMS *Virtuous* and the Royal Navy, and to conduct ourselves in the correct manner. What exactly the "correct manner" was for young matelots whilst on shore leave was open to interpretation.

It was with a sense of pride that I found myself disembarking the boat onto the dockside some minutes later. At first, the feeling of solid ground beneath my feet again made me unsteady, a feeling I found very peculiar, but I was soon right and headed towards the town with a bit of a spring in my step.

The helmsman shouted after us, 'We leave for the ship at 2100 hours. Don't be late. I won't wait for you.'

'Make the most of this,' said Wally, as we all ignored him. 'We'll soon be back onboard and on our way to the bullets and bombs. This could be our last run ashore.'

'Now there's a cheery thought,' laughed Ralph as we ran towards the road leading into the town, eager to start the festivities. We still could not believe our luck we were actually ashore with a pass to do whatever we wanted for a few hours.

We found a small pub off Line Wall Road and made it our home for the afternoon and early evening. We met matelots from other ships who had come across the same good fortune as ourselves and before we knew it we had formed something of a clique. The bar staff could not keep up with our orders and there was a point where they feared they would run out of beer. However, they found supplies from somewhere and the party atmosphere continued.

This was my first time drinking alcohol to such an extent. Again, just like I would force down the rum ration each day, I forced down pint after pint of the warm, flat beer they served up.

'Well... what do you think?' slurred Ralph after his seventh pint.

'Think of what?' I replied. I was finding it difficult to hear what he was saying above the noise in the bar, which was packed to capacity. Some sailors had been forced to stand outside on the pavement. The locals were crossing the road to avoid having to pass them.

'All of it,' he replied. 'All of it.'

Not having a clue what he meant, I decided to humour him.

'This is great,' I replied. 'I'm loving it.'

'Oh. This is great,' he replied, swinging his arms wide to indicate the pub and its current inhabitants. Beer sloshed over the side of his glass, to the annoyance of a couple of Able Seamen on the table next to us.

Oblivious to the irritation he had caused, he continued, 'But I meant the navy... All that shit.'

'I have to admit I'm enjoying being in the navy too,' I replied honestly.

'Hmm. You might not be saying that when the bombs start falling, my friend.'

'Oh, stop being such a party pooper,' said Wally on hearing this. 'We're here to forget about all that for the time being.'

All of a sudden Ralph jumped up, put his hand to his mouth and ran from the bar and out into the street. We could see him leaning against a wall, throwing up the contents of his stomach over the pavement, the puke splattering over his boots.

'Oh, shit,' said Wally, matter-of-factly. 'Looks like we're going to have fun getting him back to the ship.'

The sight of Ralph in such distress and Wally's words brought me instantly back to reality. Wally was right. With Ralph being in such a state it would be very difficult to disguise his condition when getting back onboard. We may be in for a little trouble later on.

'I think we'd better try and sober him up,' I said.

Wally burst into fits of laughter.

'Bloody hell, George. I think we'd better get ourselves sober first, don't you?'

With these words hanging in the air, he dropped his pint glass to the floor and fell forward. his head bashed onto the table, catching the edge of an ashtray, which flipped to the floor beside his shattered glass.

For a few seconds I sat there while all around me my fellow seafarers either ignored us or were unaware of the somewhat awkward predicament I now found myself in. I looked outside where Ralph had now slumped to the ground, sitting with his back to the wall of the next building, his head slumped forward with his chin resting upon his chest. His leg jutted out amongst the puke he had ejected onto the ground.

My own head was spinning. When I looked at the glass in front of me, I saw it was still half full. I realised I did not want it anymore. The very sight of it made me feel sick.

I checked my wristwatch. It was pushing 2000 hours which gave me an hour to get these two drunks back to the mooring in order to get to the launch. I put my hand on Wally's back.

'Come on, Wally,' I said. 'You need to shape yourself. We have to get back to the ship.'

He let out a groan but did not move.

This was not going to be easy.

I decided to leave him where he was and went outside to where Ralph was now lying down and snoring in the street. I kicked his boot and he jolted awake.

'What the f… Eh?… where am I?… Wha…' was his response as he looked around. He did not seem to have a clue where he was.

'Come on, Ralph,' I said, taking hold of his arms. 'Up you get. We have to get back to the ship. If we're late, we're going to be in a huge pile of trouble.'

The fresh air had also affected me and I was suddenly feeling unwell. I had not drunk like this before and I was surprised that two seasoned drinkers like Wally and Ralph had succumbed to the effects before I had. However, this gave me no sense of superiority over them. I was just thankful one of us was semi-sober.

With a bit of dragging and fumbling, I managed to get Ralph to his feet. He leaned against the wall, taking deep breaths. Then he noticed the mess his trousers and boots were in.

'Oh, God. Look at the state of me. Why have you let this happen?'

'Don't blame me,' I said, more calmly than I felt. 'This is your own doing. Anyway, we have other issues to contend with. Wally's spark out.'

Ralph looked to the doorway where he could see Wally inside the pub, his head still resting on the table where I had left him. He suddenly started laughing hysterically.

'Bloody hell,' he said. 'I thought I was bad. I don't feel so daft now.'

'This is no laughing matter,' I said in all seriousness. 'We have to get back to the dock. If we're late, we're going to be in so much trouble. If we aren't already.'

The truth of the matter was I really felt no better then these two clowns. What I wanted to do was leave them both to make their own way back. If I was to do this, then although I would escape the wrath of the officers, I would lose the respect and friendship of my two mates. When it came to a choice there was no contest. It was my friends every time.

I managed to persuade Ralph to come back to the bar. We staggered along, leaning against each other, until we made it to the table where Wally was resting.

There were a couple of other lads from the *Virtuous* in the bar who recognised us, and together we managed to lift Wally and half carry and half drag him towards the docks. At no point in this short journey did he become lucid or aware of what was happening to him. When we were almost half way there, Ralph had to stop to throw up again. Somehow he managed to keep his act together and eventually we made it to where the launch was waiting, the helmsman standing on the dockside smoking a cigarette.

Seeing us approach, he threw the cigarette into the water behind him, a big smile on his face.

HELL AND HIGH WATER

'Dear, oh dear,' he said. 'Somebody's going to be in trouble when they get back to their ship.'

'Give me a break,' I said, irritated at his demeanour. 'Can you give me a hand getting them onboard. I'd very much appreciate that.'

We were the first to arrive but gradually the rest of the party who had been allowed ashore began to appear. Some were a little worse for wear, but others, the more sensible ones, had spent their time sight-seeing around the town. It was with some regret when I realised the only sights I had managed to see were the inside of a pub and splatters of Ralph Reid's puke. I was beginning to wish I had not come out of the draw at all and been made to stay onboard.

As the boat set off I suddenly began to feel queasy. With the adrenalin starting to wear off, and, combined with the rocking of the boat and the slight breeze, I started to feel very nauseous. When I looked to Ralph and Wally, sitting there laughing and joking together, I realised the sea air was having the opposite effect on them, sobering them up somewhat. By the time we arrived at the ship, I was feeling very, very sick indeed. However, my two friends looked anything but drunk.

As we climbed aboard, I could hold it in no longer. I leaned over the side and threw up into the sea. The taste of the vomit in my mouth was disgusting and made me retch again until another load exited my stomach and mouth. For a third time I heaved, but nothing came up. I was empty. My head was spinning and all I wanted was to get to my hammock and go to sleep.

Somehow I managed to get onboard but then realised Petty Officer Singer, who was waiting on deck, had witnessed my distress. He was standing with his hands on his hips shaking his head from side to side. I looked from his angry face to the bridge behind him and could see the captain and the other officers observing us. I looked back to Singer.

'Martin,' he said in that broad Glaswegian accent of his. 'You're a bloody disgrace.'

The irony of the whole thing was not lost on me and, as Wally and Ralph walked past us, shaking their heads and muttering 'Shocking' and 'Tut, tut' respectively, I had never wanted to punch them as much in my whole life.

'Get yourself some rest,' said Singer. 'We'll have words later.'

Not wanting to argue or cause a scene, particularly when the captain was watching, I sloped off in the direction of the mess deck and into the comforting arms of my hammock.

HELL AND HIGH WATER

Six

My misdemeanour when getting back onboard did not go unpunished.

The following morning I found myself standing to attention in front of the captain, Lieutenant Commander Harrison. He was sitting behind his desk in the wardroom and did not look one bit amused. Midshipman Guthrie stood to his side and Petty Officer Singer, who had marched me in, stood behind me.

'Ordinary Seaman Martin,' said the captain, looking at a piece of paper he held in his hands I presumed to be a charge sheet. 'I really don't know what to say to you. You were given what was not only a privilege but a wonderful opportunity to enjoy some time ashore and take in the sights of this place, yet you chose to spend your whole day in a drinking establishment making a fool of yourself. I appreciate you're very new to the navy but that's no excuse for this type of behaviour. Your conduct when getting back onboard leaves a lot to be desired and will not be tolerated. Have you anything to say for yourself?'

I really did not know how to respond. What I wanted to say, to defend myself, was that I was by no means the worst of our merry band of miscreants. The ironic thing was that I had been the one who had ensured everyone else got back to the ship on time. However, my 'Good Samaritan' act had fallen at the last hurdle. If only I had managed to hang on for a few more minutes I may have got away with it. Wally and

Ralph had somehow managed this and the state those two clowns had been in, well, the irony of my situation was not lost on me.

'No, sir,' I replied. 'I can only apologise for my behaviour and assure you it won't be repeated.'

'It certainly won't,' replied Harrison, looking up at me. 'It'll be some time before you receive any privileges of this nature again, young man.'

Now, as he looked at me, I could assess the man. There was a natural air of authority about him. He was not exactly a good looking person, but he was handsome in the way he carried himself. He had a self-confidence that was evident in how he spoke. His subordinates clearly treated him with reverence and respect. He was in his early forties, clean shaven with his hair cut very short and uniform immaculate. He set the example he expected all his officers and crew to follow.

And I had let him down. And in letting him down I had let the whole ship down. His cold and unrelenting stare made me realise this and I was forced to turn my eyes away. I looked to Guthrie who instantly stood up straighter, a sudden look of awkwardness on his face.

'Don't look at me for any kind of sympathy,' he said. 'I…'

'You will report to Petty Officer Singer after each watch to be given extra duties,' cut in the captain. He had come to a decision very quickly, obviously not wanting to waste any more of his precious time on an idiot like me. 'This will happen until Mister Singer decides you've learned your lesson. Now get out of here.'

HELL AND HIGH WATER

I turned around and was surprised to see a quick wink from the P.O. as I hastily marched out of the room. Once outside he turned to me.

'You're a bloody fool, laddie,' he said. I could not be sure, but I thought he was attempting to suppress a smile. 'You got off lightly there. A couple of days jankers is bugger all of a punishment. Anyhow, we both know there are one or two of your pals who'll be breathing a big sigh of relief right now, don't we?'

'I'm not sure what you mean, P.O.,' I replied, attempting to keep my face expressionless.

He paused for a short while, examining me closely, before saying, 'Ah, begone with you, laddie.'

I turned around and headed back to the mess deck as quickly as I could.

We set sail the following day, moving in convoy eastwards. Wally and I were on forenoon watch, that is, from 0800-1200 hours, when the radio suddenly burst into life. Grabbing my pen and paper I listened intently as the dahs and dits came through the headset, the Admiralty spouting out its cryptographic message.

I listened intently and wrote down the letters. It was complete gobbledegook to me. None of it made any sense. "Dah, dah, dit" - G; "dah, dit" - N; "dah" - T; "dit, dit, dit" - S; "dah, dah" - M, and so on. GNTSM. Then DSXCV and many more five letter groups like this. When the message was completed I handed it to Wally, ready with his codebook, eager to decipher this cryptic signal as quickly as possible. We had been in enough trouble as it was and wanted to be super sharp with our work. We did not want any further criticism coming our way.

'Bloody hell,' he said suddenly, upon finishing his side of things. He pushed his chair back and repeated, 'Bloody hell!'

'What is it?' I asked, 'What does it say?'

Wally wiped his hand across his brow before responding. Normally he would not have told me what was in the signal but this time he was happy to share the information.

'The Germans have invaded Russia,' he replied. 'Can you believe that?'

I was taken aback. I thought Hitler and Stalin had signed some sort of agreement a couple of years ago. Hadn't they carved up Poland between them? It was all very odd. But then nothing the Nazis did made any sense to me.

'So,' I said. 'Isn't this a good thing? For us that is. Russia's a massive country. They've millions of people. Having them on our side has got to be a good thing, hasn't it?'

'I'm not so sure,' replied Wally thoughtfully. 'They may be big and have a massive population, but they're a backward country. This is all a bit of a shock, to be honest. This is a massive thing.'

'Well, maybe we're not going to have to fight this war on our own from now on,' I said, as Wally unscrewed the lid of a container, folded the message and popped it inside.

'Maybe not,' he replied. 'The world's gone mad.'

I could not disagree with him. Initially I had thought Russia coming into the war on our side would be a good thing, an ally to take some of the burden. But with Wally's lack of enthusiasm at what we had just discovered, now I was not so sure. And Wally was a much cleverer person than I was.

For some strange reason, as I watched him fire the signal up the pneumatic tube to the bridge, I had a slight feeling of unease about the whole thing. Would Russia coming into the conflict help us out as a nation? The answer had to be "yes" to that particular question. But what impact would it have upon me personally and the rest of crew of the *Virtuous*?

That, we would come to find out.

Seven

The weather across to Malta could only be described as glorious. The sun beat down upon the convoy as it sailed ever closer to the island. Combined with the cooling breeze that swept across the length of the ship, it made being above deck a very pleasant experience. The Mediterranean Sea remained calm and for the first part of the journey I felt quite relaxed, despite the fact we were sailing ever closer to war.

As with convoy procedures, we had to travel at the speed of the slowest ship which was a little disconcerting as this sluggish pace made us susceptible to attacks from enemy submarines. Had we been able to travel at our top speed then that particular threat would have been nullified, as there was no way Italian submarines or German U-boats could keep up with the ships of the Royal Navy. Lieutenant Commander Harrison had us on high alert the second we left the sanctuary of Gibraltar. As we travelled eastward, the *Virtuous* kept in close contact with the other five craft making up our anti-submarine hunting pack.

I looked across the water to the corvette sailing close alongside us and could see sailors on its deck. I raised my hand in greeting and one or two waved back, but most either did not see or ignored me, clearly having better and more important things to do. Beyond this ship was the huge hulking shape of HMS *Ark Royal*, its flat runway giving it a distinct appearance, dwarfing the rest of the convoy. I thought maybe one day I would sail on a ship as big as that, but for the time being I was not too bothered. Despite my recent trouble, I was beginning to enjoy my first posting. With the *Virtuous* it felt more like a family. I was sure the sheer size of the crew on the aircraft carrier would make it a little impersonal. But then what did I know? I was still very green when all was said and done.

I watched the merchant ships we were there to protect moving laboriously in lines within the protection of the Royal Navy vessels. Ships of all shapes and sizes, some with their cargoes atop their decks; crates, vehicles and even aircraft with folded wings. Smoke rose from their funnels high into the summer sky as their diesel and coal fuelled engines pushed them ever onward. I looked to the sky where the smoke dissipated as the wind took hold and wondered if our enemies could see it. We were aware that with each passing mile we were getting closer to the German and Italian airbases in Italy, Sicily and North Africa. We knew an air attack was likely to come very soon.

However, the task of the *Virtuous* was to hunt for submarines. The crow's nest was constantly manned, observers looking out for the tell-tale sign of a periscope. The E.W.O. room was also at maximum alert with trained operators monitoring their ASDIC screens, looking for the pings that would put us to action stations. For this reason I had taken my extra kit out on deck with me.

As if reading my thoughts the klaxon I had been expecting suddenly woke me from my daydreaming. Instantly men started running around deck, getting to their pre-set positions. I joined them, running towards the Oerlikon at the port side, donning my flash hood and steel helmet as I ran. I could see others on nearby ships doing the same. When I arrived I found Ralph Reid already there, positioning himself at the seat.

'Plane,' he said, before I could ask if he knew what was going on. He pointed. 'Ahead of us, a couple of miles out. You can just see it over there, ahead of the *Ark Royal*.'

I squinted my eyes and looked to where he was indicating. I could just make out a small spot in the sky which, as the seconds passed, became clearer.

'What do you think it is?' I asked as I checked his straps and fed the ammunition drum onto the weapon.

'Probably an Eyetie observation plane,' he replied. 'They'll be radioing our position back to their base. I'd expect some action pretty soon, mate.'

The adrenalin was now pumping through my body. I could physically feel it. The excitement was something I had never experienced before. All I could think was that I did not want to let anybody down. The fear of being hit by a bomb or an enemy strafing run did not come into my thoughts. All that concerned me was that I did a good job and contributed something positive.

The plane circled us, out of the range of our guns, like a vulture coveting the carcass of a wildebeest on an African plain. Waiting for the lion to finish its feed.

'Looks like a Sparviero,' said Ralph.

'A what?' I replied.

HELL AND HIGH WATER

'A Sparviero,' he repeated. 'An Italian torpedo-bomber. Can you see the humped fuselage? That gives it away.'

I squinted and could just make out what he was referring to.

'So how do you know that?' I asked.

He laughed. 'It's my job to know, George. I need to know I'm not shooting at our own planes now, don't I?'

We watched on as the plane continued to circle. Then we noticed activity on board the *Ark Royal*. We could see planes being made ready. As we continued to observe, we were pleased to see three Hawker Hurricanes rumble along the runway and take off into the sky. I understood these planes were destined for the airfields of Malta but it looked like their pilots were about to enter the action earlier than they probably expected.

The Italian pilot suddenly became aware of this threat and banked away, no doubt heading back to its base at full speed, the three RAF aircraft following behind to send him on his way. There would be no action for us just yet, I realised. I did not know if I was pleased or disappointed.

'Thank God for that,' sighed Ralph.

After a few minutes, the stand down came and we could again relax for the time being. This had been a warning to us that we had to be on our guard at all times. With the enemy now knowing where we were, an attack upon the convoy was highly likely.

I could still feel my heart pumping inside my chest as I headed back to the mess deck. I looked over to the *Ark Royal* and saw more Hurricanes being prepared for action. If the Italians came back then they would be met with a significant defensive force. As I watched them lining up on the runway, I felt quite safe. I also felt a huge feeling of pride to be part of this. I was involved in something historically significant. No matter how small my own part was in it all, I would have tales to tell my friends and family back home for years to come.

We sailed on. The huge craft cutting through the water like hot knives through butter. An immense force of metal, machinery and weaponry, pushing on to provide assistance to the defence of that small island just south of Sicily. Many of these ships had done this run before and been involved in combat with both the Italian Air Force and the German Luftwaffe. However, the chances of coming across Axis surface ships was minimal, the supply lines to Rommel in North Africa virtually cut off by the naval blockade. I had heard on one occasion, some months ago, a whole German convoy was sunk by the Royal Navy, the large aircraft carrier sailing off our port side heavily involved.

As we drew closer to our destination the atmosphere below decks became more strained. The crew did not speak much, preferring to think of other things other than the battle ahead. Some could ignore it and carry on as normal but I could see the stress on the faces of those who were new to it all.

The day after the incident with the Sparviero, action stations sounded again. Once more I found myself above deck standing next to the Oerlikon with Ralph.

HELL AND HIGH WATER

This time we could sense the convoy would not get off as lightly as the previous day due to now being closer to enemy airfields.

We looked to the skies and, sure enough, ahead were the now recognisable shape of the Italian Sparviero torpedo-bombers. They were heading straight for us. Mixed in with them was an escort of German Messerschmitts. Our own planes were already in the air heading out to meet them.

'This is it, Georgie boy,' shouted Ralph. 'This is it.'

He turned the gun towards the approaching aircraft but it soon became apparent none were interested in our smaller craft.

'It's the merchants and the carriers they're after,' shouted Ralph.

We felt a surge under us as the *Virtuous* turned to port to get closer to the ships that were now about to come under attack. I watched in horror as one of the Italian planes broke away from the pack and came in low, heading for the *Ark Royal*, its long torpedo hanging menacingly beneath its fuselage.

The Bofors and Oerlikons from the *Ark Royal* began to pound the air near the Sparviero, the flak exploding in perilous bursts around the aircraft. As the *Virtuous* got closer to the huge, hulking frame of the carrier, Ralph tried to move the gun in the direction of the Italian plane.

Before he had chance to fire we saw smoke appear from the plane's right wing, having been hit by the *Ark Royal's* guns. Almost immediately, the pilot began to struggle to keep it on course, the plane listing dangerously to the right.

JOHN McKAY

We watched in silence as the Italian plane, too low for the crew to bale out, began an attempt to turn to save itself. But we could see clearly it was mortally wounded. It continued to veer to the right as something fell from the wing. As it hit the water it cartwheeled viciously before coming to rest, where it floated for a few brief seconds before giving up the struggle to stay on the surface and sank beneath the waves. It all happened so quickly.

We could hear cheering from the gunners on the aircraft carrier and one or two of our crew joined them, shouting whoops of joy. However, I could not find it within myself to celebrate the passing of my fellow man. I felt a sadness at the killing of the Italians. They were probably young men, no older than I, who, through fate and global political machination, had found themselves in strange looking aircraft sent out to attack a large fleet of ships on another man's order.

Noticing the look on my face Ralph said, almost solemnly, 'Don't worry about it, George. It's them or us, pal. That's the size of it. This is what war is. Them or us.'

I knew he was right. I could not argue with him. But it did not make me feel any better for it. And watching my comrades cheer and pat each other on the back did not sit right with me at all. Men had died before our eyes and I found no joy in it.

The bravery of the pilots of the Royal Air Force and Fleet Air Arm as they fought to keep the enemy planes from the merchant ships was breathtaking. They flew into the face of danger without hesitation and with a gusto and enthusiasm that had my eyes

HELL AND HIGH WATER

glued to the skies as they engaged in aerial combat with their counterparts from Italy and Germany. A lot of these pilots were veterans of the conflict that had taken place above the skies of southern England not twelve months before and so this was nothing new for them. "The Few", Churchill had called them. A tag that had been appropriate. Whereas during the battle for Britain, when these men had been responsible for saving the lives of thousands of my fellow countrymen, and for keeping the war against Hitler's tyranny alive, above the skies to the west of Malta they had saved the convoy and the lives of the men on the ships. Their contribution and sacrifice could never be underestimated. They were true heroes in my eyes.

The battle did not last long. Soon those Axis planes still flying were turning away, their fuel and ammunition spent, to make their way back to their airfields wherever they may be.

A few of the planes got through and dropped their bombs close to the ships but there were no significant casualties, apart from a small merchant trawler to the rear of the convoy some distance from us, the name of which I did not know. It had taken a direct hit from a bomb from one of the Italian planes. Smoke billowed from its foredeck, rising into the clear Mediterranean sky as it struggled to keep afloat. However, the ship did not sink immediately and all the crew were evacuated safely to one of the destroyers on the port side. Once everyone was safely boarded, the convoy continued, leaving the stricken vessel to sink in its own time.

JOHN McKAY

As we drew closer to Malta we witnessed a large number of Hawker Hurricanes leave the two aircraft carriers heading for the RAF bases on the island. It was clear they were needed as quickly as possible as it was under sustained aerial attack from Axis forces. How the island had managed to avoid succumbing to the pressure they were under was unbelievable.

It was imperative they did not give in. Malta was of massive strategical importance to both sides in the battle to control the Mediterranean Sea. To lose it would mean a future invasion of Italy would be totally impossible and that whole theatre of war would be lost. Our forces currently fighting in Africa would be in trouble too as the enemy would have virtual control of the sea.

We arrived just off Valletta the following day and could see immediately the battles raging in the skies above the island. From where we were anchored the damage to buildings along the coastline and at the docks was obvious. German bombers flying overhead were engaged by British planes. As the merchant ships sailed into the harbour to unload the much needed supplies, we came under more air attacks from the Nazis and fascists.

Ralph finally managed to get to fire the Oerlikon at the Messerschmitts and dive-bombers. He even claimed a couple of hits but I think this may just have been adrenalin and bravado.

During the afternoon our group patrolled a mile from the port entrance, searching for submarines that may be attempting to get close enough to torpedo the ships, but we failed to locate any. Whether they were

HELL AND HIGH WATER

aware of the power we had at our disposal and held back for fear of being sunk or if they simply were not there, we did not know. After witnessing the devastation the enemy was wreaking upon this small peaceful island my initial melancholy at seeing the Italian pilot die a couple of days ago was now fading fast.

We did not hang around in port for too long as we were becoming sitting ducks. After the last of the cargoes was unloaded, we immediately set sail on the return trip to Gibraltar.

As we got further away from the island the air attacks became less frequent until eventually they stopped altogether. However, our guard did not drop at any point, the captain having us at a constant state of alert; the threat of attack from Nazi U-boats was still very real, especially in the half light of dusk and dawn.

We made two more runs to Malta over the next couple of months and both of them were filled with the same dangers as our maiden trip. I would not say we became complacent or less fearful but I suppose you could say we grew accustomed to it. There was a sense of "just getting on with it" and I never heard a single man complain about the situation. I was able to suppress my own fears and developed the attitude that whatever would be, would be. As I did not have much control over whether the ship got hit or not I thought there was no real point in worrying about it. However, I was always mentally prepared that in the event of it ever happening then I would try to conduct myself with some dignity.

JOHN McKAY

I always felt most vulnerable when on duty in the radio room as I could not see what was taking place outside. This "not knowing" made me nervous when at action stations when I could hear the sound of the ship's anti-aircraft guns pounding the skies around us. During these times Wally would look at me with a reassuring smile when he saw I was nervous or concerned. This simple gesture was a comfort to me.

'Don't worry, George,' he would say. 'If we get hit, we get hit. We'll just deal with it if it happens. I'll see you all right.'

I did not get much sleep during those days. This was the same for the whole crew and it was something we just got used to. When not on duty we would man our action stations or sit in the mess deck playing cards and drinking cups of kye or coffee. Although the lack of sleep made some jumpy and others quite cranky, the majority of the crew went about their duties confidently, without complaint, accepting this was what it was like to be part of a naval crew during times of war.

After the third Malta run we were ordered back to our home port in Northern Ireland and so set sail with the other ships in our group. We would learn later we were to have the Hedgehog anti-submarine weapon fitted to the foredeck and so there was a small sense of relief we would be out of action for a short while.

When we reached the relative safety of the English Channel we started to relax a little and the alert state among the ships was reduced.

'Here you go,' I said, turning to Wally with a signal one afternoon when on watch.

HELL AND HIGH WATER

'Cheers, mate,' he said taking it from me to begin his decoding duties. He turned his back and put his arm across the desk to keep me from seeing what he was writing. He reminded me of a young boy in school whenever he did this, trying to prevent his classmates from copying his work.

'Hmm,' he said after a while. 'Looks like we're on the move again, George, my friend. And it'll be a little cooler than where we've just been.'

He put the decoded message into the tube and turned back to me.

I knew he revelled in holding these secrets to himself for a while. I had long since decided not to give him the satisfaction of showing any interest. After all, if it was of any real importance then I was sure to find out in due course.

As it turned out, this signal, which Wally thought was fine to have a little fun with, turned out to be the beginning of what was to become a very significant period in the lives of every man onboard HMS *Virtuous*.

Eight

Due to the refit, we were granted shore leave and I managed to make the ferry across from Northern Ireland to Liverpool. After spending an eventful time at home I returned to Belfast a few days later, earlier than I had initially intended.

I now felt more at home on board the *Virtuous* than I did back on Egerton Street. The familiarity of the crew, and the fact we had been through something quite unique together, gave me a sense of affinity closer to them than it did to my blood siblings. These men, from all corners of the British Isles, whom I had not known that long in real terms, were more my brothers than Jimmy and Francis could ever be.

We were due to sail for Loch Ewe, a large inlet in the north-west highlands of Scotland, to rendezvous with other ships to form a convoy to Iceland. From there we would make our way to Murmansk in Russia, escorting a large group of merchant vessels for the delivery of war cargoes to our new Russian allies. There had already been a few of these voyages and from what we could gather from matelots we met from other ships whilst on leave, some of whom had done the run, we knew we would be in for a rough ride.

It was now March,1942, and the Americans had finally joined the war after the Japanese had bombed some place in Hawaii the previous December. For the most of us, we felt they had joined us a little late, but now we had both the Americans and Russians as allies, we felt the victory we thought impossible only a few months before was now very achievable.

We arrived in Loch Ewe and anchored near the centre of the inlet amongst an ever growing fleet. The radio traffic during the next two days was frantic as preparations were made for the journey and more and more ships arrived.

But this was nothing new. The Russian convoys had commenced only two months after the Germans invaded the Soviet Union. We were not sure if this was more a political thing than an effective military strategy. I supposed that if they were under attack and ill-prepared, then as an ally, we had to do something to assist them. However, this did not sit right with some of the crew, myself included. Britain had been left to its own devices after France had fallen and the Soviets had been if not an ally or friend of the Nazis, then certainly an indifferent observer. As for the Americans; they had at least lent us war equipment, the ship in which we were sailing included, as well as keeping us supplied with food and raw materials. But, we supposed, having the Russians on our side was probably good for us as a nation. However, at this point in the war it did not look too good for us as individuals.

The politics of it all was not something we would dwell on for too long and our thoughts turned to the logistics of the journey ahead and not the reasons why we were doing it. Whilst in Belfast, we had each been given cold weather uniform. Finding the room to store this extra gear had been a problem at first but, after much pushing, shoving and adjusting, we managed it.

JOHN McKAY

We spent downtime stitching our names into the extra uniform as the last thing any of us wanted was for some of it to go astray. By the look of what they had given us, it was clear that where we were going, the weather would be as much an enemy to us as the Germans. This clothing could possibly save our lives.

We had been issued with padded, hooded duffel coats that were lined with lambs wool and an extra hood with only slits for the eyes and mouth. We had also been given underwear so thick you could have turned it into a sweater. As I was a part time gunner, I was also issued a knee length sheepskin jerkin. We were also provided with mittens that had a separate thumb and index finger along with scarves, helmet liners and balaclavas.

The distribution of this kit had a twofold effect upon us. On the one hand, it gave us comfort to know the top brass were looking out for us and were making sure the gear we had would do the job. On the other, it made us realise where we were going would be extremely cold.

During the evening of the second day at anchor, I was leaning against the starboard gunwale smoking a cigarette when I was joined by Wally. He was wearing a balaclava and rubbing his hands against the cold. I turned to offer him a cigarette but he shook his head.

'A few of us are going to have a game of cards, if you fancy joining us,' he said. 'Come inside, it's freezing out here,'

He was quite right. It was very cold and there were black clouds in the dark sky above us which looked like they were about to open up and throw down a hard cold rain. I had thought it a good idea to attempt to acclimatise myself to being cold because I knew I would have to operate and potentially fight in hazardous and extreme conditions.

With nothing better to do, and feeling there was no point in being out in the cold when I did not need to be, I threw my half smoked cigarette over the side and followed him back to the mess deck where we found a small group in the corner sitting around a table, tin cups of tea and coffee in front of them. I was surprised to see Petty Officer Singer among them, shuffling a well worn deck of cards. It was not often you would find him in the lower ranks' mess deck. He had a cigarette hanging from his mouth and a woollen cap upon his head which he had pushed back. If I was not mistaken, he looked a little drunk, but I could not be sure. A half eaten ham sandwich was on a plate in front of him.

'Ah, here you are, laddie,' he said on seeing me. 'Are you coming to join us for our little game?'

'I'e a couple of hours before my shift, so why not?' I responded sitting down opposite him.

Wally sat down beside me and I looked around the table. To my right was Dave Higson, one of the cooks, who looked as though he really could not be bothered with it all, chewing his nails absent-mindedly. He occasionally looked at them as he took them from his mouth, before spitting out what he had bitten off to his side. I really hoped he did not do this when he was cooking our food.

JOHN McKAY

Sitting opposite him was Alf Thorne, a Petty Officer stoker who had formed a friendship with Singer. Thorne was a youngish looking, dark haired fellow from Manchester who had a somewhat gruff countenance but was well respected by all on board. He nodded a greeting to me as I sat down.

John Steadman, an ASDIC operator from Birmingham who reminded me a little of Charley Chaplin as he walked in a rather comical way with his feet sticking out and big Dougie Sears, who worked in the sickbay, a huge, softly spoken man from Ipswich, made up the rest of the players.

'Okay, all right,' said Singer, enthusiastically, 'Let's get started then shall we. Come on boys, make room for the cards now. Move those cups.'

The cups were pushed to the side as Singer dealt out the cards.

'I take it everyone knows how to play gin rummy?'

'There's too many of us,' said Steadman in his thick Birmingham accent. 'You can't play gin rummy with seven people. There's not enough cards.'

Singer scratched his head for a few seconds.

'All right. You have a point. How about poker then?' he said after much thought.

We all nodded our heads. Personally I did not really care what we played. I was just happy to be inside out of the cold.

'We can't play poker if it's not for money,' said Alf Thorne. 'There's no point if it's not for a few bob.'

Singer looked around the mess deck suspiciously.

HELL AND HIGH WATER

'We can't have any officers catching us,' he replied. 'We'd all be for the high jump if we were caught gambling. And I'd be in more trouble than you lot put together.'

'They never come down here,' said Wally. 'When was the last time you saw an officer down here?'

Singer shrugged his shoulders. 'Good point, well made, laddie. Get your pennies out and let's have some fun.'

Myself and Dougie Sears decided to sit the game out. I was not into gambling after seeing my Uncle Stan succumb to the vice and end up in a whole load of trouble with my Aunt Margaret a few years ago. In my opinion, gambling was for mugs and was an easy way to make yourself destitute. By the state of Singer's cards, they looked like they had seen some action and I was not prepared to pit my wits against a professional.

As they played I observed them.

Singer was very confident and he and Alf Thorne won the first few hands. They were not playing for too much, only pennies, but as the game wore on I could see Wally was more adept with cards than he had initially let on. He quickly won back the money he lost and I noticed Singer and Thorne getting a little agitated as their losses started to mount. Steadman decided to quit early after losing more than he was prepared to and Dave Higson sat nervously biting his nails as each hand was played.

'Ah, laddie,' said Singer to Wally, when he lost two shillings in one round. 'You've played this game before.'

JOHN McKAY

I could tell he was not happy. I guessed the two Petty Officers had thought we were easy prey and now that it was not working out for them they were not best pleased. I could not help smiling but tried my best to suppress it. I did not want them losing their temper with me.

'Maybe a time or two, P.O.' replied Wally noncommittally. 'I suppose I'm having a bit of good luck tonight.'

'A bit of good luck?' said Thorne. 'You could say that.'

Thorne was starting to get annoyed. He kept looking at his wristwatch, knowing there would be a shift change in a few minutes time and Wally would have to leave, giving them little time to win their money back. I could not see this ending well.

'This will have to be my last hand,' said Wally. 'We've got to go in a couple of minutes.'

'You'll go when I tell you you can go,' said Thorne, glaring at him. 'And not a second before, you Geordie bastard.'

'We can't leave Harry and Jack,' I pitched in. 'They'll want to get to their bunks. It's not fair on them. And if Mister Guthrie gets wind that we're late, then he'll want to know why. We can hardly tell him we were playing poker for money with two Petty Officers and they wouldn't let us leave, now, can we?'

I knew I was treading on thin ice but I did not really care. I was looking out for my mate and I did not want them to use their rank to bully him. There was no need for Thorne to speak to Wally in that way just because he had lost a few bob on a game of cards.

HELL AND HIGH WATER

Singer put down his cards and placed his hand on Thorne's arm. At first I thought he was about to blow his top but instead he spoke to us calmly.

'You've got a point, young laddie,' he said softly. 'I think we've had enough fun for one night. Off you all go, now.'

Thorne seemed about to say something but I saw Singer squeeze his arm slightly and he stopped.

Without giving him time to change his mind I stood up, Wally following. Bidding them all good night, I grabbed my kit from the corner of the deck and made my way to the radio room, followed close behind by Wally. I could hear the others muttering as we left.

An hour later, sitting in front of the radio, the headset around my neck, I looked at my friend and contemplated him. He had not spoken much since the card game and looked deep in thought. Singer had put his head around the door earlier to see how we were doing and to bring us both a cup of coffee, which I took to be a sort of peace offering. Maybe he was slightly embarrassed his friend had not taken losing so graciously. When he was happy we were both fine he left us to it.

Although I had been onboard for many months now and considered myself part of the furniture and somewhat of a seasoned sailor having done three convoys to combat zones, I realised I did not really know too much about the man with whom I had spent most of my waking time. The man I considered to be my best friend in the navy.

Walter Honeyman was something of an enigma. Outwardly he came across as a bit of a joker, someone you could have fun with, a bloke who did not take life too seriously despite the dangerous world we now found ourselves to be living in. However, he divulged anything about his private life. Whereas every other sailor I knew received letters from home and carried pictures of family members, girlfriends or wives, Walter did not seem to have any of that.

Looking at him I could sense all was not well. He was exceptionally quiet, not having said two words to me since we came on duty. I decided to see what I could find out. However, I felt I should broach the subject with a certain degree of care. I had the impression that whatever his story was, he probably did not want to tell it.

'So, Wally,' I said, taking off my headphones. 'Are you all right? You've been very quiet. Did Thorne piss you off a bit back there?'

'Not really,' he replied. 'I'm used to his sort. If he wants to be an idiot then that's up to him. It's his problem, not mine.'

We sat in silence for a little longer. For the first time since I had known him the atmosphere between us had become a little awkward. I could sense he was feeling a little low and if I asked the right questions he would possibly open up and tell me what was making him so melancholy.

I leaned over to grab one of the mugs of coffee Singer had brought in. As I did so, I caught his eye.

'You've never really told me about yourself,' I said. 'You know all about me. All about my family and what's been happening to me back home recently, but

HELL AND HIGH WATER

you're a bit of a mystery to me, Wally. You never give anything away.'

My boldness in what I said came from the fact he had been something of a confidant for me. During my time alone with him, I had spent many hours talking about my life, my family, my father and most of all, Glenda. There were no secrets I had that I did not share with this man.

'There's nothing really to tell you,' he replied after a while. 'I'm an orphan and was brought up in a home with loads of other lads just like me. When I was old enough to leave, I left. I joined the merchant navy a few years ago and then transferred to the Royal Navy just before the war started. That's it, pal. Nothing more to it. Pretty boring stuff.'

'So what was the home like?' I asked. 'What happened to your parents?'

He sighed and ran his hands down his face.

'If you really must know, you nosey bastard, they were murdered by my mother's lover when I was about five years old. Or so I've been told. Apparently she'd been having an affair with some fella from Washington…'

'Washington?' I said, raising my eyebrows.

'Not America Washington, Tyne and Wear Washington, you thick so and so… When she left him to go back to my father he didn't take too kindly to the rejection. He bludgeoned them both with a club while I was asleep in the next room. I never heard a thing… I found them the next morning.'

'Bloody hell, Wally,' I said, in total shock at what he was telling me. 'I had no idea.'

JOHN McKAY

'How would you?' he said, almost matter-of-factly. 'It's not something I really like talking about, to be honest with you. But you did ask.'

'So what happened then?' I asked, intrigued by his story.

'Well, the bloke handed himself into the police and admitted what he did... He went to them the next morning... told them where the bodies were. They came straight around and found them... me too... I was sitting on the edge of the bed amongst their blood and stuff. He told the police he couldn't handle the rejection and was shocked at what he'd done. A crime of passion and all that.'

'Jesus, can you remember it? You being so young?'

'It's not something that you're likely to forget, now, is it? Saying that, not really, if I'm being totally honest. I have a vague recollection and can remember the policeman who found me being very nice to me. My main memory of it is having a glass of milk and a biscuit at the police station while they decided what they were going to do with me.'

I was shocked at what I was hearing. Wally always gave me the impression of a fun-loving fellow with not a care in the world. A man who got along with everyone. It seemed a lot of his character was something of a front. All this time he had been hiding his sadness and hiding it well.

'Didn't you have any relatives that could've take you in?' I asked.

'I've relatives all right,' he replied. 'But none of them wanted anything to do with me. Those on my father's side couldn't be sure if I was the bastard son of this murderer and those on my mother's are all a bunch of arseholes. They were quite happy to see me sent to the orphanage.'

'That's terrible,' was all I could think to say.

'I was in that shithole of a place for over ten years,' he continued. 'I hated every second of it.'

I could sense he was now beginning to struggle with the story. Memories he had long since buried now being dug up by my prying questions. I felt I did not want him to continue but he carried on nevertheless. I suppose it was probably good for him, cathartic even, to let it all out. To let out all the pent up anger and sadness he had suppressed for years.

He told me of the times, from a very young age, when the care workers or whatever they were called, would abuse him both physically and mentally. The late night visits from the principal and his deputies. To him and the other boys. He told me of things I could never imagine happening to small children, perpetrated by those in positions of trust and power. I felt physically sick hearing it. And all this had happened to my very good friend who sat beside me and whose positivity had got me through three combat operations so far.

I felt an enormous sadness for him, but most of all I felt an enormous respect. Here was a man who was able to put all this behind him and act in a professional and supportive way to myself and the others on the ship.

'Now promise me you'll never repeat any of that,' he said, once his story was finished.

'Of course,' I replied. 'Of course, Wally. I had no way of knowing. You come across as so positive all the time.'

'Yes. Well it would be stupid to dwell on it now, wouldn't it?' he replied. 'What good would that do in the long run? It's over now and I'm quite happy to forget about it and move on with my life. So if we never mention it again then I will thank you for it.'

'Of course,' I repeated. 'If you ever…'

'I won't,' he cut in.

Then, as if on cue, to signal the conversation was well and truly over, the radio burst into life. I put on my headset again as the familiar sound of Morse code started to beep into my ears.

HELL AND HIGH WATER

Nine

Liverpool

Lying in my hammock a few hours later my mind drifted once again to thoughts of Glenda Bradshaw. My trip to Liverpool on leave had been eventful to say the least but my brain chose a more happy memory to place at the forefront of my thoughts. Our time together before the start of my military service.

I had recently been given notice that the Royal Navy was to require my services and I was to report for training in the new year. At the time I did not know how an eighteen year-old apprentice printer could possibly help Britain win the war. Nevertheless, this made me feel very important and proud that I would be doing my bit.

This was something my father had missed out on when he was younger. He had never been called up for service during the Great War due to the leg injury he had picked up at a disturbance at Juvenal Street back in 1909. He had been nineteen years old at the time and had always blamed the Catholics for this, although, from what I could gather, it was the police who had been the cause of his wound. I also heard a rumour that he spent a few nights in prison because of it.

My father was a member of the Orange Order and his hatred for all things Papist was quite lost on me.

JOHN McKAY

The days of sectarian rivalry in the city were fast fading and the two factions integrated wholly now, joined together by a more political commonality. The days of throwing stones at each other were long in the past, but some people, my father included, could not let things go. Maybe this was due to the injury that had held him back over the years and the cause behind it, or maybe it was ingrained in him from his own father who had himself been very much the anti-Catholic.

Myself, well I was beyond this prejudice. My own views were a lot more liberal. I put this down to my mother and how she shielded us children from my father's intolerance.

Despite what he claimed, his injury had not caused him any particular problems in gaining employment. He was a supervisor down at the docks and had worked there all his life. When war broke out, the Bootle dockyards became as active as they had been in the nineteenth century when Liverpool had been the busiest port in all Europe. With supplies coming across the Atlantic from America, he was constantly there, working all hours to get inbound ships unloaded, and loading cargoes onto vessels destined for export to foreign shores. In spite of all his failings, he was a very proud man who loved his family and was not afraid to express that love to us. It did not embarrass him. Regardless of his sometimes odd characteristics, I was proud of him and loved him dearly.

After the dance in the Catholic club and Glenda's kiss later that night I was unsure whether this would be a one-off thing or if she was interested in seeing me again. My mind was put at rest a couple of days later when I was leaving work. As I came out of the gates I spotted her standing under a lamppost on the opposite side of the street.

'Hello, Glenda,' I said as I approached her. I was glad to see her smiling. 'What drags you over here?'

'Oh, I was just passing and thought I'd see if you wanted to walk me home,' she replied.

I smiled. 'Of course.'

As I walked alongside her, she grabbed my arm and linked me just as she had done on the Saturday night. I could smell a nice scent coming from her neck and when I looked down at her I so wanted to kiss her.

'Have you had a busy day?' she asked.

'Not really,' I replied. 'Still learning the job, to be honest. Mister Johnson says I'm doing well, but I'm not so sure.'

'What makes you say that?' she asked. I was not sure if she was truly interested or whether she was just making conversation.

'Oh, I don't know,' I replied. 'Maybe my heart isn't really in it now I know I won't be there for much longer.'

'It's a good trade, George. You should make sure you continue with it when you get back.'

'I know. You're probably right. My mam says I need to carry on with it, but with the war and everything, I might not have much choice. Who knows what's going to happen?'

Instinctively we both looked in the direction of the docks. The Germans had not just concentrated their bombing raids on London and the southern ports. Our own city had been hit pretty hard by the Luftwaffe too. We had been raided quite heavily in August and September and there had been intermittent raids in October. As Christmas approached, we could not see any sign of it stopping. The noise of the air raid sirens had become a familiar sound to us and we dreaded hearing it, particularly when my father was at work, as the docks were the target of the bombers. We always feared the worst and breathed a huge sigh of relief when he arrived home unscathed some hours later.

Mother was a nervous wreck. She feared him getting killed and worried for her children. She had asked him about sending the youngsters out to the countryside as was happening throughout the country, but for some reason he was dead against it. He wanted the family to stay together and would not let some arrogant Nazis break us up.

'It's all a bit frightening, isn't it?' said Glenda as we sauntered along.

'It's certainly that,' I replied. I was not lying. Every time I heard the sirens I was filled with dread. It was the indiscriminate nature in the way the bombs and parachute mines fell. But it was the incendiaries that scared me the most, setting fires all over the city and stretching the emergency services to breaking point.

'Did you enjoy yourself the other night?' she asked, casually changing the subject and casting me a cheeky glance.

I felt my face redden but I did not want to show she was making me feel uncomfortable, which she was able to do quite easily.

HELL AND HIGH WATER

'I did,' I replied. 'It's good to get out now and again. Or do you mean what happened later?'

'I'm not too sure what you mean,' she replied coyly.

We continued along in silence for a few moments. As people passed they looked at us and smiled, no doubt thinking we were a young courting couple and pleased to see some happiness in times such as this. As we walked I thought about the girl on my arm. Did how we looked to others reflect what was actually taking place? Were we now a courting couple? Did that kiss mean we were? I was not so sure, but this was something I needed to know.

'What are you doing tonight?' I asked.

'Nothing much,' she replied. 'I think Iris wants me to patch one of her dresses for her... But if I get a better offer, I'm sure I'll be able to find an excuse.'

'Well if you find one I'll take you out."

'Yes,' she said, without hesitation. 'That would be nice.'

Eventually we got to her street and agreed to meet later that evening at half past seven. She reached up and gave me a kiss on my cheek and as she pulled away she stroked her hand down my face lightly. I immediately I felt goosebumps rise on my arms. It was not a horrible sensation.

She laughed lightly to herself as she turned away. I understood she knew exactly what she had done, and had done it on purpose to produce this reaction in me. I was unsure if the girl was playing with me but at that moment I did not care too much. I would go along for the ride and see what happened.

As I strolled back to Egerton Street, I thought more about Glenda. I knew it would be a problem if we were ever to become serious, due to my father's irrational hatred of all things Catholic. I made the decision not to mention her religious persuasion to him. As I strode on I decided, even better than that, I just would not tell him about her at all.

After all, it was still very early days.

Ten

We set sail for Reykjavik on a very cold morning, a couple of days after my conversation with Wally regarding his troubled childhood. We were to form up off the Icelandic capital for onward journey to Murmansk, escorting nineteen merchant ships carrying war supplies to the Soviets. Much needed cargoes including tanks, planes, coal, food, machine parts, clothing and other essential equipment would be carried in the holds and on the decks of those ships to allow the Red Army to continue its fight against the Nazis. It was obvious to us all by now that the Russians were to play a significant part in how this war was to turn out. We could not have them succumbing to Hitler's attacks due to a lack of supplies the British and Americans could have provided. It was beneficial to all of us these convoys got through.

The route would take us around the north coast of Iceland towards Norway. Then it would move around the Norwegian coast and over the top of Scandinavia, taking a course between Spitzbergen and Bear Island, continuing to the Kola Inlet and into Murmansk.

This was not a good time of year to undertake such a journey. Although winter was starting to fade, summer was still a few weeks away, meaning we would need to sail relatively close to the coast to avoid the ice further north. It would be necessary to keep clear of the frozen wastelands of the Arctic Circle and this would bring the convoy within easy range of German airbases in Norway. Added to this, the increasing number of daylight hours would make it difficult to avoid the Kriegsmarine and Luftwaffe. The odds seemed stacked in our adversaries' favour. With more daylight hours for them to operate, to seek and attack us, we did not expect an easy time of it. There was much trepidation among the crew when we finally set sail.

The journey to Reykjavik was to take almost six days and the first couple were largely uneventful. However it was not a nice experience to spend any time out on deck. If you needed to be out there then it was prudent to make use of the cold weather clothing we had been issued in Belfast. It was clear the further north we headed, the colder it got. With the rain blowing into our faces as we carried out our duties, it did not make for good working conditions.

Although we did not feel particularly vulnerable to enemy attack on the journey up to Iceland, I much preferred the warmth of the Malta convoys despite the frequent attacks we had experienced. However, there was still the constant threat of Nazi U-boats to contend with but we put that particular thought from our minds as much as we could.

And then the weather hit us.

On the third day a violent storm erupted. An Atlantic tempest that threw the ship around as if it was a small toy. The low hull of the *Virtuous* did nothing to help with its stability as we rolled and pitched, fighting the growing threat of the weather sinking us, nature doing the Nazis' job for them. The fear of going down was obvious in the faces of every matelot I

HELL AND HIGH WATER

saw; pasty and ghostlike, as though some had died already.

Anything not riveted or tied down was thrown around mess decks and working areas, crashing against bulkheads, doors, gantries and worst of all, people. Sailors clung to whatever they could to stop from losing their footing and hurting themselves. However, injuries were unavoidable and the sickbay was beginning to fill with people with a range of problems, some of them quite serious.

It became impossible to sleep. If you were lucky enough to make it into your hammock without falling onto your backside then, once in, you swung around so violently that you had to cling to the sides for dear life, bashing against your mates who hung in theirs beside you, all trying unsuccessfully to avoid each other.

Although many of us had not succumbed to seasickness before, there was no escaping that particular curse on this journey. Some sailors became so ill that all they could do was lie wherever they could find a space, rolling about and moaning loudly as the pots, pans, random pieces of kit and other ship paraphernalia flew around them, uncaring or oblivious to the danger they were in. These foetid mess decks, where we now found ourselves having to live within, ran with condensation and seawater, mixing with rotting food, broken crockery and dirty clothing as they sloshed about the floor, adding to the rancid stench and general discomfort. We could not go outside to throw up, our bodies too weak to make the short journey and for a fear of losing our footing and going overboard into the freezing North Sea. Instead, we vomited where we were and this, mixed with the other detritus and waste, made for a very disgusting mess deck.

However, we still had to work. The ship still had to make its way northward to Iceland.

It seemed sometimes the sea was above us and not below. The mountainous waves would reach to forty or fifty feet high and hang threateningly over us like a sea titan, before the ship would then rise on another wave and crash down again into the watery valleys created by the storm. The spray covered the open decks making them slippery and treacherous underfoot. Suicidal dashes across open decks to carry out duties became common. It was a wonder nobody found themselves in the sea at times. If they had they would have been done for. There was no way the ship would have been able to pick them up.

On the second day of this relentless storm, I found myself once again in the radio room on duty with Wally. We dared not speak for fear of opening our mouths and vomit pouring out. A couple of uneaten corned beef sandwiches lay on the desk in front of us. These had become the staple diet of the ship during the bad weather, the cooks finding it impossible to cook anything of any real substance due to the danger of having boiling water slopping around the galley. It was pointless.

I looked at the sandwich, too scared to put it into my stomach in case I brought it straight back up again. I could not have puke over the equipment. That would be a disaster. Drinking anything was also extremely difficult and I had not had a hot drink since the storm began, it was simply too dangerous. And so water was all I had consumed in that time. In fact, it was the only liquid any of us had drunk.

Wally looked at me and offered me a half smile.

'I bet you wish you'd joined the army now, don't you?' he said. 'I bet they never told you about this in the recruitment office.'

'You're dead right there, my friend,' I replied. 'This is shocking. I've never experienced anything like it.'

'Don't worry too much,' he said. 'This can't last for much longer and with each passing hour we're getting closer to Iceland. It'll be calmer closer to land.'

Being within the confines of the radio room and having no horizon to fix our eyes upon, the rolling and yawing of the ship increased the feeling of nausea twofold. I struggled desperately not to give in too much to the seasickness. I tried the trick of taking deep breaths and then holding it for a few seconds. It seemed to work for a while but I am not sure if this was just mind over matter.

I still had a job to do and so had to fight it. I was not the only one suffering. There were many of us in the same position. Whereas I could sit in a chair and hang on to the side of the desk and the bulkhead to steady myself, my fellow sailors in the boiler rooms would have it much more difficult than I. This was the reason none of us complained. We all had our own difficulties to endure. No matter how bad you thought your lot was, there was always somebody else in a worse situation than you.

'That's what I'm worried about,' I replied, gripping the side of the desk as the ship suddenly lurched to starboard. 'If the weather is bad here, what's it going to be like the further north we get… when we go from Iceland to Russia?'

'No point concerning yourself with that now,' said Wally. 'Worrying about something that may not happen. Anyway, with the weather this bad it'll keep the Germans away. I can't see any planes flying in weather like this. And if they did, they'd find it extremely difficult to hit any of us. Not that they've bases within our range yet anyway. And as for U-boats, if there are any in the area they'll be suffering as much as we are if they rise to attack depth… Worse even.'

This was true. Although the weather was atrocious and we were all suffering, it kept the threat of enemy attack at bay and I, for one, would sooner suffer this than have a torpedo slam into our hull.

'Did you hear about Ralph Reid?' Wally asked after a while.

'What about him?'

'Nearly went overboard a few hours ago. Apparently he had to go out on deck and a wave washed over and dragged him to the side. He managed to hang on to something and his mates got him back inside but only after a lot of messing around. He was out there for twenty-five minutes. Bloody frozen stiff when they got him back in. He's in the sickbay now.'

'Bloody hell. Poor Ralph,' I said, shocked this had happened to a friend of mine. 'Can't say I'm surprised though. I think I'm more amazed we haven't lost anyone yet.'

'The sickbay's quite full, you know,' Wally informed me. 'Anyone with seasickness is being told to bugger off but there's been loads of knocks. I saw one poor sod with a huge gash on his head earlier on.'

Again the ship pitched to the side, causing Wally's codebook and pencils to drop to the floor. He stooped down to pick them up and as he did so, Petty Officer Singer appeared at the door. His face was as white as a sheet and he had what looked like a puke stain down the front of his chest.

'You laddies all right?' he asked. 'Bearing up?'

'Not so good, to be honest, P.O.,' I replied, as Wally scrambled around the deck on all fours, struggling to retrieve his stationery.

'Aye, laddie,' he replied. 'We'll soon be out of this so keep up the good work. You're all doing fine.'

And with that he was gone. Probably heading back to the sanctuary of his bunk if he had any sense.

The shift continued without any incident and we both managed to get our corned beef sandwiches down and keep them there. When Harry and Jack arrived to relieve us, I could see they had probably not managed to get any decent rest before they took over. I feared the same would happen for the two of us.

Thankfully, a couple of days later, we arrived in Whale Bay at Hvalfjödur to the north of Reykjavik. The hills and mountains around the city now protected the ship against the elements to a degree. The storm that had caused us so much grief over the previous few days finally abated.

JOHN McKAY

This left the ship's company with the gruesome task of cleaning up the mess it had caused. When not on duty, we were made to mop up all the puke, filth and debris that had mixed on the mess decks, and swab and clean up the floors, bulkheads and outside decks. The stench was atrocious but we went at it with a vigour. None of us wanted to continue to live and work in those conditions and we needed to be back to normal as soon as possible. Whatever normal was.

We were anchored some way off the city but, from where we were, we could see the lights of the buildings from the deck. It was good to see land again, even if we would not be setting foot upon it. It gave me a sense of safety. When I saw the ships of the convoy forming up, and the impressive naval destroyers docked a few hundred yards from our starboard bow, I determined we were a formidable and capable fighting force.

Convoy procedures meant the merchant ships were to arrange into columns with each column separated by approximately a thousand yards of open sea with each column spaced five hundred yards apart. The escorting military vessels would sail at the sides, and front and back, thereby protecting the lesser armed merchant vessels from enemy attack. The destroyers would also patrol between the columns to provide added protection.

Our job, as an anti-submarine frigate, was to patrol ahead of and outside this perimeter, searching for enemy U-boats that might wish to take a pot shot at the merchant ships, who were their ultimate target. By using the ASDIC system we hoped to spot them before

HELL AND HIGH WATER

they had chance to wreak their havoc, and hit them with depth charges and the newly fitted Hedgehog mortar. I worried that with the convoy being so large and spread out, it may not be too difficult for a German submarine to breach the cordon.

Each convoy was given a codename. PQ, followed by a sequential number, for outgoing voyages, and QP for returning trips back to Iceland or Great Britain. I was not sure what these particular letters stood for but was told they did not really mean anything, and were merely the initials of the fellow who had thought up the whole procedure.

The day after we arrived off Iceland, having refuelled and taken on more provisions, the convoy set off for Murmansk. Although I always felt nervous at the start of a voyage, for some reason, this time if felt a whole lot different. The trip up from Loch Ewe had not gone well and if it was to be a portent of what was to follow in the next phase of the voyage, then we had a lot to be worried about. This time I really did not have a good feeling about how this journey was going to play out. And, what was worse, I could see the same trepidation upon the faces of all my shipmates.

Eleven

We had not gone more than half a day out of Hvalfjödur before action stations were sounded. Although this had become a regular thing for us, it never failed to cause butterflies entering my stomach and fly madly around inside whenever that piercing, whooping klaxon reverberated around the ship.

We were patrolling at the starboard side of the convoy, the hills and mountains of Iceland barely visible to our right and fading fast from sight as we headed north-east. Immediately we rushed to our pre-set positions and, with Ralph still being in the sickbay following his episode on deck during the storm, it was up to me to man the Oerlikon. Once strapped in and the weapon made ready, I cannot deny I was suddenly hit with a serious bout of nerves. This was not my primary role. I just hoped I would be able to perform my duties with a degree of capability and success. I had never fired the weapon in anger and was scared I might not be up to the task.

Despite wearing the sheepskin jerkin and flash hood, the cold penetrated through as if I was naked, and being unable to move around to keep warm, I soon began to shiver. The cold was piercing. With each exhalation my breath formed like fog in front of my face.

Word soon got around that a U-boat had been spotted on ASDIC. The ship picked up speed as we sailed

HELL AND HIGH WATER

out to meet where the pings had indicated the submarine might be. I realised my role as a gunner would probably not be tested in any combat operation and I felt a small sense of relief my skills with an anti-aircraft gun would not be put to the test just yet. An Oerlikon was little use against a U-boat.

I could see two sailors in front of me setting the timers on the depth charges housed on the runs at the side of the ship. I strained my neck and could just about make out activity at the Hedgehog mortar at the bow. Marines and more sailors were making the weapon ready for firing, working hard despite the sea spray soaking them as the *Virtuous* moved closer to its target, dipping into the water then rising again as it lurched forward in search of its prey.

'Twenty yards,' shouted a leading hand whose name I could not quite remember. 'Be ready, lads! Don't balls this up!'

Approximately five hundred yards away I could see another anti-submarine ship, the trawler HMS *Blackfly,* coming around to join us. The nerves I initially felt were giving way to a feeling of intense excitement. To be involved in such a hunt was thoroughly exhilarating. I would not have wanted to be anywhere else. The professionalism of my shipmates in carrying out the orders of the officers was commendable. I genuinely feared for the Kriegsmarine submariners who were about to feel the full weight of the Royal Navy tumbling down upon them.

The *Blackfly* headed to our wide left and then started to come to bear at right angles to us. Almost simultaneously both ships cut their engines and fired their Hedgehog mortars, the operators winding the dial as the twelve bombs from each weapon flew into the air to come crashing down into the sea in front of the ships. For a couple of seconds there was complete silence as the mortars travelled down to the set depth before suddenly exploding at the same time with an almighty whooshing noise. Watching closely, I could see the vibration in the waves.

This tremor was immediately followed by a huge eruption of seawater which shot what must have been eighty feet into the air. No sooner had the water settled back into the sea than the captain ordered the *Virtuous* forward again and five depth charges from the rack in front of me were rolled out into the ocean. As we made our way past the site and out of damage range from our own weapons, again the seawater shot into the air behind us as the barrels exploded beneath the waves.

The adrenalin pumped through my veins. I watched on in awe as my shipmates prepared more charges for another run at the Nazi submarine.

Midshipman Guthrie paced along the foredeck with another officer, attempting to look efficient and in command, his ears and nose glowing red with the cold. Like the other officers he was wearing a camel coloured duffel coat with a polar-necked pullover. Rather than make himself more comfortable by putting a scarf around his mouth and nose, he was choosing this quite ridiculous red-faced look instead. I really could not take to the man and my dislike for him was growing all the time. I just could not see the point of him. He did not seem to do anything other than hang around with the other officers trying to look important.

I decided to unstrap myself from the Oerlikon to get a better view of what was happening. I was not really deserting my post as I did not go further than six feet from the gun and merely stood against the gunwale to watch proceedings. I found it all very fascinating. And anyway, we were still probably some distance from the range of any Luftwaffe patrols.

Looking out into the water I was astonished to see hundreds of dead fish, all killed by the depth charges and mortars.

As if following my gaze I heard a shout to my right, 'We can pick those up later. It'll be a nice fish supper for us all tonight, boys.'

I turned to see who had made the comments and was joined by Dave Higson. I had not seen him to speak to since the card game.

'That's if they'll let us,' I said. 'We have a much bigger fish to catch before we can even think about picking up any of that.'

'This is all a bit exciting, isn't it?' he grinned.

'Yes,' I answered. 'But you have to feel a bit sorry for them down there. They must be shitting themselves.'

'I wouldn't worry too much about that,' he replied, sullenly. 'They're Nazis at the end of the day. They started all this. The bloody war. And anyway, my younger brother was on the *Lancastria*. With what the Germans did that day, I really have no sympathy for them.'

'So what happened to him,' I asked, intrigued.

'He tells me the ship went down in under half an hour, just off the coast of St Nazaire during the evacuation. Bombed by the Luftwaffe. Thousands died he tells me. Thousands. Probably twice as many as went down on the *Titanic*. And when the survivors were in the sea trying to stay alive, to stop from drowning or burning in the oil, the buggers strafed them. Machine gunned defenceless people as they floated there. And there weren't only military personnel on that ship, you know. There were women and children too. Civilians. He managed to cling onto some wreckage and was pulled out of the water almost dead a few hours later. He spent over a month in hospital and I don't think he's right yet.'

I had not known this about Dave's brother. With the thought of what he had just told me I was able to reconcile myself with the fact that what we were doing, despite it probably causing the deaths of many men, it was completely justified.

'And let's face it,' he continued. 'They're here to sink these ships. Do you think they give a toss about any of our sailors? I don't think so.'

'You're right,' I replied. I could not argue with him. In fact this made it extremely important to find the U-boat and sink it.

The ship sailed on for a minute and then did an about turn to starboard, heading back to where we had dropped the charges. I could see the *Blackfly* doing the same, as both vessels prepared for a second run.

I then heard a bout of laughter from the bow. I looked over to see what was so amusing. I observed one or two sailors pointing out to sea. As the ship got closer to the area we had attacked I saw something extremely large floating in the water ahead of us. I could not make out what it was at first and squinted my eyes to try to see better. Even when we got closer I could not understand what it was I was looking at.

Although I did not know what it was, I certainly knew what it was not. It most definitely was not a German submarine.

'A whale,' I heard a voice say from behind me. I turned around to see Midshipman Guthrie standing behind us looking out at the large, dead sea mammal floating a couple of hundred yards ahead of us. 'It's a bloody whale.'

Looking at it again, I could see he was right. I could now make out the shape of the animal floating belly up, the sun reflecting back off the white of its thick blubbery skin.

'So, no sub then?' asked Dave, grinning at me, but so Guthrie could not see.

'It appears n... not,' he stammered by way of reply. 'Carry on.'

And with that he walked away.

With the panic now over, we were stood down and a detail was sent out on a boat to retrieve as much of the dead fish as they could. Just as Dave had predicted, we would be eating well that evening.

Apparently this was not the first time a whale had been picked up on ASDIC and it probably would not be the last. Each time it happened it would have to be assumed to be a submarine. The captain would more than likely have been unconcerned about the false alarm and was probably happy with how the ship's company had reacted. It had been like a live training exercise in the end.

As I stood on the deck watching a group of sailors rowing out to collect the dead fish, I was suddenly taken by the sheer magnitude of the ocean. I had lived by the sea all my life and had somewhat taken it for granted. But what did I really know about it? What did anybody really know? The ocean was a mystery. The ocean was a world within a world of which we knew nothing about. We did not know what lay beneath its waves, what creatures inhabited it, or geological structures were contained within it. We could build mighty ships with equipment that could detect large objects beneath it, but we could never know for certain what they were without actually seeing them. I wondered if mankind would ever be able to explore it to any great degree, to discover the massive array of marine life that lived below its surface. I was of the opinion it was as likely as flying to the moon.

As I watched the boat return a few minutes later full of cod, I overheard one or two shipmates discussing how this voyage may not turn out to be so bad after all.

They could not have been more wrong.

HELL AND HIGH WATER

Twelve

The convoy powered on relentlessly, heading ever closer to the Norwegian coast and our destination in the Soviet Union. The incident with the whale had caused much merriment among the crew. The lads who worked in the E.W.O. room, including my friend, John Steadman, took some friendly stick from their shipmates. They argued back that a U-boat and a whale looked exactly the same on an ASDIC screen. I think it was more from the relief it turned out to be nothing unfriendly that prompted the banter. It gave us a comical break from what was becoming a tense atmosphere about the ship.

As we moved northwards the chill in the air became more severe, to a point where it was quite painful when you breathed in, hurting your lungs and nasal passages with each breath. I had known cold before, in the Liverpool winters when the freezing January wind would blow up Chapel Street from the River Mersey, but this was something else. It was now impossible to be out on deck without wearing the thermal gear issued to us in Belfast. We only set foot outside if it was absolutely necessary. Inside, the mess decks were not much better. Sometimes the heating would fail and we would be left wearing all our cold weather gear whilst eating our dinner, or on shift carrying out our duties. The steel bulkheads would transfer the freezing temperatures from outside to the inside. There was a growing sense things were not going to get better any time soon.

This was confirmed a day later when we received a signal from the Admiralty.

Wally was sipping a mug of coffee, blowing over the top of it and holding it close to his face with both hands, when I handed him the message to decrypt.

He put down the cup and picked up the codebook.

'Oh shit,' he said, after a while. 'This isn't good.'

The days of him holding the deciphered signals to himself had been and gone. He handed me the slip of paper to read as he reached over for a container in which to send it up to the bridge. It was a weather report informing us there was a strong chance of a storm headed our way. After what had happened on the journey from Scotland to Iceland, this was extremely bad news. The ship and crew had struggled to cope with the high wind and rough seas and I could see this being much worse if it did hit us.

I handed the signal back to him and he put it in the container and fired it up to the bridge.

A couple of minutes later the captain's voice crackled over the public address system.

'All crew are to be aware we are expecting some more inclement weather. Fix down or stow away anything that's likely to break and prepare yourselves for another bumpy ride.'

That was it. Again, like all the captain's messages, it was short and to the point. We were getting to understand that Lieutenant Commander Harrison was a man of very few words.

HELL AND HIGH WATER

Almost as soon as he had finished than the radio burst into life once more. This was quite a lengthy message and it was some minutes before the final letter group was transmitted. I handed the signal to my friend. As he worked to decode the message, I pushed my chair back, stretching my hands behind my head.

It was close to the end of our shift and, as I stretched, Jack and Harry arrived at the doorway.

'Time's up gentlemen,' said Harry. 'Make way for the real signallers.'

I smiled. 'You're both very welcome to it. My hammock awaits. I'm knackered.'

Wally let out a sigh and we all turned to look at him. He had finished decoding the signal and was putting it into a container. When he pressed the button to fire it to the bridge, he found it was not working. He pressed it again but nothing happened.

'Bloody hell,' he said. 'That's all we need.'

'Don't worry about it,' I replied. 'If you give it to me, I'll take it up. You can contact the mechanic and get it fixed while these two sit down and save England for us.'

'Fair enough,' replied Wally and handed me the container.

As I walked along the gangway and up the ladder to the bridge I began to feel a little nervous. I had not read the signal and from Wally's demeanour I was sure it was another load of bad news. He was normally happy and cracking jokes at the end of the shift but this time he had behaved quite the opposite. And here was I, about to deliver a potentially bad signal to the most senior officers on board. I just hoped they would not shoot the messenger.

I reached the gangway outside the bridge and stood at the door. Through the window I could make out four people inside. The captain stood with the Executive Officer, Lieutenant Mitchell. Midshipman Guthrie was standing closest to the door with his back to me and an able seaman, Johnny Spencer, whose job I was never too sure about, was seated at a table looking at a chart.

I tapped lightly on the window and Guthrie turned around. Upon seeing me he frowned and with a condescending motion of his right hand, he waved at me, as though to tell me to go away and not to bother them. I knocked again and held up the container.

He came to the door and opened it. The others on the bridge looked over.

'Wha… what is it, Martin?' he asked. He appeared instantly irritated by my presence.

'Hello, sir. I have a signal for the captain,' I replied, holding up the container. 'The system has broke so I thought I'd bring it straight up.'

'Oh… Okay,' he replied. He held out his hand. 'You can give it to me. I'll see he gets it.'

As I was about to hand it to him, Lieutenant Commander Harrison called over.

'Mister Martin, isn't it?' he said.

I was shocked the man remembered my name. The last time we had spoken directly to each other was during my charge after the debacle of the run ashore in Gibraltar some months ago.

'It is, sir, yes,' I replied.

HELL AND HIGH WATER

'Come inside,' he said. 'You can give it to me yourself.'

'Yes, sir,' I replied stepping past Mister Guthrie, who looked more than a little put out that the captain had asked me inside. I would have laughed at him but felt the situation warranted I behave myself.

I approached the captain and handed him the container. He unscrewed the cap and took out the signal.

As he read it, I looked around the room. It was typical of all bridges on this size of vessel. It was a lot smaller than you would expect for what was essentially the hub of the ship. It had excellent vision on three sides due to the huge thickened glass windows. Although we were at virtually the highest point on the vessel, the sea spray was such that it occasionally splashed against them. Guthrie moved back to his original position before I had disturbed him, which seemed to be to stand with his hands behind his back looking out of the window, trying to look as important and authoritative as he could. Lieutenant Mitchell stood behind Johnny Spencer as he did something with the chart he was pondering over. I noticed to his right a Hallicrafters Model HT4 radio transmitter. This was the *Virtuous's* contact with the rest of the convoy. When Johnny saw me looking he caught my eye, quickly glanced at Guthrie and then raised his eyebrows, as if to reflect my own thoughts on the man. I very nearly laughed and so moved my eyes away from him.

Through the windows I could see some of the other ships of the convoy, the afternoon sun's rays reflecting back off their hulls. I was surprised at how far away they appeared. If a decent U-boat commander could get his submarine past the military cordon they could probably have a field day with the merchantmen. I hoped the number of Royal Navy ships were sufficient to deal with any enemy attack upon them and had to believe they would be, but it gave me a strange chill nevertheless.

The sea was quite choppy and I thought maybe this was the beginning of the storm we were heading into. I could clearly see the rise and fall of the waves as the ship rose then dipped into them, seawater splashing over the bow as we cut through the water, soaking the decks before exiting back into the ocean through the scuppers.

'Hmm,' said Harrison after reading the message. 'I think you'd better take a look at this, Charles. You too, Donald.'

Immediately, the two officers moved over to the captain, Lieutenant Mitchell taking the note from his outstretched hand. Guthrie stood to his side and they both read the message together.

I was beginning to feel a bit like a spare part and then felt the captain's gaze upon me.

'I take it you've read it,' he said.

'No, sir,' I replied. 'I haven't. You see Wally... Able Seaman Honeyman... Well, he decrypts them after I've taken down the letter groups. He puts them straight into the system and fires them up here.'

'Hmm,' he said again. I could not tell if he believed me. To be honest, I was not altogether too bothered if he believed me or not.

HELL AND HIGH WATER

'Hand the message to Mister Martin here when you've read it,' said Harrison to his two subordinates.

Almost reluctantly, Mitchell handed me the signal and Guthrie looked at me as though I was something he had trodden in. The captain clearly noticed this small exchange but chose to pretend not to.

I read the signal and had an instant feeling of dread. The information it contained did not make good reading. The Admiralty were informing the convoy that three German surface destroyers were believed to be patrolling the area we were headed for. A Nazi U-boat wolf-pack was also believed to be operating in the area.

I handed the message back to the captain.

'What's your view on this?' he asked. It took me a few seconds to realise he was directing the question towards me.

'My view sir?... I'm just a telegraphist,' I replied.

'You're not *just* a telegraphist, young man. You play an important role on this ship. Every man on board does. Don't underestimate your contribution. If you have an opinion then please voice it.'

'Sir... Do you feel this is appropriate?' asked Mitchell.

'Ye... Yes, sir. I am of Mister Mitchell's opinion...' added Guthrie.

'I would merely like to know what the ratings on board this ship are thinking,' replied the captain. 'Like I've just told Mister Martin here, every man on board has an important role to play in how this ship functions. From the cooks who keep us nourished, to the stokers who keep the ship afloat and moving.

From the shipwrights and mechanics who ensure that everything is in order and working properly, to the gunners on deck who keep the enemy planes at bay. Every man… Cooks, writers, gunners, stokers, medics… and telegraphists and decoders too. We're all as important as each other.'

This seemed to silence them and so I looked at the signal again before I replied.

'To be honest with you, sir, I'm not really qualified to answer for everyone but I can offer you my thoughts if I may.'

'Go ahead.'

'I believe there's a respect for the officers on board this ship. We trust them. We know we're probably heading for a bad time on this journey but we'll do it nevertheless and without complaint. And that's because we know it's necessary. We know we wouldn't be asked to do it unless it was important and we'll do it to the best of our ability. I also believe this is a happy ship. The crew get on well with each other and it's rare you see anybody falling out over anything. And when they do, it's quickly sorted and forgotten about. There's a determination amongst the crew to do a good job. To make you proud of us, to make our country proud of us and to make our families proud of us too.

'As for this,' I added, nodding to the signal now back in the captain's hand. 'This is just something we'll have to deal with as and when it happens. You can rely on us, sir.'

HELL AND HIGH WATER

'Very good,' said Harrison, nodding to me with a small smile. 'It makes me glad to hear it. Now you can return to your duties.'

And with that he turned around to continue with whatever he had been doing before I interrupted him.

As I reached the door to let myself out I sensed someone behind me.

Guthrie had followed me and, as I opened it, he said, almost in a whisper: 'Ensure that the tu...tube gets fixed as a matter of p... priority. I don't want you... you disturbing the cap... captain unnecessarily again.'

Then he turned around and was gone.

I closed the door behind me. As I made my way through the ship to the mess deck where my hammock was waiting for me, I wondered exactly what part of my visit to the bridge had been unnecessary.

It was not long before we were being put to the test once more.

Only an hour after I met with the captain on the bridge the familiar sound of action stations shrieked throughout the ship and again we found ourselves running to get into position. I had been lying in my hammock trying to get some well earned sleep when the klaxon went off. As I fumbled into my cold weather gear, desperately trying to wake up and be as quick as I could, I felt an immense sense of doom. The deployments to the Mediterranean and the skirmishes we had been involved in there had never really given me an overwhelming sense of anxiety, despite the danger we had clearly been in. For some reason, this time it felt very different.

As I left the the mess deck and rushed onto the open deck, the cold hit me like a train. Instinctively I pulled the lower part of my flash hood up and over my nose and mouth, and squinted my eyes to prevent them from freezing. There was a mild wind that, although not strong, pierced through the thin cloth and made my teeth chatter.

I found Ralph making ready at the Oerlikon. He had recovered from his mishap on deck a few days ago and was back to full duties. Using my mittened hands as best I could, I assisted him with the straps and, after a few moments, he was ready to go. I ensured the ammunition drum was in position, fixed firmly on top of the weapon, and then looked around to see where the danger was coming from.

We could see, to the rear of the convoy, a plane flying towards us in the mid-afternoon sunshine. It was quite high, some distance away and looked to be posing no immediate threat.

'Heinkel... or a Junkers,' said Ralph. 'I can't quite make out. It'll be a spotter recce-ing us. Expect trouble soon, pal.'

I knew he was right. It was clear that now we had been seen it would not be too long before the weight of the Luftwaffe would fall upon us, their planes flying from bases along the Norwegian coast.

I looked out across the waves to the other ships as they rose and fell in the swell and was again astounded at how far away they appeared. The *Virtu-*

ous, along with the other escort ships, had an extremely big responsibility to keep those ships safe and it weighed heavy upon us. No doubt the boys in the Electronic Warfare Offices would have their eyes glued to the ASDIC screens, keeping look out for any U-boats that may attempt to sneak through unnoticed, like a fox attempting to get into a hen-house when the farmer has his back turned.

It was not long before the foxes appeared. Not from the depths of the ocean but from the sky.

They came at us from the south east, flying a direct line from the coast. We had no air protection and would have to rely on the skills of the gunners on the destroyers with their heavy 4.5 inch guns, Bofors and Oerlikons to put up a barrage to stop them. The merchants themselves were lightly armed, each with a small contingent of marines on board to man their weaponry for incidents such as this.

They were Junkers Ju88 bombers. Looking at them, as they filled the sky to our rear, bearing down on the convoy like falcons, I was once again hit with the familiar feeling of adrenalin entering my bloodstream. It was exciting but at the same time absolutely terrifying.

The escort ships began to move tighter to the merchantmen, closing up to allow their guns to assist in their defence. It was not long before the German planes started to drop their bombs. They did not risk getting too close due to the barrage put up from the gunners but, before long, the noise of gunfire and the swooshing of bombs as they exploded in the sea around the ships was soon filling the air around us.

Suddenly, I felt the deck near me vibrate violently as Ralph fired the Oerlikon in the direction of a Junkers that had broken away and was attempting a strafing run upon us. Despite the Bofors at the stern firing its ack-ack in the air, where it exploded in dark clouds around it, the German pilot guided his aeroplane with expert skill, firing his machine guns as he got within range.

I could hear the bullets striking the superstructure and the deck and I instinctively bent down for cover. Then it passed over us at extreme speed, all the time Ralph blasting away with the 20mm cannon. Then it was gone, as quickly as it had appeared, looking for another ship to target.

'Bloody hell, that was close,' said Ralph, and, as I stood up straight again, I was able to look at the damage the plane had caused.

Luckily it did not look too bad. The majority of the bullets had hit the superstructure, causing no damage at all but one or two lanterns and a couple of windows had been smashed and the deck had many bullet holes. Other than that there was no other damage I could see. Most importantly, there had been no casualties.

'That pilot must be on a death wish,' said Ralph when he stopped firing. 'How we all missed him is beyond me. His luck won't last if he continues to attack like that.'

I looked across the water to the merchantmen and could see the sea erupting around them as the bombs rained down from the German planes. The bombers remained in the cover of the clouds, not daring to get in too close unlike the plane that had just strafed us.

For some odd reason, as the bombs exploded, the music of Tchaikovsky's 1812 overture entered my head. I watched as the seawater flew skywards as the bombs detonated. As if in time with the music in my head, I was able to mask out the screech as they fell and the thunderous roars of their explosions with my own odd thoughts and fantasies. It somehow made it all easier to bear.

I looked again skyward at the circle of Nazi planes above us and realised they were remaining at this distance for a very good reason. If any of them were damaged by our guns and had to ditch into the sea then there would be no survivors. The cold of the North Atlantic would surely do for them.

The gunners of the escort ships continued to fire their weapons at the German aircraft and after around fifteen minutes we could see they were beginning to turn back. They were either out of ammunition or running low on fuel. It did not concern me as to the reasons they were leaving, I was just glad they were.

In the distance, in the middle of the convoy, I could see thick black smoke billowing skyward and realised one of the ships had been hit. Judging by the amount of smoke pouring into the sky, it was clear it had been damaged badly. From my vantage point on the port side, I could not quite make out which one it was, but it looked like a large merchant vessel. I hoped that nobody was hurt and they would be able to evacuate everyone before it went down, which looked inevitable.

I turned to Ralph who, despite the severe cold, had moved his flash hood to the side and was wiping sweat from his brow with the back of his glove.

I grimaced. 'That doesn't look good.'

'You're not wrong there, George,' he replied. 'Do you know which it is?'

'Can't make it out, pal,' I said, squinting my eyes. 'But it looks a large one.'

'Looks like it's done for.'

I could not help feeling a small sense of responsibility for the merchantman's fate. We were there to protect them but for this particular vessel we had failed. The ship would surely sink and take down with it all the essential cargo needed by our Russian allies. I just hoped all the boys on board would be able to get off before it happened.

The convoy seemed to stop in the water as we looked at the stricken ship. I could make out a couple of smaller vessels heading out to it to pick up the survivors including what I presumed was the official rescue ship, the steamer, HMS *Perth*. As they got closer I again felt the ship lurch slightly beneath me as we picked up speed. The convoy was not going to hang around when another air attack was possible. With what I had read in the signal I had taken to the bridge earlier, even though I felt for my comrades on the ship that had been hit, I understood we could not hang around and be sitting ducks for the Kriegsmarine and U-boats that may be operating close by.

We were not stood down until an hour or so later and, after grabbing a quick bite to eat in the galley, I again found myself in the radio room with Wally,

HELL AND HIGH WATER

having taken over from Jack and Harry who had spent the duration of the attack on duty there. Jack told me he preferred to be on deck when under attack.

'I know it's probably much more dangerous, but at least you can see what's going on. It's being cooped up in here that gives me the chills. And, if the ship gets hit, I think you'll have more chance of making it off if you're up top when it happens,' he explained.

I could not argue with him. This made total sense to me as I felt the same way. I hated being below decks when we were under attack. Wally and Harry nodded their heads in agreement.

'You laddies all right?'

We turned to the doorway to see Petty Officer Singer standing there. He looked harassed.

'Yes, fine,' we replied.

'Good, good. Keep up the good work, boys. Keep your guard. These bastards will be back before you know it. Looks like the *Imperial Star* has had it. Won't be long before she's at the bottom of the sea, unfortunately.'

Before we could respond he turned and walked away.

'Okay,' said Harry, drawing out the word. 'I'm off. See you boys later.'

After Jack and Harry had left us, Wally said, 'He seems to take all this personally. Singer, that is. There's no point in that, if you ask me,'

'Maybe it is personal,' I wondered. 'Maybe that's the only way to look at it. For each of us out here, we have our own stories, our own thoughts and hopes for the future. It's probably the same for them too. The

Germans. I don't mean the Nazis, but the normal fellows like you and me…'

'Don't ever compare us to them,' interrupted Wally. I was slightly shocked at his curtness. 'Don't do that. Don't say we're all basically the same, because we're not. We haven't blindly followed a madman and his warped ideology that's led the world into a second major conflict barely twenty years after the last one was over. We're not the same as them, George. In no way are we remotely like them.'

I did not reply. Instead I turned away from him before the tense atmosphere I had just created could get any worse. And then the radio beeped into life and I put the headset over my ears.

Thirteen

Liverpool

'So who's the lucky girl, then?' asked my father.
'Excuse me?'
'You know full well what I mean, young man,' he replied.

He was sitting in his favourite chair by the fireplace, the battered one that my grandfather used to sit in before him, and no doubt his father before that. He had taken off his shirt and was wearing only his trousers and a vest that was more grey than the white it had originally been. He had a pair of old slippers on his feet to complete his usual evening "home from work" attire. He tapped his pipe against the wooden chair arm, brought it to his mouth and sucked at it, the tobacco glowing orange, lighting his face slightly.

I could not tell if he was having fun with me or whether he was asking the question because he already knew the answer.

I did not know how to respond.

'Cat got your tongue?' he asked as he blew out the smoke.

Out of the corner of my eye I could see Jimmy, who was sitting on the couch, looking at me with an inane grin upon his face. When I turned to him his grin grew bigger.

'Yeah,' he said, repeating father's words, 'Cat got your tongue?'

'Shut up, Jimmy,' I said and turned back to my father, who was waiting for my answer.

'She's just someone I met last week,' I said. I realised there was no point in lying about going out with a girl.

'Oh, yeah,' he replied. 'And where did you meet this young lady?'

'In a pub in the city,' I lied. 'I was out with Billy from work. He knew her and introduced us. I thought I might take her out tonight.'

I could tell by his frown he thought I may not be telling the truth, but he did not push it, thankfully.

'Hey, mam,' said Hilary, who was sitting on the floor playing with a doll as mother walked in from the kitchen. 'Our George is going out with a girl.'

'Is he now?' she replied. She sat herself down in the chair opposite my father. 'Well isn't she a lucky girl then.'

Mother looked at me and smiled. I could always rely on my dear old mam for support.

Father continued to tap at his pipe and I could sense he wanted to ask more questions but now that mother was in the room he became quiet. However, it was she who continued the interrogation.

'So who is she?' she asked innocently.

'Some girl I met in the city last week,' I lied again.

'Oh, yes,' she replied, taking her knitting needles from a bag to the side of her chair. 'And what's her name?'

'Glenda.'

'Glenda?' she replied. 'That's a nice name. Don't you think, Eddie?'

HELL AND HIGH WATER

'Nice enough,' replied father, once more blowing out the awful smelling smoke into the room for us all to breathe in. I often thought that if I wanted to smoke a pipe then I would buy my own, but the whiff of father's awful habit made that particular vice one to which I would never bother with. I would stick to the odd cigarette.

There were a few moments of silence. I looked at my watch. I had told Glenda I would meet her outside her Aunt Ida's house at half past seven and it was now only a quarter to. I was wishing the minutes away.

'Glenda,' said mother thoughtfully. 'Isn't that the name of the young girl who's just taken up with the Shepherds?'

'I've no idea,' I replied, and then realised I had been too quick to answer.

Instantly, father sat up straighter in his chair.

'The Shepherds?' he said. 'Those Catholics you used to knock around with when you were younger?'

'That's who the Shepherds are,' I replied. Even to me it sounded insolent and defensive.

I was starting to sweat a little and becoming very uncomfortable. I wished I had made up a name, but how was I to know that mother was aware the Shepherds had taken in their niece from Wales?

'It wouldn't be the same girl, now would it?' asked father, thankfully ignoring my insolent tone.

'No,' I lied again. 'There's more than one person in the world called Glenda, you know.'

He seemed to accept this and sank back into his chair.

'Good job,' he replied. 'You know what would happen if I caught you going out with a Catholic, don't you?'

'I'm aware of your thoughts on the subject,' I replied.

'Good. I'm glad we're clear then.'

I glanced at my mother who looked down at her knitting as our eyes met. I knew I would get no support from her as far as this subject was concerned as she had put up with this type of thing from him for as long as I could remember. Whether she agreed with him or not was irrelevant.

I realised at that moment that should I get serious with Glenda there would be a whole load of trouble ahead. But, as the relationship was still in its infancy, if it actually was a relationship, then there would be no point causing trouble at this early stage. If it developed into something more deep then I would have to cross that particular bridge when I got to it.

A half hour later I walked onto her street and found her standing outside her Aunt's front door waiting for me. Instinctively I looked at my wristwatch.

'Don't worry, George,' she said, as I got nearer, 'You're not late. I thought I'd have a bit of fresh air and wait for you out here. All that cigarette smoke in Aunt Ida's front room isn't good for my asthma.'

'I didn't know you had asthma,' I said.

'How would you? I never told you. It's something I can control as long as I don't exert myself too much.'

There was a twinkle in her eyes as she said this and I felt myself redden again. Quickly I turned away and started to walk, taking her arm as she held it out to me. Again, I was not sure if she was playing with me, saying slightly odd and quirky things to see if she could get a reaction. I was not sure about her, but I was certainly intrigued by her. Most of all I was very much attracted to her pretty looks and there was something about the awkward way she could make me feel that I found oddly endearing.

We moved along the cobbled streets heading towards the city centre. As we walked we looked around us. A group of children, perhaps seven or eight years old, were playing with balls and sticks, dogs chasing them happily as they played. They looked like they had no cares at all and as I turned my gaze towards the docks and the barrage balloons that had been raised there, their long cables snaking down to the ground beyond my view, I was struck by the contrast of war and innocence within the same area of my vision. As I looked at these children, laughing and chatting together, no doubt up to a myriad of mischief, I thought it was not that long ago since I was doing the same.

'What are you thinking?' asked Glenda, breaking me from my nostalgic thoughts.

'Nothing really,' I replied. 'Nothing interesting anyway.'

'Go on.'

'Well, I was just looking at those kids over there and how they remind me of myself when I was that age,' I replied. 'Then I looked over at the docks, and thought that I'll soon be involved in all that... The war, you know. Just a silly thought really.'

'It's not silly at all,' replied Glenda. 'I think that it's quite profound really. The contrast between the two and how you've noticed it... Do you ever get scared?'

'What do you mean?'

'Do you ever get scared you'll lose it all? That you'll forget about what it was like to be a child and to have no worries. To lose that innocence.'

I laughed but I don't know why.

'I can't say I've given it much thought,' I eventually replied. 'I suppose only time will tell. One thing's for sure though, and that's I'm joining the navy soon. But after all the bombing here, I'm not too sure whether staying in the city is actually going to be any safer than being on the front line.'

Eventually, we found a small quiet pub where I ordered us both a drink and we sat in a corner.

'So,' I said, as I handed Glenda the small glass of beer she had asked for. 'Why does Liverpool appeal to you? I don't understand why you'd leave the safety of Wales to come here.'

'Like I told you the other night,' she replied, 'I needed a job and thought I'd come and stay with my Aunt and cousins for a while. I didn't see enough of them when I was growing up.'

I could not tell if she was being fully truthful with me. The way she shifted her head away as though she was observing the room around her, her eyes not able to meet with mine.

'What do your parents think about you coming here?' I asked. 'Surely they're worried about you, aren't they?'

'Maybe,' she shrugged. 'Who knows?... Who cares?'

This flippant remark seemed odd. I was about to question her further when she interrupted.

'Anyway, enough of this boring talk. I thought you were more fun than this, George Martin. Iris told me you were very funny. You know, I think she's a little bit in love with you.'

'Don't be daft,' I replied. 'She's just Iris. And anyway, I think she's quite happy with Billy.'

'Oh, I think she's just playing with him. Having a bit of fun.'

'She's all he talks about since the other night,' I replied.

The conversation turned to other matters and our hopes for the future. I felt I could not offer any kind of fulfilling conversation as I could not envisage my life beyond the war. However, Glenda told me of her hopes to become a teacher and to one day marry a handsome man and have many children. When she spoke of the future, she turned her head away and I thought for a moment she was avoiding my eyes. I took it that she was embarrassed about speaking so frankly about a quite intimate subject when we hardly knew each other. But, when I looked harder, I could see a small tear in her eye which she quickly wiped away. I was about to ask why she seemed so sad when she quickly took control of herself and cracked a joke.

I found Glenda to be extremely good company. I was totally relaxed in her presence although I had the sense she was not telling me everything. She seemed to be holding something back. Something she did not want me to know, or something she did not trust me with. I was not totally sure about he,r but this mysteriousness only added to my growing fondness for her.

We had a couple more drinks and I could feel my head getting slightly fuzzy. After a while we collected our coats and set out for home.

Being late November it was dark when we got outside, but the evening air was remarkably mild. Glenda took hold of my arm and pulled herself tight in to me, which instantly made me feel warm inside and out.

We walked on and as we moved out of the city centre the deserted streets gave me a feeling of peace and solitude. But for the distant sound of traffic on the main road and the dull rumble of a train pulling into Lime Street station, we could have been forgiven for believing we were the only two people in the world.

This thought was broken by the familiar sound of air raid sirens. We looked back to the Liverpool skyline and could see searchlights criss-crossing the night sky, occasionally reflecting back off the barrage balloons that served to protect the port. After a minute or two we could make out the faint outline of German bombers and hear the sound of anti-aircraft guns as they pounded the skies, trying to prevent the Heinkels and Dorniers from dropping their parachute mines, high explosive and incendiary bombs. Despite the mild weather conditions, I shivered momentarily as I thought of those poor people underneath the rain of shrapnel and fire the Nazis were sending down upon them.

We continued on our way, our strides quicker now and with a purpose, desperate to get as far away from the raid as possible and back to the safety we felt in more familiar surroundings.

As we passed an alleyway, Glenda suddenly pushed into me with such a purpose that I almost fell over. Then she forcibly guided me into the entry and, before I had chance to say anything, to ask her what the hell she was doing, she pushed me up against a wall. With my back pressed against it and her face only inches from mine she looked deep into my eyes. I could see that from the roadway we would not be seen by anyone who may be passing. But then there was nobody around to see us anyway.

'What are you doing?' I asked. 'We need to get to a shelter.'

She did not reply instead forcing her lips onto mine, kissing me with an urgency I could not understand, as though the world was about to end and she had to do this before it did.

I had not experienced anything like this before and I could hardly respond due to the shock of it all. As she bit my lip and put her tongue into my mouth, I felt her hand around the small of my back. Then she was turning us around so that her own back was now against the wall and I was leaning into her, our positions suddenly reversed.

I soon started to relax and to kiss her back, as furiously as she was kissing me. I kissed her face, her mouth, her neck, her ears and she did the same, the both of us lost in the moment.

And then she took hold of my hand and placed it inside her coat and over the next few minutes, whilst people only three or four miles away were experiencing hell, I myself discovered heaven in a dimly lit back street in Liverpool.

'Where the hell have you been? said father as I closed the front door behind me. 'We've been worried sick about you. What happened to you?'

Although I knew he would have been in the Anderson shelter during the raid, it looked to me as though he had never left his seat the whole time I had been out, as he was sitting in the same position he had been in when I had left almost four hours earlier. When I laughed, I was not sure whether I was laughing at his comment or at the ridiculousness of the whole situation.

'Short raid tonight, thank God,' said mother as I sat down on the sofa next to Jimmy. My brother looked annoyed that I was disturbing him from the book he was reading, wriggling to the side to get away from me, not wanting our bodies to be touching in any way. 'Thank God it lasted only a few minutes. We were worried about you. We thought you might have been caught up in it.'

'No,' I replied. 'I wasn't, thankfully. We could see the bombers as we were walking home. They were targeting the docks again. I'm just glad you weren't working tonight, dad.'

The younger ones, Dorothy, Hilary and Francis were no doubt tucked up in bed, leaving the four of us in the front room together.

I looked around the room at my mother and father sitting in their chairs, father smoking his pipe and mother knitting something or other. What it was I could not quite make out. The glow from the flickering fire providing them with the light they needed, which gave the room a warmth that matched the mellowness I felt within.

Watching my family settled like this, I felt at that precise moment that life could not get any better. I had a wonderfully close family, I had a good job, I was about to join the navy and I had met the most wonderful girl in the whole world.

Yes, I thought, as I joined my father in watching the flickering flames of the coal fire on the other side of the room, life really could not possibly get any better.

Fourteen

Life could not possibly get any worse.

That was what I thought as I watched in total helplessness as the Junkers dived towards us, its guns blazing ferociously like the Angel of Death, the pilot ignoring the flak bursting in perilous clouds all around him.

'Bloody hell, they're mad!' screamed Ralph. He fired the Oerlikon at the approaching aircraft as if his life depended on it, pumping round after round into the sky.

Which it did. All of our lives depended on the skill of the gunners.

They had come a half hour after I had finished my shift, arriving like a swarm of locusts, hell-bent on wreaking havoc amongst the convoy. This was the worst attack yet. There seemed to be three times as many planes in the sky as compared to the previous day. Whether this was because we were sailing closer to the Luftwaffe bases where more squadrons would be within our range, or whether the Germans had decided they would throw everything they could at us, we were not quite sure. Whatever it was, it meant these attacks were becoming more frequent, more sustained and more violent.

Ralph continued to fire and as his shells burst around the incoming bomber his ordnance was joined by more from the other guns, in a desperate attempt to stop the plane from dropping its bombs onto the ships.

Suddenly smoke appeared from the engine on the right wing of the aircraft and instinctively the pilot pulled back on his control column, attempting to gain altitude to prevent from losing control. As the Junkers ascended higher into the air, its underbelly became exposed and was immediately hit with more rounds, raking huge holes into the fuselage. Frantically, the pilot struggled to keep control but it was a fruitless task as it was now too badly damaged to stay in the air. Suddenly it twisted, almost like a dying bird in mid flight, and came crashing down into the sea to the side of the ship.

I could see the pilot and co-pilot in the cockpit as the bomber lay on top of the water. They were still alive and I looked on in morbid fascination as they struggled to release their straps in a desperate attempt to escape, their aircraft quickly becoming their coffin. However, the damage to the plane was too severe, the holes too large, and I could see clearly the seawater entering the cockpit around them. For a brief moment the pilot's eyes met mine and then, with a sudden lurch, the water took hold and dragged the battered aircraft beneath the waves. A few seconds later they were gone, all traces of their existence banished to the sea bed.

There was no time to celebrate the saving of the ship as more planes swooped down. Like kestrels attacking their prey they came at us. We fired our guns in a relentless barrage to keep them at bay. There was no time to look around and see how the rest of the convoy was getting on, but I could hear explosions in the distance and a strong smell of burning filled the air. I was conscious of the need for the *Virtuous* to carry out its primary task of protecting the convoy from U-boats and hoped these constant air attacks did not cover the German submarines breaching the flimsy cordon around the merchant ships.

Then, as quickly as the attack had started, the German planes turned and headed for home, their fuel and ammunition exhausted.

The sun was getting low in the sky as the nights drew in quicker the further north we sailed. I prayed it would not be too long before we rounded the northernmost part of Norway and could then sail across the Barents Sea to the Kola Inlet and Murmansk. The enemy planes would not attack when it got dark, but we knew it was at this time the convoy was most vulnerable to attacks from the deep. The German U-boat commanders preferred to use the half light at dawn and dusk. It was easier to see the ships silhouetted against the sky and harder for our lookouts to spot them in the fading light, their surfaced hulls blending into the shadows of the black water.

Exhaustion was becoming a problem for the crew. When not involved with our primary duties, there was always something we had to be doing. Whether this was repelling enemy air attacks or cleaning and preparing weapons, the killicks, P.O.s and Chiefs always seemed to have tasks for us, something else with which to occupy our time.

HELL AND HIGH WATER

We got our sleep wherever and whenever we could. Sometimes I found it hard to keep my eyes open in the radio room. On occasion, it was only due to Wally's constant banter that kept me awake. Somehow I knew he was doing this for that very reason, to stop me from falling asleep and landing myself in trouble.

'Do you think they'll ever stop?' I asked him that evening. 'Do you think we'll soon be out of their range?'

'Probably when we get back to Iceland, yes,' he said glumly, which was no comfort to me. 'They've bases all over Norway, George, and some not far from Murmansk too, where we're headed. And the U-boats haven't even started yet. We know they're out there, don't we? You read that signal yourself.'

'I know,' I said, reluctantly agreeing with him.

I was hoping he would be able to offer me some words of comfort, but he could not. I realised it was unfair of me to constantly lean on him when I was anxious. It was very selfish on my part and he was probably feeling as worried as I was.

'Looks like we lost another,' he said. 'Not sure which it was, but a merchantman went down in that last attack. With all hands too.'

'I thought as much,' I replied. 'Didn't see it but could smell the burning in the air.'

'It's horrible,' he replied. 'Can you imagine it. Most of those blokes would've been sailing long before the war, probably thinking it was a nice way to earn a living. Getting to see a bit of the world and all. Then this bloody Hitler goes and spoils it and they find themselves on ships heading to places they never thought they'd ever go to. Then they get shot at and killed because of it. I'm sure none of them signed up for this.'

As I contemplated his words, I thought back to my own excitement at being called up and my enthusiasm to get started. I felt a little foolish now.

'You see, George,' he continued. 'We can't really complain, now, can we? Most of the lads on board are probably volunteers. We made the conscious decision to join the Royal Navy and even if we did it before the war started, we knew that one day we may be in situations such as the one we find ourselves in right now. My point is, those merchant lads out there, they probably have a more dangerous job than we do. It's those the Nazis need to sink, more so than us.'

Wally had a point. It was ironic those not in the uniform of the military were in the most peril. But then, we were all in danger and one life was as valuable as the next ,in my opinion.

Suddenly the ship shook violently and I was thrown from my chair, my head hitting the desk as I fell. As I tried to right myself, Wally was thrown on top of me as the ship lurched savagely from side to side.

'For Christ's sake!' shouted Wally. 'This is all we bloody need.'

Quickly I scrambled back into my chair and put on the headset that had been yanked from my head, which was already starting to throb from the whack I had just received.

At first I thought the ship had been torpedoed but it soon became apparent we were being hit by a sudden

HELL AND HIGH WATER

and ferocious storm. In all the excitement of the air attack I had quite forgotten about the recent signal advising us more bad weather was on the way.

Again, just like on the trip from Scotland to Reykjavik, the ship was tossed around wildly and savagely, the sea lifting it up and throwing it down again like an angry rollercoaster, pitching it from side to side in its attempts to do to us what the Nazis were yet to achieve. With each roll, each climb to the top of the mountainous waves and each dip into the watery valleys, we were thrown around, cracking our heads against bulkheads, doors and ladders, sliding us along decks and throwing our equipment and gear all around us. This lasted for the remainder of the day and deep into the night.

It was impossible to do our jobs to any kind of acceptable standard and, for the main, we simply clung on for our lives, convinced that at some point, the ship would turn over and we would all be dragged down to a watery grave. Men hung on desperately to any piece of furniture that was riveted or screwed down, unwilling to move for fear of being thrown violently against the bulkheads.

But the ship did not turn over. It did not sink. For some reason, probably known only to him, God was on our side that night and with his protection we managed to keep afloat. By the morning the storm that had hit us so hard for those few hours had vanished, almost as quickly as it had appeared. The two extremes in the weather was difficult to comprehend.

I wandered out onto deck and looked around. The stillness of the sea, compared to the tempest that had struck the previous night, was incomprehensible to me. I could not understand it. I could not believe that this very ocean that had tried to kill us all the night before now looked so peaceful and tranquil.

It soon became clear the convoy had been dispersed by the storm. I scanned the horizon and could not see a single merchant ship anywhere. Word soon got round that two merchant ships had been sunk by the weather and the convoy was scattered over a very large area. It was obvious we had to form up as soon as possible as the danger from U-boats and enemy aircraft was still very real. Whilst they were somewhere out there unprotected, they were extremely vulnerable.

'Let's just hope that if we don't know where they are, then the krauts will have even less of an idea,' said Wally when I met him in the galley. 'Sit down and have something to eat. I bet you've not eaten anything for hours.'

'I've not slept for hours, either,' I said, taking a corned beef sandwich from his plate.

'Oi,' he said as I bit into the bread. 'Go get your own. There's loads over there.'

I pulled my tongue out at him.

'Do we know which ships were lost?' I asked.

'I know as much as you,' he replied. 'No idea. But the rumour is two have gone. Maybe Jack and Harry have a better idea. They might have had a signal about it.'

'Yeah,' I said. 'Maybe.'

The news that two more of the ships we were supposed to protect had gone to the bottom of the sea was

HELL AND HIGH WATER

instantly depressing. I knew we were doing the best we could but it was still not good enough. The Nazis were having success against us and I wondered just how many more would be lost before we made it to the sanctuary of the Kola Inlet, still some days away yet.

Seeing the look of despondency on my face Wally said, 'Don't take all this to heart, George. There really isn't a lot we can do about it, when all's said and done. Those two ships were taken by the weather and there's nothing any of us can do about that. We just have to keep doing what we're doing and see where it takes us.'

As always, I knew Wally's words were correct. Nevertheless, they did not stop me from feeling gloomy.

As the sun began to rise higher we were aware we were in a very precarious situation. The half light of dawn was the opportune time for the U-boats to attack. With the convoy being dispersed and struggling to get back into a formation that could be better protected, any enemy submarine commander worth his salt could use this time to launch an attack on any straggling merchant ships, or Royal Navy vessels they came across. We prayed the spotters in the crow's nest would be highly alert and be able to see any submarines that ASDIC may miss, or the tracks of enemy torpedoes fired in our direction. We hoped the current calm sea would assist them with their task.

I left Wally sitting at the table in the galley and made my way to the mess deck. There were a couple of hours to kill before our next stint in the radio room and I wanted to use the time to try and get an hour's sleep.

When I arrived, I was surprised to find the room almost empty. The quietness suited me and, as I made myself comfortable in my hammock, my mind once again drifted to thoughts of home.

Fifteen

Liverpool

Glenda and I could not get enough of each other. Every spare hour and every spare minute we had, we would try to spend together. We were desperate to pack as much as we could into the few weeks we had before I had to head off to the navy.

I managed to persuade Mister Johnson to let me lock up the printshop three nights a week, telling him I wanted to stay late to complete my qualification before I left for the military. He was more than happy for me to do this and thought my conscientiousness was commendable. However, the real reason was so I could sneak Glenda into the building when the place was empty. This was the only time and place where we could really be alone. I would look forward to it all day, thinking about nothing else.

My demeanour on these days did not go unnoticed by Billy.

'What the bloody hell's the matter with you?' he asked one afternoon during our tea break.

'What do you mean?' I replied. 'There's nothing the matter with me.'

'You've been walking around with a big cheesy grin on your face all day. And, if I can be frank, you've been bloody useless too. It's slightly irritating, to be honest with you.'

'Oh, don't be so miserable,' I replied. 'It's better than walking around with a big frown.'

'I suppose it is,' he replied, taking a sip from his teacup. 'But there's not a lot to be happy about these days, is there? There's a war on. The Germans are routinely bombing the city and I'll be off to the army soon. And you the navy.'

'I know. So that's why we have to make the most of things, don't we?' I replied, smiling at him. 'None of us know when a bomb might fall on us. And who knows what's going to happen to us when we join up.'

'Okay,' he replied, reluctantly agreeing with me. 'I see your point. But stop with that bloody inane grinning. Like I said, it's bloody irritating.'

'I've a lot to grin about.'

'Glenda?' he asked, raising his eyebrows.

'Yes,' I said. 'What about her.'

'What do you mean "what about her?"' he replied coyly. He had what I could only describe as a contemptuous look upon his face.

I placed my cup on the small table in front of us.

'The way you said her name just now. Is there something wrong? Have you something to say?'

He sighed and sat back in his chair.

'Oh, it's nothing, George. Nothing to worry about.'

'I'll be the judge of that,' I replied. 'Come on. Out with it.'

I was starting to get a little irritated by his comments and the way he was saying them. It was as though he knew something about my girlfriend I did not. Whatever it may be, he looked not to be too impressed with it.

HELL AND HIGH WATER

'Just something that Iris said to me the other day,' he replied.

I stared at him and could tell he was beginning to feel uncomfortable. He was moving into territory he was not content with, an area of conversation he had not expected.

'What did she say?'

'Oh, it's probably nothing, George. I was just saying that the both of you look good together and that… And then she said something that concerned me a little.'

'Which was?'

'That maybe Glenda isn't all she seems,' he said boldly, sitting up straighter in the chair. 'Her life isn't as straightforward as you'd think, George. There may be a little secret lurking there somewhere, you know. The reason why she left Wales.'

'She left Wales to find work here.'

'That's what they're all saying but I think there may be more to her story than that. Think about it,' he continued. 'Why would anyone want to head to a city where bombs are falling almost every night, when most people here just want to leave? She's done the opposite of what they're doing with the children. Where we're shipping out our kids to safety in the countryside, she's come in the other direction. Does that make any kind of sense to you?'

Although I was getting annoyed with Billy for casting doubt on Glenda's character, I felt there could be something in his words. What he was saying made sense to me. Now that I thought about it, Glenda being in Liverpool seemed more than a little odd. Why had her parents been so happy for her to leave Flint and why had Iris's parents been equally happy to take her in when there was barely any room for the family as it was?

'Come on, boys, tea break over.'

I looked up and saw Mister Johnson at the doorway, the clipboard he carried everywhere held at his side and a pencil balanced behind his good ear.

'No problem, Mister Johnson,' replied Billy standing up immediately. The relieved look on his face told me he was happy with the sudden cessation of our conversation. 'We'll be right there.'

Reluctantly I took my cup to the sink and rinsed it before placing it on the draining board. As I followed Billy out of the break room, I could not help thinking about what he had just said to me. For the first time since I had met her, I was starting to feel a little uneasy about Glenda Bradshaw and I did not like the feeling.

I did not like it one bit.

'What's the matter, George. You've been very quiet.'

We were lying on the threadbare couch in the printshop rest room, the same piece of furniture I had had my rather awkward conversation with Billy a few hours earlier. I grinned to myself at the difference in the two situations. If he only knew what we had been up to, more than just a few times on this very spot, I don't know what he would have said.

I had waited for the workshop to empty, telling Mister Johnson I wanted to do a few more things before I

HELL AND HIGH WATER

left for the evening. Thinking I was a dedicated employee, he was happy to give me the keys to the building again. I then waited for twenty minutes before going to the back door and letting Glenda in. By locking us both inside I knew we would not be disturbed.

This had all been Glenda's idea. The first time we had done it, it had gone so well that we realised it was a foolproof plan. And so we had embarked on what was to be a fairly full-blooded, energetic relationship, all held within the walls of Johnson's Printworks Limited.

We simply could not keep our hands off each other, the attraction between us magnetic and extremely physical. We took some mad chances. We were young and in the heat of the moment things could sometimes go a little too far. But then we would laugh at our foolishness and hold each other until we dozed off. On one occasion we had fallen into a deep sleep and it had been nearly eleven o'clock by the time we had woken, dressing quickly and almost sprinting back to our homes. I had told my parents, who had stayed up waiting for me, that I had gone for a drink with friends after work and had lost track of time. I do not think for one second either of them believed me. They had just been thankful I had not come to any misfortune.

However, that night I had been a little subdued afterward and as we lay there, holding each other, I realised this was due to the conversation I had earlier with Billy.

'It's nothing,' I eventually replied.

She was not convinced.

'I can see it's not nothing,' she said, sitting up, holding the blanket we had been lying on to cover her naked body. 'What's the matter, George? You don't seem yourself tonight.'

I absentmindedly ran my finger along her hip, which remained uncovered, tracing my fingertip along the silvery lines that ran vertically along the tops of her legs. She quickly pushed my hand away and covered her hip with the blanket.

'It's just something that Billy said earlier,' I replied. I did not really want to tell her, not wanting her to develop any animosity towards my friend, but there was something about being in her presence that made me speak openly and frankly.

Immediately she sat up straighter and leaned over to the side of the couch for her underwear, which she had earlier thrown in a heap with her other clothes.

'And what did he have to say about me?'

'It wasn't what he said, more the way he said it,' I replied. I was now starting to feel very uneasy and wished I had simply kept my mouth shut. This must have been how Billy had felt earlier when I quizzed him.

Her face had taken on a serious expression. Even though she had not yet heard what I was about to say, that she was annoyed nevertheless. This defensive attitude did nothing to allay my concern.

'Come on, George, spit it out. What has he been saying about me?'

I leaned over for my trousers and as I put them on, I replied, 'He was just wondering the reasons why you left North Wales for here. He seems to think there may be more to you than what you've told us. He can't see the reason for you coming to Liverpool when you were safe in Flint.'

'Does he now?' she said.

Her eyes were starting to fill with tears and I immediately felt guilty for telling her. Guilty that my thoughtless words had caused this reaction.

'And what do you think?' she asked, turning her head away from me as she put on her blouse.

'I don't think anything,' I replied. This was partially true. I had not given it any thought until my conversation with Billy earlier. I had taken everything at face value. Maybe I was too trusting, maybe I was naive, or maybe I just had no reason to worry and all was well with her.

'You clearly do. I can see it in your face,' she said sternly and then rose to finish off getting dressed.

I did not know how to reply and so said nothing, dressing myself in the now awkward silence that had developed between us.

'Take me home, George Martin,' she said once we were both fully clothed.

The walk back to Russell Street was completed without any words being spoken between us. I began to worry this was it for us, that the relationship was over. Despite her petite size, I struggled to keep up with her as she marched purposefully along, ignoring all around her. The early evening was quite pleasant and normally we would have strolled along, her arm linked in mine, but after the conversation we had just had it was clear she was not pleased with me.

As we reached the corner of Russell Street, she turned to me.

'George,' she said softly, looking up at me as I faced her. 'If you're to continue courting me then I really must insist you close your ears to idle gossip and speculation. I'm new to this city and am just finding my way. I don't want anything spoiled because you choose to listen to tittle-tattle.'

'I don't choose to listen to tittle-tattle,' I responded, affronted. 'I was merely letting you know what Billy said.'

'Well, Billy Jones is a bloody idiot,' she said sharply. 'What does he know about me? What gives him the right to cast doubts upon my character?'

'I don't think he was trying to do that,' I replied. 'He was just…'

'Like I say, he's an idiot,' she interrupted. 'Anyway, it's time I got home. Aunt Ida will be wondering where I am. I don't want to get into any trouble again, like last week.'

With that she turned and walked away.

I watched as she got to the door, opened it and walked in, closing it behind her without looking back or giving me a wave or a cheeky smile, something she would normally do.

I could not help thinking that something had just been lost between us and I had been the cause of it.

I walked the remainder of the journey home somewhat sullenly. As I hung my coat on the hook in the hallway I became aware of my father standing in the kitchen doorway, my mother behind him.

'You lied to me,' he said.

HELL AND HIGH WATER

'I'm sorry…'

'Don't come that with me, you little sod,' he said. 'You lied to me. That girl you've been seeing. She's the same Glenda who's living with those Catholics around the corner. The Shepherds.'

I was not in the mood for this.

'So what?' I almost shouted. 'So what? What does it matter what religion she is? She doesn't even go to church anyway. And neither do you for that matter. So what's all the fuss about?'

'How dare you speak to your father like that!' he said, approaching me, menacingly.

'What's going on?'

I looked up to see Jimmy coming down the stairs.

'Nothing to concern you, young man,' replied father. 'Go back upstairs.'

'Yes,' I said. 'Go back upstairs, Jimmy.'

Putting his attention back to me, father said, 'You know full well why I can't stand them. Look at this leg,' he tapped his knee. 'This is because of them. The reason I've had this bloody limp all my life. It's all their fault.'

'I thought the police did that to you,' I replied insolently. 'And even if it was a Catholic's fault, like you want to believe, then what has it got to do with Glenda? She wasn't even born when it happened. And she's from Wales.'

'You cheeky little sod. I ought to give you a good hiding.'

'Eddie!' shouted my mother. 'Please stop this…'

'Anyway,' I said. 'You have nothing to worry about anymore. I doubt I'll be seeing her again anyway.'

'Good,' said father, suspiciously. 'That prevents me from having to ban you from seeing her.'

'You couldn't have stopped me,' I replied. 'I'm eighteen now and I can make my own decisions about who I see and who I don't.'

'Not while you're living under my roof, you can't,' he replied. 'I'm your father and I'll be the one who decides what goes on under this roof… And who lives under it, come to that.'

With that, he turned around and walked back into the living room to no doubt sit in his chair by the fire, as he did every evening he was not working.

Mother stepped out of the kitchen.

'Try not to hold this against him,' she said to me softly. 'You know what he's like.'

'I do,' I replied. 'But all that was so long ago and things have changed in this city since then. People don't have the same religious intolerance anymore. People don't care about it. Those divisions are long gone. There's a war going on and we should all be pulling together now, not arguing over ancient differences. And, let's face it mam, there's not really much difference between what Catholics and Protestant think anyway. And we're all scousers too. It makes no sense to me.'

She listened but did not reply.

'So is it true then?' she asked.

'Is what true?'

'That you've stopped seeing this Glenda girl?'

'Yes,' I replied. 'I think so. We had a bit of an argument earlier and I doubt she'll want to see me again.'

HELL AND HIGH WATER

'Okay,' she replied. 'Maybe it's all for the best.'

Then she brushed past me and joined my father in the living room.

I stood in the doorway for a few moments watching them sitting there together. I hated falling out with them. I loved them both very much and knew they loved me back and just wanted the best for all of us. But my father's bigotry was something I found extremely hard to accept.

As I lay there that night struggling to sleep, my thoughts went back to Glenda and what had happened. Was there anything in what Billy had told me? Was she being too defensive? Many questions were running around my head, but the one I wanted an answer to most of all was did she want to see me again? After what we had been doing in Mister Johnson's building, then I sincerely hoped she did. Otherwise there may well be something more to her than I originally thought and Billy may have been right all along.

Sixteen

I was awoken sharply by someone shaking me quite violently. At first, I thought I was back in my bed in Liverpool and it was my younger brother Jimmy larking about.

However this feeling of disorientation was quickly gone as I looked into the now bearded face of Petty Officer Singer. 'Come on, laddie,' he said, almost apologetically. 'Your services are needed. Get your gear on and follow me.'

With a sigh I clambered out of my hammock and grabbed the leather jerkin I had left on the table beneath me. We now slept fully clothed, not daring to take off any of our gear other than our heavy coats, due to the penetrating cold that now infected the ship. Sometimes we had to shake ice from the blankets we used to wrap around ourselves when attempting to get some rest. It was like sleeping inside a refrigerator.

We had reached the northernmost tip of Norway and were now heading along the Barents Sea south of Svalbard near Bear Island. The first leg of the journey was nearly over and it would only be few more days before we arrived at the Kola Inlet, where we would leave the merchant ships to make their way along Kola Bay to the port of Murmansk to offload their cargoes. Outside temperatures were reaching minus twenty degrees centigrade. It was torture to stay on deck for any length of time, particularly when the sea was rough. The moisture on our skin quickly turned to ice and, if we did not cover ourselves up well, there was a danger of developing frostbite. After only a few minutes, ice would form on our beards, eyelashes and eyebrows and the irritation and pain we endured when we returned indoors was shocking as our eyelashes thawed and dropped out.

A group of seven sailors had gathered near the doorway to the foredeck. As I joined them, Singer was just starting his pep talk.

'Okay, laddies. It's a bit bracing out there today. I understand the temperature has reached a low of minus twenty. In short, it's a tad fresh. Keep yourselves covered at all times and on no account touch anything with your bare skin unless you want to stick to it.' He indicated a pile of tools that had been placed near to the exit door. 'Grab a pick, crowbar, axe, anything you can find. We need to clear as much ice and snow off the deck as possible.'

I walked forward and took hold of a crowbar. Placing it under my armpit, I took off my gloves and pulled my scarf over my mouth and nose. I then put up my hood, put my gloves back on and followed the others outside.

If I thought the cold inside the ship was barely endurable, it was nothing compared to what greeted us as we walked outside. Although the sea was calmer than usual, it was still quite choppy. As the ship rose and fell in the swell, rhythmically plodding forward, I struggled to keep my footing. I was extremely glad the rubber-soled boots we had been issued had a strong grip, as to slip and fall overboard would mean certain death. There was no way anybody could survive for too long in the water.

For this reason, Singer tied a length of rope around each man, securing him to a main hawser line that stretched from fore to aft. If any man slipped and fell, then he would only slide the length of his rope and would be prevented from going overboard.

The whole of the ship seemed to have turned white. I could not see a single spot not covered in snow or ice. The bulkheads, funnels and guns were caked so thick it would probably take a number of shifts to get rid of it all.

'If we don't get this cleared, the ship could capsize,' said a killick stoker to my right, his scarf muffling his words. 'The ship's hull is very shallow and if we get top heavy then we could quite easily flip over. And the guns and fire control systems are bloody useless if they're all iced up… Shit me… It's bloody cold.'

This was not an understatement. I had never known anything like it in all my life. I decided there and then I would sooner do ten Mediterranean convoys than a single Arctic run. This was no way to live. This was not sailing.

'Let's get to work then,' I replied.

We walked forward and I started to smash at the ice covering one of the 3 inch heavy gun barrels, huge chunks dropping to the deck. Another group of sailors followed behind, sweeping the ice overboard. I squinted my eyes against the cold wind and found it slightly more bearable if I turned my back to it as I worked, hacking and bashing at any ice I could see, smashing huge lumps from the barrel. Everything was frozen solid. The anchor chains lay beneath nearly a foot of ice, and pins frozen in their shackles had to be beaten free with the mauls and hammers. It was totally exhausting. Each breath was an agony as the icy air filled our lungs. I made a promise to myself that I would never moan about the British winters if I ever made it home again.

Occasionally, as we worked, I heard someone shout out in pain as a badly aimed mallet struck the hand of a sailor, the gloves giving little protection against the heavy tools and the intense cold.

It was not long before we were soaked to the skin. The spray from the sea drenched our clothing. The towels we had put around our necks for added protection became sodden after only a couple of minutes and then started to freeze as the seawater quickly turned to ice. We were all shivering but we knew there was no escape from it. This was important and essential work we were carrying out. We had to do it to stay alive.

It was slow progress but eventually we could see we were having an effect. As we soldiered on, clearing the deck, gunwales and anchor chains, we started to reveal the ship beneath its icy coating.

The sea spray washed over as the ship lurched forward, freezing the instant it landed upon the deck and our clothing. We would brush it off our soaked bodies with our cold, mittened hands whenever we could. It was tiring work and the sweat that formed on any exposed skin would sparkle in the Arctic sunlight, as though we had glitter on our faces. The mucus that ran from our runny noses stuck to our stubble and scarves, gluing the fabric to our skin. And how my ears throbbed beneath my ineffective hood!

We could not do this for too long. It was impossible to stay outside for more than a few minutes for fear of getting frostbite or losing concentration and doing ourselves an injury. After only twenty minutes of hard graft we were ready to go back inside and let some other unfortunate buggers take over for a while.

As I was chipping away at an ice covered anchor chain, I suddenly heard a piercing scream behind me.

I turned around and saw Singer striding over to a tall sailor leaning against the 3 inch gun turret.

'What the bloody hell have you done, laddie,' I heard him shout. 'What did I tell you? You stupid bastard.'

The lad screamed again.

'I'm sorry P.O.,' he whimpered.

'There's no point in saying sorry now, is there?' replied Singer. 'For Christ's sake, what the bloody hell were you thinking?'

I followed Singer to the sailor. He was a young lad, probably no older than I was, whose name was Howard. He was leaning against the turret with the palm of his bare hand against the metal structure, clearly stuck fast.

'It won't come off,' he cried. 'My hand's stuck.'

'I can bloody well see it's stuck,' replied Singer, clearly exasperated at the man's stupidity.

'How has this happened?' I asked him.

'I had something in my eye and took my glove off to get it out… Then I slipped and put my hand out to steady myself…'

HELL AND HIGH WATER

'Jesus,' I replied, not knowing what else to say.

'Well we're going to have to get you off it,' replied Singer.

'Maybe you could get some lukewarm water and pour it over?' suggested a sailor to my right. 'Maybe that will free it up.'

'We can try,' replied Singer. 'But it'll probably freeze on his hand as soon as we pour it.'

One of our group was despatched to get some water but I knew even then that this would not work. It was clear to me the lad would just have to bite the bullet and pull it free. Whatever of his hand was left on the turret would just have to remain there.

After a minute, the sailor returned and handed the cup to Singer. Although it had only been out in the open for a matter of seconds, I could see that it was already starting to freeze.

'This is no good,' said Singer and I could see tears forming in Howard's eyes as he realised his situation was becoming hopeless. 'I'm afraid you're just going to have to yank it off.'

I could see his tears starting to freeze and knew we needed to get him inside as soon as possible. His hand was beginning to turn blue and if he was not careful, he would lose it completely.

'Don't thing about it,' I said. 'Just do it. Just yank it away. Your hand looks numb anyway. You probably wont feel a thing.'

'I can't,' he groaned. 'I can't...'

'Come here,' said Singer taking hold of his arm. 'I'll do it for you.'

'No. Please...'

Before he could protest any further, Singer tucked himself under Howard's armpit and, using the full weight of his body, pushed forward firmly and sharply.

Howard let out an ear piercing scream and when I looked at the turret, I could see most of the skin of his palm and fingers had remained on the metal structure. It was so cold the blood and skin quickly froze over, the frost evident immediately on the abandoned flesh.

'Get this bloody fool inside,' said Singer turning away from him.

I took hold of his good arm and the killick who had told me of the importance of clearing the ice took the arm with the damaged hand.

As we assisted Howard into the forecastle he began to weep quietly as he clutched his damaged hand to his chest. It would be extremely painful once it started to thaw. I did not envy him the suffering he was about to endure.

'I can't believe he's done that,' he said between sobs. 'I can't believe he's just ripped my hand off.'

'Oh, shut up with your bloody blubbering,' said the killick, sternly. 'You should be thanking him. He's probably just saved your life, you idiot. What on earth were you thinking?'

We dropped Howard off with a very annoyed doctor at the sickbay and returned outside.

As we got on deck, we met Singer coming in the other direction.

'Don't worry about it, laddies,' he said. 'We're done for now. Another group is coming out in a few

HELL AND HIGH WATER

minutes. Get yourselves a bite to eat and a hot drink and thanks for all your efforts.'

I was grateful my stint clearing the deck had come to an end although I knew this would not be the only time I would be called upon for such duties. This was an important job that needed doing and required keeping on top of. The last thing we wanted was to avoid the German U-boats and aircraft only to sink because we did not clear the ship of ice. It would be the ultimate irony. If it meant a few hours out in freezing temperatures, then so be it.

Once inside I went in search of Wally who had somehow evaded Singer's little ice clearing party. It always surprised me how he managed to get out of difficult tasks and duties, but after nearly freezing myself half to death, I did not blame him.

I found him in the galley reading a dog-eared paperback, a cup of hot tea sitting on the table in front of him.

'Ah, George,' he said, on seeing me approach. 'Why don't you get yourself a nice beverage and come and join me?'

I had to smile. There was something about being in Wally Honeyman's company that made everything seem a little brighter and more bearable. He had a natural gift of being able to uplift me even in the direst of circumstances, which this journey certainly was. And all this despite his own troubled background. I was slightly in awe of him.

A minute later I sat opposite him, a cup of sweet steaming tea in my hands. Behind him, over his left shoulder, a porthole had frozen solid, ice and snow covering the outside making it impossible to view out.

'Not a real lot to see out there anyway,' he said, noticing my gaze. 'It's just water and ice and stuff. Pretty boring really.'

'It's okay for you,' I said. 'I've just been out in it. Breaking ice.'

'I would have joined you,' he replied. 'But I wasn't invited. Always seem to be left out of the parties, me, you know.'

'Hardly a party,' I smiled. I nodded to the book in his hand. 'What's that you're reading?'

He held it up so I could see the title.

'This thing,' he replied. '*Oliver Twist* by Charles Dickens.'

'I didn't know you read books,' I said, sipping at my brew.

'A man of many surprises, me, George,' he smirked.

'Never a truer word spoken,' I said.

'It's quite appropriate, this story,' he said quietly, looking down at it. 'In a way you could say it's about me. Dickens could have written this book with yours truly in mind. A young orphan gets mixed up with the wrong sort and lands himself in a bit of lumber. Pretty much like my life for the past couple of years, don't you think?.'

I laughed. 'So you consider me the wrong sort, do you?'

'No, not you, George. Although I'd say you're like the Artful Dodger to my Oliver. What do you reckon?'

HELL AND HIGH WATER

'Hmm, I'm not too sure about that,' I responded. 'Wasn't the Dodger a little bit of a scallywag?'

Wally burst out laughing.

'Scallywag. I love it. You don't half make me laugh, George. Yes, I'd say you were a bit of a scallywag on the quiet, after what you've told me.'

I was glad my face was still red from being outside in the elements so Wally could not see me blushing.

'I've read this book a thousand times,' he said. 'I love it. I think maybe it's because of the happy ending. The kid goes through all sorts of problems and dangers, but in the end everything is all right. Everything turns out fine for him. Maybe I'm just a bit of a romantic at heart.'

'Can't say as I've ever read it,' I told him.

'You can borrow this, if you like,' he replied, offering the book to me.

'That's very kind of you,' I replied. 'But please finish it first.'

'Like I said, I've read it a thousand times. Please... Take it.'

There was a look of excitement in his eyes as I took the book from him. I was taken by his enthusiasm and decided I would definitely read it. If nothing else it would give me some escape from all that was happening.

Suddenly I felt a pain in my eyelids. The thawing out process had begun. As I rubbed my eyes I could feel some of my eyelashes falling out. I had seen this happening to others and they had complained about how much it hurt. Now it was happening to me I could fully understand the reason for their complaints. It was very sore and, after much rubbing, I could sense my eyes were beginning to redden.

'Bloody hell, George,' said Wally. 'Be careful. You'll rub them out altogether if you carry on like that. Then how are you going to read the book?'

Despite the discomfort I was in I smiled at him.

'Maybe I just need some rest,' I replied. 'I'll be all right in a few minutes.'

'We're on duty in an hour, so if you're going to shut your eyes for a bit, then you'd better be sharp. Go on. Try and grab a few minutes and I'll come and get you when it's time to relieve Jack and Harry.'

Taking his advice, I stood up to leave. As I reached the exit I turned and looked back at him. As he raised his hand in a gesture of farewell, a thought crossed my mind.

He looked like the loneliest person I had ever seen in my life.

HELL AND HIGH WATER

Seventeen

That evening, in the half light of dusk, I found myself again clearing ice and snow from the forward deck. It seemed every spare minute away from the radio room had to be spent doing something active and I, along with many of my shipmates, was getting extremely exhausted. The constant air attacks and ice clearing duties, interspersed with our main roles, was beginning to take its toll on all of us.

It was too cold to spend very long on deck so the work was done by a number of teams, spending only fifteen minutes at a time, chipping at the ice with picks, axes and mauls and then sweeping it overboard into the Arctic Ocean. The fear of capsizing made us work doubly hard. As we worked we could see progress being made, which did give us a slight uplift in our battered morale.

I looked out to the north. The ships to our port side, silhouetted against the evening sky, stretched out for many miles. It had taken the best part of twenty-four hours for them to form up in convoy again following the storm that had dispersed them the previous day. In the far distance beyond, I could make out the shapes of icebergs and floes, the avoidance of them the sole reason for us sailing this far south and putting us within range of the German bombers. I wondered if future convoys, those that would take place during the summer months, would be any less dangerous. Surely we were travelling during the worst time of year. The bad weather, extreme temperatures and the route which took us closer to the enemy was more hazardous than what our colleagues would face when summer arrived, I was sure. However, the arrival of summertime would bring more daylight hours and therefore more chance of prolonged enemy air attacks. I was not sure which I preferred. I realised I favoured neither. Joining the navy had initially been an adventure and although we had been in constant danger during the Malta convoys, I had still found it strangely enjoyable compared to what we had had to endure on this voyage. There was nothing enjoyable about any of it. This was hell.

As I looked out at the ships as we sailed eastward, I suddenly felt an inner peace. A calmness within me that I had not felt in many days. This remote area of the world looked for the most part one of the most tranquil places you could imagine. The clear sky, calm sea and emptiness of the place could make you think all was well in the world if you did not know any better. If you took away all the ships from this scene and disregarded the freezing cold, then it may not be such a bad place to be. A place where you could find a real peace.

We were invaders, after all. All of us. Both us and the Germans should not be here. This place did not belong to any of us.

As I chipped away at the ice, I suddenly heard a strange noise. A sound that made all of us stop what we were doing for a moment and listen. Amongst the rumbling of the ship's engines and the splashes it made as it propelled forward, we could hear an odd sound reverberating across the ocean. It was similar in tone to that of a foghorn, deep and vibrating, yet more rhythmic, rising and falling in an almost tuneful way. And it was coming from more than one direction, as though one was calling and another replying, singing to each other in the early evening.

I felt a shiver run down my spine and goosebumps grow on my arms but knew it was nothing to do with the freezing temperatures.

'What the hell is that?' asked a sailor to my right.

'I've no idea,' I replied.

'Don't worry your heads, boys,' said the chief mate who was leading our party. 'It's just the whales calling out to each other.'

We listened for a minute longer. The sounds seemed so peaceful and calming. We became lost in the relaxing atmosphere they had created. It was wonderful to hear, beautiful even. As we listened to these magnificent animals calling out to each other, the irony of the situation was not lost on us. Here we were, human beings invading their environment with our weapons of war and death, and yet they still sang their songs of peace amongst us, giving us an alternative viewpoint of the world. As though they were telling us we did not have to do what we were doing, that there was an alternative way. They had given us a yearning for a brighter future in a world where there was no longer any conflict, no longer any death.

'Come on, boys,' shouted the chief mate, breaking us from this reverie. 'Back to work. The sooner this ice is clear the sooner we can get back inside. If…'

JOHN McKAY

He was interrupted by a flash of light that lit up the night sky. Where for a few moments we were all taken away to a place of peace and of hope, we were immediately brought back to our own reality.

A couple of miles out to sea the fading light was brought back to full brightness, an explosion of orange flame illuminating the sea and sky all around, as if the the sun was rising again before it had fully set. For a second I was transfixed, not fully understanding what had taken place. I caught myself looking over my shoulder to the bridge where I saw the captain and Mister Guthrie looking out of the window. For a brief moment my eyes met with Guthrie's but he quickly turned away to talk to the captain, who had a telephone receiver to the side of his head and was no doubt barking orders into it.

Then the noise hit me, the unmistakeable roar of an explosion and although it was some distance away, it filled my ears and shook me to my core.

The *Virtuous* suddenly lurched to port and I turned my head back to the light, which I now realised was one of our ships. It was obvious to me that whatever had happened to it was catastrophic. We could see further explosions taking place along the length of the vessel. I could not tell if it was a merchantman or a warship but, as we started to gain on it, it became clear it was the latter.

We began to slip and slide along the deck as the *Virtuous* gained speed and had to grab onto whatever we could to steady ourselves.

'Inside, everybody,' shouted the chief mate and so we immediately headed to the forecastle door, freeing our lines from the hawser as we did so, slipping and knocking into each other as we raced to the door. The action stations klaxon was now sounding throughout the ship and I realised that instead of going inside I would have to take up my position at the Oerlikon with Ralph Reid, exposing myself to the freezing cold for much longer than I had initially anticipated.

As it was clear the threat was not from the air, I took my time, first visiting the mess deck and swapping some of the drenched clothing, stuffing dry towels inside my jerkin and wrapping another around my neck like a scarf. It was obvious this was a U-boat attack and we were now heading out to hunt and kill it.

A minute later I was standing beside Ralph as he chipped away at the gun with a claw hammer, attempting to remove the ice that had set in a solid block over it.

'Bloody hell, George,' he said. 'I'm not sure I'll be able to get this thing to work. It's frozen solid.'

'A bit like me,' I replied humourlessly. 'You're probably wasting your time, Ralph.'

He glanced at me for a second but continued to hack at the ice nevertheless. I wrapped my arms around my body and shivered.

As we drew closer to the stricken vessel we could see it was a corvette, HMS *Dreyfus*, and it was in terrible trouble. We were still some distance from it but it was obviously in massive distress. Fires burned along its decks and the bridge was bent at an angle away from the ship. It looked like the torpedo had hit amidships and exploded in the engine room below the water line. Fires had quickly spread and without the engines, it was moving very slowly in the water, merely its momentum keeping it moving at all. It was a sitting duck for another shot. We could see matelots scrambling to the lifeboats to escape the sinking, their senior officers probably dead from the damage to the shattered and twisted bridge.

And then time seemed to stand still for a moment. The night sky was again lit up as the *Dreyfus's* magazine exploded, ripping the ship in two before my eyes. I could feel the heat cutting through the ice cold of the Arctic night despite it being almost a mile away and it made me press myself into the bulkhead at the side of the Oerlikon. Even from this distance I could hear the screams of the wounded and dying, as in a panic, they abandoned ship, some of them jumping from the sides, choosing to freeze to death in the icy waters of the Barents Sea rather than burn aboard the ship.

I thought about the Germans who had done this. Did they care about the lives they were taking? Did the U-boat commanders have any compassion for their fellow sailors as they fired their torpedoes into the sides of the Allied shipping. They could not have. They did it all with an evil efficiency. I supposed it was the same for us as we dropped our depth charges on top of them whenever we had the chance. I supposed they were doing their jobs just as we had to do ours. The whole thing made me sick to my stomach.

The *Virtuous* was now getting closer to the *Dreyfus* and I could see men who had jumped or been blown into the water thrashing manically in an attempt to keep afloat. Oil burned around them and we could

HELL AND HIGH WATER

clearly hear their screams across the waves as their heads and torsos burned in the fiery water whilst their legs and bellies froze beneath the surface.

We could see some had made it to a lifeboat, around ten sailors all huddled together, two of them frantically rowing the oars in a desperate effort to get away from the doomed ship that was clearly sinking fast, only a few yards from them. More sailors, those too slow to make it to the lifeboats were now jumping into the freezing sea. Fear and despair forcing them to carry out this suicidal act. Clinging on to life if only for a few minutes more.

As we got nearer we could clearly see their faces looking towards us, calling for us to stop and assist them, to pluck them from the sea and rescue them.

But we did not stop. We carried on past them as though they were not even there. Heading out to the open sea to join the other anti-submarine vessels to hunt and destroy those who had done this. I had never felt so helpless, so useless and so powerless in my entire life.

We passed a hundred yards from them and could feel the heat from the burning ship as it started to sink, the air turning to steam as the seawater hit the red-hot superstructure. I could see it burning underwater for a few seconds before the water extinguished the flames, something I could not understand, a phenomenon my brain had no way of processing. It was all as in a dream; a nightmare.

Ralph and I looked down into the water. A lot of the men were clearly dead, their bodies already frozen, their faces covered in ice. The whiteness of their faces akin to ghosts, to spectres that would haunt my dreams for the rest of my days.

And then the *Dreyfus* suddenly lurched and let out a loud groan as though it was still alive, the steel hull twisting and resisting to the last, as it was dragged beneath the waves, the gods of the seas pulling it under. We watched on as those in the lifeboat, those desperate souls who had seen a glimmer of survival, a faint hope of making it out alive, were suddenly sucked back by the pull of the ship's sinking, overturning the wooden boat and throwing them all into the water. We watched on as only three of them resurfaced. One, a young lad no older than myself, managed to crawl onto the overturned lifeboat and cling on. But as we passed I saw him slowly slide back off the hull and into the water, his frozen hands unable to hang on, not having the strength to stay afloat. He slipped beneath the water and was gone forever.

I looked at Ralph and it was obvious to me he was feeling the same as I. I could see in his eyes that he too felt just as helpless, just as useless and just as ashamed as I did. Ashamed that we had borne witness to this and had done nothing about it.

There was a designated rescue ship at the rear of the convoy but we both knew by the time it arrived they would all be gone. All of them. There would be no-one left to rescue, no lives to save, no young men to return back to their mothers, wives, sweethearts. The sea would be their burial ground. The sea had claimed them and the sea would keep them. All eighty five of them.

HELL AND HIGH WATER

I knew that we could not have stopped. Had we done so we too could have been in the sights of the U-boat, that invisible killer that had carried out this heinous act. We had a duty to protect the rest of the convoy and to protect our own crew. But it did not feel right. How could it feel right? We had passed them, watched them die, then sailed on as if it all was unimportant, as though their lives did not matter.

Again I looked at Ralph and realised, through my bleary eyes, that just like me his tears had frozen to his face.

We don't know if we got the U-boat. Not really. We could never be sure.

We rallied with the *Blackfly* and dropped a few depth charges but were never sure if we had damaged it or not. What we did succeed in doing, at least, was to chase it away as there were no more attacks that night.

As I lay in my hammock some hours later, I thought about why they were nicknamed "wolf-packs". They stalked the edges of the convoy, looking for an opening to attack. And when they attacked they did it quickly, violently and efficiently, just like a pack of predators hunting a feed.

My hatred for my enemy was growing. I saw submarine warfare as a coward's way to conduct a sea war. They did it all secretly, killing from a distance, not facing their enemy in a straight one on one fight, firing their torpedoes and then running away. To me, it was the complete opposite to those of the Luftwaffe who braved our anti-aircraft fire and had to come in close to get a kill. At least those pilots stepped forward and faced us and, although we tried to kill them, we had some respect for them.

But not the submariners. They had no honour. They had no shame.

I tried to sleep but thoughts of those men who had died in front of me would not leave my head. Although I was both physically and mentally drained, exhausted like I had never been before in my life, sleep did not come easily. Too many images were running around my head.

I thought back to the final thing I had seen of the *Dreyfus* as we had moved into position to take on the U-boat. There had been nothing left. Nothing other than that one overturned lifeboat bobbing up and down in the water, all the bodies having sunk beneath the waves just like the ship itself. It then occurred to me that they had not even had the time to put on life jackets, the torpedo taking them all by surprise and the destruction of the ship happening so quickly. Not that life jackets would have helped them. The cold would have done for them all, long before the rescue ship would have arrived.

As I lay there with my hands over my face I understood that conflict on the oceans is somewhat different to that on land. There is no detritus of war left behind for others to see. Nobody can view the dead or the twisted, mangled wreckage of corvettes, frigates, destroyers and merchantmen. Whereas on land, where the dead can be collected, buried with ceremony, and monuments raised at the spots where they fell, for the Navy dead it is very different. There are

HELL AND HIGH WATER

no bodies to bury, no towns for relatives to visit later or a place to go to collectively mourn their passing, other than the ports from which they sailed. The sea takes care of all that. The sea cleans it all up and swallows it whole, takes it all away as though it never happened. As though to have carried out these appalling acts is a sacrilege to the very water on which it took place and the sea is having none of it, erasing it from all earthly memory. The battlefield of the ocean looks no different before or after the action takes place; it remains the same, shrouding the evil and horror beneath its waves; all evidence gone. A ship can be sailing along peacefully but within minutes it could be lying at the bottom of the sea, its hull ripped apart by an enemy torpedo, as though its very existence was a lie, all flames extinguished, all engines silenced and the screams of the dying consigned only to haunt the memories of any unfortunate soul who may have borne witness to it. Yes, war in the seas of the Arctic looks cleaner, there is no pock-marked earth left as a visual reminder. But the horrors and suffering are as equally violent and heartbreaking.

Yet still the whales sing.

Eighteen

One thing that could be relied upon, one thing the clocks could be set by; the air attacks.

Between 1400 hours and 1600 hours was the time the Luftwaffe would come. Wave after wave of Heinkel He-111s and Junkers Ju-88 bombers, coming in low to attack the ships with their torpedoes and bombs, strapped to their wings and undercarriages.

From the radio room we could hear the thud of the Bofors guns as they pounded the sky above us and the lurch of the ship as it zig-zagged across the water, causing us to have to grab onto the desk to stop us falling from our chairs.

I hated being inside the ship when it was under attack. It was the not knowing what was going on above us, not being able to see what was happening or to do anything positive to help the situation that got to me. That and the fear of an explosion occurring at any time without any warning that could potentially sink the ship, just like the way the *Dreyfus* had been hit.

I now carried my extra cold weather gear wherever I went. I wanted it within an arm's length as I never knew just when I would have to make an emergency exit. I did not want to freeze to death, the temperatures outside being in the minus twenties. To survive a sinking only to die of hypothermia awaiting a rescue ship brought the fear of God into me, particularly after watching those poor buggers perish the previous evening. Rescue ships could only save those who

HELL AND HIGH WATER

were able to make it to the lifeboats. Anyone in the water would be doomed.

Wally took all of this with an amazing calm.

'Whatever happens, happens,' he would say. 'If you have no control over it, then there's really no point in worrying about it. Worry about the things you do have some control over if you have to worry at all.'

His logic made sense but it did not help me. I worried about it anyway.

Suddenly the ship lurched to port and I fell from my chair, knocking my hip sharply on the floor. A moment later, Wally landed on top of me causing me to painfully bang my head on the wooden deck.

'Jesus! That was close,' said Wally. For the first time I sensed panic in his voice. As he picked himself up, he succeeded in treading on my leg. 'Sorry, George.'

After some struggling, I managed to right myself and get back into my chair.

'Don't worry about it,' I replied. 'Not your fault.'

My head and leg hurt like hell but I put a brave face on it. We could hear the guns increase their rate of fire outside. We both realised the *Virtuous* was being targeted but neither of us said it.

Petty Officer Singer appeared at the door. He looked harassed, sweat at his brow despite the very low temperatures.

'Better get your gear on, laddies,' he said. 'Nothing to worry about, but you better get it on anyway.'

And then he was gone.

'Nothing to worry about, eh?' I said. 'Doesn't sound like it.'

'I think we'd better do as we're told, George,' said Wally. 'Better to be safe than sorry.'

Taking off my headset, which had been pretty much redundant during the last few hours, I put on my leather jerkin and a balaclava, ready to pull down over my face should we need to go outside.

There was a sense of inevitability about it all. We could hear German bombs landing in the sea around us and I felt it was just a matter of time before one of them hit us. This was probably the worst attack we had come under since I had joined the *Virtuous*. I was starting to get very concerned.

Even below deck we could clearly hear the ship taking hits from the machine guns of the enemy aircraft. The shouts and screams of our shipmates as they desperately tried to ward off the attack could also be heard, and again I wished I was above decks despite the obvious danger that would bring. At least then I would know what was going on. At least then I may be able to do something about it.

Then there was an almighty shudder. The whole ship seemed to lift out of the water and vibrate violently. Wally and I clung on to the desks in front of us as all our stationery, cups and hardware fell to the floor. The noise was terrific. A loud shuddering explosion shook the ship and I thought my ears may burst. I looked at Wally and, for the first time ever, I saw terror in his eyes.

'Shit, George,' he said. 'We've been hit.'

I stood up.

'Come on, Wally,' I said. 'We're doing no good in here. Let's see what's happening.'

HELL AND HIGH WATER

Somehow it did not feel as though we were abandoning our posts as we entered the passageway. It felt like the right thing to do. Sailors were running in both directions, some panicking and others with a more ordered purpose.

Grabbing hold of a rating as he barged past me I asked, 'What's happened?'

'Direct hit near the stern,' he said. 'Bomb from a Junkers, I think. Went straight through the deck and exploded. Christ knows how many have been hurt.'

'Are we sinking?' I asked.

'How the fuck should I know?' he responded. 'Now let go of my arm, you idiot, I've got things to do.'

Releasing him I turned to Wally.

'Let's get above deck. If we're going down we need to get to a lifeboat. I'm not going into the water, Wally. I'm not going out that way.'

Wally followed me along the passageway. As we climbed the ladder to the next deck, the boat shuddered again and I nearly fell back onto him. I was starting to panic and had to take a deep breath before I could find the strength to carry on.

The battle was still raging in the sky above us. Despite being damaged, the crew of the *Virtuous* were still firing the Bofors and Oerlikons at the enemy aircraft. As I stepped out onto the foredeck, I saw a Junkers 88 crash into the sea ahead of us.

Looking behind me, I could see thick black smoke billowing from the stern, rising high into the afternoon sky. Planes circled overhead as they waited for an opportune moment to come in to give us the coup de grace. However, all was not lost just yet. The ship was still afloat and not listing to any side. We were still high in the water and with a huge sense of relief I realised the bomb that had hit us had not breached the hull. We were not sinking. Not yet anyway.

'You two,' I heard someone shout and when I turned around, Mister Guthrie was standing just behind us, a group of sailors with him. 'Come… come with us.'

We followed them along the side of the ship, heading towards the bombed area. Upon reaching it the full damage was revealed to us. There was a huge hole in the stern deck, just in front of the rear gun turret. One of the two 3 inch guns was bent, now useless, the turret itself badly damaged and scorched. We could see sailors lying prone on the deck, clearly dead, and others were being assisted away from the area by their shipmates. All around, the air was filled with the sounds of wounded men moaning in pain, the crackle of flames, and persistent gunfire.

We approached the gaping hole and could see a fire burning below decks, some of the smoke entering the passageways. Luckily, with the hole being so big on the top deck it acted as a chimney, sucking most of the smoke outside and into the air above us.

'Grab those hoses,' shouted Guthrie above the din, indicating towards firehoses that were kept in cabinets attached to the superstructure to our left. 'Let's get that fire out before it spreads.'

Taking the hose from the cabinet, we awkwardly coupled it to a nearby riser and, as Wally turned on the main, the hose began to charge. Pulling back on

HELL AND HIGH WATER

the nozzle, I was happy to see water spray out, relieved that the system had not frozen.

Directing the water into the hole, aiming for the base of the fire, we were joined by another two teams and, before long, with the assistance of our shipmates below who were tackling the fire from within the ship, we quickly had it under control.

We had to disengage ourselves from what was happening around us. On more than one occasion we could not avoid it and had to fling ourselves down as a German plane came in low to attack, bullets ripping at the deck in front and around us. This was dangerous work but we knew if we did not get the fire out then we were done for. We could not let it spread.

I could see another ship to our starboard side using their firepower alongside our own to drive off the enemy planes and after a while the pilots decided there were easier targets nearby and headed off to harry those instead. I felt a sense of relief but at the same time a sense of dread for those who were now coming under attack instead of us.

After fifteen minutes of firefighting, we had managed to contain the blaze and it became evident we were no longer needed in this particular role.

'Okay, Honeyman and Martin,' yelled Guthrie. 'Get yourselves away from here and see if you can help with the wounded.'

I was surprised by how Guthrie had behaved during this crisis. Where I had always taken him for a bit of an idiot, he had shown decisive leadership. He had taken control of a situation and not panicked, making strong decisions and getting the job done. He had finally shown to me why he was an officer and I had a new found respect for him.

As we rushed along the deck towards where the wounded were being tended to, I heard a sound behind me that instantly filled me with terror. I turned my head to see a lone Heinkel bearing down upon the ship and it looked as if it was headed straight for me and Wally. Immediately the gunners started to fire at it and I could see pieces of its wing flying off as their bullets found their target.

Yet still it came at us.

Suddenly the air was filled with the sound of enemy machine gun fire as the aircraft's machine guns opened up on us. I could see them ripping up the deck behind us, the line of bullets gathering pace as the plane flew over.

For a reason I did not initially understand, I found myself flying through the air. I could see the forward gun turret getting ever closer and my eyes became transfixed by mark on the steel structure. I could swear I was almost laughing as I hit the turret, my face striking what remained of the skin of young Howard's right hand that still clung to the spot where it had been left a couple of days ago.

And then I found I was lying on the deck, my eyes looking up towards the clear blue Arctic sky. I remember thinking that it was all so very odd. All this was so far removed from Mister Johnson's printshop back in Liverpool that I just wanted to laugh. How had I got here? Why was I involved in all this? What did any of it have to do with me?

HELL AND HIGH WATER

The pain hit me some seconds later. I was aware of people rushing towards me, sliding and slipping along the deck to get to me.

It was only when I saw Wally's face looking down at me I realised I had been hit. My shoulder felt numb and I could not lift my left arm.

'Am I dead, Wally?' I asked him.

'Not yet, fella,' he replied. 'Not yet... Looks a bit sore though.'

Again I almost laughed, but the pain was too great. It felt as though I had been repeatedly kicked by a horse and my whole body ached with it.

'Let's get him inside,' I heard someone shout and then, recognising the Glaswegian accent, I realised it was Petty Officer Singer. 'Make way, laddies.'

They helped me to my feet and I was surprised I was still able to walk. Wally took my right arm and put it around his neck and between him and Singer, they got me inside and to the forecastle mess deck. I could see other sailors lying around as their colleagues tended to their wounds, overseen by the medics from the sickbay.

I noticed Dougie Sears walking among the wounded. When he saw me, he looked shocked, which I did not take as a good sign. He came straight over.

'Okay,' he said to Wally and Singer. 'You need to get his kit off. We need to look at the damage.'

It was extremely cold and I dreaded them taking off my clothing. It was obvious there was no heating, the damage caused by the bomb had probably put paid to that ever working again, and I feared freezing to death. However, I had no say in the matter and they both did as they had been told. Before too long I was laid on the deck, topless, my bloody clothing being used to cushion me against the hard, cold floor.

Without saying anything, Dougie took out a morphine ampoule from his medical bag and stuck it in my arm.

'This'll help, George, mate,' he said. 'Try not to think about the pain.'

'I wasn't,' I replied. 'Not until you just mentioned it.'

Dougie smiled at me. 'That's it, lad. That's the spirit.'

He turned away and indicated to a doctor, a harassed looking man of around forty years old, who was tending to other wounded men, assessing each of them in turn.

'Sir,' he said firmly. 'I could do with your help here, if you don't mind.'

As the doctor approached, I could tell by the look on his face and the urgency in Dougie's voice all was not well. I looked to my friend, Wally, and was shocked to see him sitting with his back against the bulkhead some feet away, his knees tucked up to his chin. He had a desperate look on his face.

It was then I noticed all the blood. There was a lot of it on the deck around me, bright red against the light brown wooden floor, flowing away from me. I realised at that point it was my own. It had all come out of me.

'Don't look at it, laddie,' said Singer, who was still at my side, pressing a towel against my shoulder. A very red towel, I noticed.

The last thing I remember, as I lay there on the deck of the damaged HMS *Virtuous*, was the medical officer looking at my shoulder then turning his worried face to an anxious Dougie Sears and saying, 'Get the theatre prepared immediately, Douglas. Immediately.'

It was then that I fainted.

Nineteen

Liverpool

Fortunately Glenda wanted to see me again but she was not very happy with me. She made her feelings known when I saw her the following weekend.

Billy was also in Iris's bad books for what he had said to me. It turned out Glenda had fallen out with Iris over it and Iris had taken this out on Billy. I cannot say I felt sorry for him because I did not. He deserved it. The bloke was an idiot.

He turned up for work on the Friday morning with a note from Glenda, which he handed to me sheepishly.

It simply said, "*Meet me outside Aunt Ida's tomorrow at 12, Glenda*".

'To the point, I suppose,' I said, putting it in my pocket.

'Sorry about all that,' said Billy. 'But I was only passing on what Iris told me.'

I nodded at him and turned away. Things were starting to get a bit strained between us and he was beginning to irritate me. He was my friend, but he was a pain in the arse at the same time.

The following day, at precisely twelve o'clock, I stood across the road from the Shepherds' house and waited as I had been ordered to by Glenda.

HELL AND HIGH WATER

She made me wait for fifteen minutes and it was only when I started to walk away that I heard her shout from across the road.

'George... George.'

I turned and saw her trotting towards me. I had the distinct feeling she had been watching me all along. I was not into playing these games and although I wanted to continue to see her and carry on with our relationship I would not be messed about like this.

'Sorry I'm a bit late,' she said smiling, grabbing my arm and linking me, as though we had never had crossed words. As though what had happened only a few days ago had never taken place.

'That's okay,' I replied as we walked along.

There was a chill in the air despite the sun shining, winter starting to take a firm hold.

'So,' I said, 'What do you want to do?'

'We could go for a walk in the park,' she suggested. 'Or we could...'

'I don't have the keys,' I replied, knowing what she was about to suggest. The truth was that I did have the keys but I had left them at home on purpose. I was not in the mood and I was worried it was becoming too much of a habit. I did not want to become somebody's bad habit no matter how much I enjoyed it.

We walked for a while, all the time Glenda chatting away. I could not understand this change in her attitude towards me. I honestly thought she would not want to see me again but here she was, carrying on as though all was well. It made me wonder if there really was something in what Billy had said.

JOHN McKAY

We came across a small cafe and I guided her towards the door.

'Come on,' I said. 'Let's get a cup of tea and some lunch.'

We sat at a table near to the window and after the waitress had delivered a pot of tea, two cups and some rather unappetising looking ham sandwiches, I asked her, 'What's the matter Glenda? You seem in a strange mood.'

'Do I?' She acted surprised I would say such a thing although I could tell she was putting it on. Her raised eyebrows and high tone of voice gave her away. It seemed too much.

'You do,' I replied. 'I thought after what happened the other day you wouldn't want to see me again.'

'Well I thought the same thing about you,' she replied. 'I thought you were thinking bad things about me and I was too much trouble.'

'Oh, you're too much trouble, all right,' I joked. 'But there's something about you that draws me to you.'

'What do you mean?' she asked, wrinkling her nose.

'Oh, I don't know,' I replied. 'I've never met anyone like you before. You seem to live for the moment... take chances... make me take chances I would never have dreamed of taking before I met you.'

'There's a war on,' she said. 'Who knows what's going to happen to us? There's no point in dilly-dallying and being cautious all the time. We could be dead at any moment. How many are dying right now? The Germans are bombing everywhere and we can't seem to stop them. Look at London. It's getting hammered. And Liverpool too. Look what happened the other day on Bentinck Street. All those people taking shelter from it, yet they still got hit. They still died. We've no power over any of it, George, apart from what we *can* control... If that makes sense.'

'It kind of does,' I replied, sipping at my weak tea. 'But I still don't understand why you would leave the safety of Wales to come here. If you'd stayed in Wales then you wouldn't have to worry about any of this, would you?'

'Of course I'd worry. I have relatives here, as you know. I'd worry about them.'

'But you wouldn't be in any personal danger.'

She was quiet for a moment.

'Maybe. But I couldn't stay there,' she almost whispered.

I did not want to push her. I could tell there was a reason she had left the safety of Flint, other than coming to visit family. I felt to press her would cause her to clam up again and maybe start another argument which I wanted to avoid.

'So how are your parents?' she said suddenly, the change of subject catching me slightly off guard.

'My parents?'

'Yes, George. Your parents?'

'They're fine. Why do you ask?'

'Well... I was thinking... If you and I are getting serious, then don't you think it'd be a good idea for me to meet them?'

I nearly spat out my tea. It caught at the back of my throat and I started to cough, which made Glenda laugh nervously. An old couple sitting at a table in the corner looked over, but became uninterested as soon as they saw me, turning back to face each other to carry on with their silent lunch.

'I'm not sure that's such a good idea,' I replied, after controlling myself once more. 'You do know about my father, don't you?'

'Not really,' she replied. 'Aunt Ida tells me that he's a bit of a funny one…'

'Well, that's one way of putting it,' I said. 'He hates Catholics. He wouldn't approve. In fact he doesn't approve.'

'So he knows about us?'

'He does. But he thinks we aren't seeing each other anymore. We had a bit of a row the other day and I told him you probably wouldn't want to see me again.'

'Oh…' she looked slightly upset for a moment but then her face changed and she smiled again. She shrugged. 'Not to worry, eh?… This sandwich is disgusting.'

An hour later I walked her home and as we reached the top of her street she kissed my cheek before turning and walking the rest of the way on her own.

I watched her go and, although I wanted her to, she never looked back.

She confused me. She was an odd girl and I was beginning to wonder if she was right for me after all. It was clear she was holding something back. There was something she was not telling me and until she did, then there was no real future for the relationship.

But there was something strangely magnetic about her. Something I could not quite put my finger on that drew me to her. She had given everything to me physically, but emotionally, well that was not happening. And I needed that. Was this physical approach to the relationship some kind of smokescreen? Did she think by giving herself to me in the manner a wife does to a husband, it somehow compensated for what was lacking elsewhere?

She was an enigma, that much was true. However, I did not know if I had the capability, or the energy, to solve her.

Twenty

My shoulder hurt like hell. The pain was like nothing I had ever experienced before.

Apparently the round had ricocheted off the bulkhead and hit my back to the side of the shoulder blade exiting under the collar bone. Thankfully it had missed all my major organs but the exit wound had caused a lot of tissue damage and broken two of my ribs high up the rib cage. It had then grazed the collar bone as it came out. All the blood on the deck, and the fact the wound looked to be in my chest, had caused the doctor to react the way he had, thinking the injury was much more severe than it actually was. I was relieved to find out it was not life threatening but I would need rest and recuperation for a while to allow it to heal. I would be in a lot of pain whilst this happened and be left with significant scars for the rest of my life.

I had been unconscious for nearly five hours and it was dark when I awoke. My left arm was strapped across my chest and the bandages around my shoulder seemed a little tight. I could hear activity throughout the ship. When I tried to raise myself to observe what was happening, I fell back on the bunk and so did not try again. I was cold and exhausted. Totally and completely.

I looked around my surroundings and saw I was in the sickbay. Every bunk was taken by an unfortunate such as myself who had been wounded in the air attack. Dougie Sears and another medic stood near the doorway smoking cigarettes. There was no lighting in the room, the electrics presumably damaged by the German planes. However, I felt a big sense of relief. After all, I was still alive, and the ship was not sinking.

I tried to twist onto my side to make myself more comfortable. A huge pain shot through my body and I involuntarily cried out. Upon hearing me moan, Dougie looked over. He took one last drag of his cigarette before flicking it away and then came over to me. He knelt down to my side.

'Try not to move too much, George,' he said. 'You're all stitched up and the doc won't be too pleased if you burst them.'

'It bloody hurts, Doug,' I said.

''Course it does, George,' he said. 'You've been shot, fella. You didn't expect it to tickle now, did you?'

I started to laugh but it made the pain worse.

'What's going on?' I asked when I had composed myself.

'The ships buggered, mate,' he replied. 'We only have limited power and we're currently being towed by that big bloody destroyer. Apparently we're not too far from the Kola Inlet so hopefully we'll be in Murmansk sometime tomorrow before them bloody planes come back. We're having to dock there to carry out repairs before we can head back. The captain's hoping to get you all to a hospital on land while the repairs are being done.'

JOHN McKAY

I looked around the room but could not see too much due to the lack of light.

'How many?' I asked.

'Eight dead. Fourteen wounded. Some not so bad and some pretty banged up. I'd say your injuries are somewhere in the middle of that particular spectrum.'

'Could've been worse, I suppose. But then could've been better too,' I said.

'That's about the size of it. Let's face it, you're lucky to be alive.'

Dougie left me alone and went to check on the other patients.

I closed my eyes and tried to sleep again but the cold and pain made it impossible. Instead I thought about the situation I found myself in and started to get a little depressed. I prayed my injuries would fully heal. I did not want my arm to be left useless for the rest of my life. I was still very young and I did not deserve it. As I started to feel more and more sorry for myself I looked around the sickbay at my shipmates who had also been injured and my mind went to those that had perished. I had seen a whole crew go down the previous night, watched men burn alive and freeze to death at the same time. I had witnessed the *Dreyfus* breaking in two, its twisted hulk disappearing beneath the icy waves, taking all eighty-five souls with it, and now eight of my own shipmates had also lost their lives. Men I knew. Men I had worked with, laughed with and lived with for the past year. Men no older than I, dragged into this war to stop an evil tyrant from forcing his warped ideology onto the world.

HELL AND HIGH WATER

I decided the pain in my arm should serve as a reminder to me that I was lucky. Whenever it caused me distress and discomfort I would be glad of it. It would make me realise I was alive, that I had survived. And when the pain eventually left me, which it would surely do, then the scars that remained would be a visual memento to stop me from feeling sorry for myself ever again. Self-pity was not only pointless, it was completely selfish and mentally draining.

Eventually I found the sleep I craved and when I awoke some hours later there was much hustle and bustle about the place. Medics and volunteers were moving the most seriously wounded from bunks to stretchers and taking them out on deck, wrapping them in blankets and trying to keep them warm. I tried to turn onto my side and, after much wincing and gritting of teeth, I managed to do it. I pulled the thick woollen blanket up to my chin with my good hand to keep the draught off.

Through the open door I could see more sailors on deck. Beyond them I could make out land and realised we had finally made it to the Kola Inlet. I knew the threat of U-boat and surface ship attack was now gone, as we had reached our final destination.

Apparently, we should have moored up at Polyarny, at the mouth of the inlet to await the return voyage back to Iceland, but, due to our battle damage, the *Virtuous* would have to dock near to Murmansk to make repairs. The cargo ships that had survived the journey were to make their way to the docks at Murmansk for unloading.

There was no doubt in my mind that although we were safe from the Kriegsmarine for the time being, they would probably be lying in wait outside the inlet, ready to hit us again when we set off for home.

I could hear the distant sound of bombing, getting ever louder as the ship sailed along the inlet and realised the Luftwaffe were probably bombing the port. The danger was by no means over and I shuddered slightly. When would I ever be safe again? Even at home, in Liverpool, I had witnessed attacks from the German air force and I was starting to get sick of the whole thing.

A familiar figure appeared in the doorway.

'Hello, George,' said Wally, approaching my cot and sitting down on the floor beside me, 'How're you feeling?'

'Bloody awful,' I replied.

'I'm not surprised,' he said. 'I shit myself when I saw you get hit. Thought you were a goner, that's for sure. But then I thought it'd take more than a Nazi bullet to see off my young pal.'

'I thought I'd had it too,' I replied. 'I didn't understand what had happened at first… It doesn't half hurt, pal. The pain is shocking and I can't really feel my arm. It's gone kind of numb.'

'What's the doc said?'

'Not had chance to speak to him yet,' I replied. 'But Dougie Sears reckons I'll be all right. Reckons I just need some rest and relaxation. Take it easy for a while. Probably going to offload us wounded in Murmansk.'

Wally frowned, which did not inspire me with confidence.

'That sound you can hear,' he said forlornly. 'That's the bloody Luftwaffe bombing the port. I don't think you'll get much rest, I'm afraid.'

Murmansk was a quick plane ride from the German's northern Norway bases. It was not surprising they would make the somewhat short journey to disrupt the offloading and attempt to destroy the ships and cargoes we had escorted. It made sense they would do this. However, I felt I was safer on land and wanted to get off the ship as soon as I possibly could.

The doctor who had operated on my shoulder the previous day, Mister Greaves, walked over to us.

'Can you sit up please, Martin,' he said. 'We need to change your bandages. Do you think you can walk?'

'I think so, sir,' I replied. 'I'm sure I can manage.'

'Good,' he continued. 'You'll hopefully be getting off the ship for a while. The Russians are willing to take the wounded. There's no room here and the ship has to go into dry dock for a couple of weeks at least, while we carry out the repairs.'

'Thank you, sir,' I replied. 'For saving my arm.'

'Don't thank me just yet, young man,' he said, looking up at me as he unwound the bandage. 'We're still a long way from home just yet.'

Once the fresh bandage had been applied, with the assistance of Wally, I stood up. For a second I stumbled and nearly fell back onto the cot, suddenly dizzy, but after a moment I managed to clear my head and felt strong enough to stand. The effects of the anaesthetic had not quite worn off but I knew that with some fresh air I should be okay.

Wally helped me to dress, putting on as many layers of clothing as he could find, the temperature outside still well below zero. He did it delicately, careful not to cause me further pain. Whenever I winced or cringed, he would stop, check if it was okay to continue and then, after a nod from me, carry on.

'We've no idea how long you're going to be standing out there in the cold for,' he said. 'We need to get as many layers on you as possible.'

I looked out through the open doorway. It was snowing. The land to the port side was covered in it and again I shivered. I was not sure if being off the ship would be a good or a bad thing.

Eventually the *Virtuous* pulled into port and I joined a line of walking wounded gathered on deck. The snow was falling heavily and it coated us within seconds. Six stretchers were laid out before us where medics and volunteers, including Dougie Sears, stooped down to try and shield the wounded men from the bad weather. Occasionally they brushed snow from the blankets but it was quickly replaced by more as it rained down thickly upon them. The captain, and the ship's senior officers were gathered before us.

I looked around and studied the port of Murmansk.

We were secured to a dock next to a narrow railway spur that jutted out in front of the ship. The train line stretched into the distance, beyond a huge granary, its doors open to the elements where I could see workers

HELL AND HIGH WATER

coming and going. For as far as I could see along the dockside, huge iron derricks, cranes and pulley systems had already begun to lift the cargo from the merchant ships that had completed the journey. Tanks, wagons, medical supplies; crates of munitions and food, all lifted to the dockside where rows of trucks waited to take them away. Many of the dockers were females, labouring hard with remarkable efficiency. There was also a gang of women cutting up huge tree trunks and heaving the logs to the damaged ships to assist with shoring up their battered hulls and superstructures. This was something I had never seen before. I wondered what my father would think if women were allowed to work on the docks at Bootle.

Further out in the water rested a couple of abandoned, sunken ships, their masts and funnels jutting out of the surface as though pointing an accusatory finger to the heavens for allowing them to perish in this awful place.

Although the snow made vision difficult, further inland I could distinguish a large number of bombed out buildings. Mounds of rubble had been shifted and piled up at the sides of the roads to allow wagons and other vehicles to pass, to keep the routes to and from the docks open. Localised fires burned in bomb damaged buildings and amongst the rubble on the cratered streets. To the right of a single storey port building, I noticed a small pack of wild dogs, scrawny and malnourished, roaming in the debris, scavenging for whatever food they could find. Black smoke rose high into the sky from these damaged, grey buildings. Above, German planes attempted to break away from

JOHN McKAY

a group of Russian Petlyakov Pe3s to dive down and drop their payloads on the ships offloading at the docks and surrounding buildings, where some of the cargoes were initially being stored. Anti-aircraft guns on the roofs blasted their ordnance skyward and I noticed some of these were being crewed by women. I was both taken aback and impressed with the large amount of females actively involved in the Russian war effort.

Murmansk was not a nice looking city. It appeared ugly, dirty and grey. After viewing it from the deck, the last thing I wanted was to step foot off the ship, but I did not really have a choice. The captain had an agreement with the Russians that the wounded would be accepted and looked after in one of their hospitals, one of which I could see just behind the granary. I hoped this was not where they were thinking of sending us as it did not look to be in a safe location at all. Christ alone knew what kind of care we would receive there.

In fact, I was not sure if it would be safer to stay on the ship as the city looked to be under constant bombardment.

'Jesus, George,' said Wally. 'What a shithole.'

'You're telling me,' I agreed sombrely. 'A bit like Newcastle, eh?'

He snorted at my poor attempt at a joke.

We watched as a gangplank was lowered to the dockside and Lieutenant Mitchell walked down it. He was met by three Russian officers, each one of whom was dressed in more effective looking cold weather

HELL AND HIGH WATER

rig than we had. All three appeared serious and unfriendly in equal measure. It was obvious only one of them spoke English, a man in a well worn uniform with a large, furry hat and even larger moustache that hung down the sides of his face like a Mexican bandit. A red star was on the front of his hat and for some reason I could not work out, he held a small pistol in his hand. Why he felt the need to have it unholstered was beyond me. It made me feel slightly uneasy.

I could see Lieutenant Mitchell gesticulating back to the ship. Although I could not hear what he was saying, he was clearly frustrated. After a couple of minutes he came back aboard and approached the captain.

'What's the problem, Charles?' asked Harrison.

'They're refusing to take our wounded, sir. The gentleman said they've had no instruction to do so and he's not prepared to take them. They've enough wounded of their own,' he added, somewhat awkwardly.

'Oh, did he now?' replied Harrison raising his eyebrows. 'I think it needs to be explained to him that these boys lying around here have gone through hell to get these supplies here and they need to be treated with a little more respect. You can tell him from me. No, wait... I'll do it myself.'

Brushing past Mitchell, he strode down the gangplank and walked up to the three Russian officers. One had now lit a cigarette and was assisting his comrade in lighting another, covering the flame of the match with his gloved hand to protect it from the wind and falling snow.

JOHN McKAY

'Now just what the bloody hell is going on here?' I heard him say loudly. The Russians did not change their expressions but smoked their cigarettes as though this was the most normal thing in the world. The rest of the conversation I could not make out, but after five minutes of gesticulating, pointing and negotiating, Harrison turned around and waved to Mitchell to bring down the wounded.

Immediately there was activity on deck as the stretcher bearers picked up their charges and carried them down the gangplank to the dockside, followed closely by the ambulant casualties.

As I was about to set off at the end of the line Wally tapped me on the shoulder.

'Here, George,' he said as I turned around. He handed me a small package which I did not recognise at first. Noticing my bewilderment he continued. 'It's my copy of *Oliver Twist*. I took it from your hammock. It might give you something to do while you're away.'

'Right,' I replied. 'Thanks.'

I took the book from him and pocketed it.

'I'll return it to you once I've finished it,' I told him.

'Don't worry,' he said. 'There's no rush.'

He patted me on my good shoulder and turned around. He walked back to the sanctuary of the ship, out of the cold, which was now starting to penetrate through my clothing.

We waited almost half an hour before five battered looking trucks with huge red stars on the doors arrived and we were told to get into them. Again, I noticed a couple were driven by women and there was a

HELL AND HIGH WATER

nurse to every vehicle. Once the stretchers were loaded I was assisted into the back and settled onto a bench and before long, we set off. Through the back of the truck I could see the crew who had loaded us walking back to the *Virtuous*. I had been told it would be heading to dry dock in a place called Rosta, further down the coastline to carry out repairs. We had been assured that those casualties fit enough would be picked up on the way back but anyone too badly injured may have to wait until their wounds had healed sufficiently before they could be repatriated. Those men would have to travel home on another ship as and when one became available.

I felt a huge sadness at having to leave the ship. It had been my home for a long time and I had come to love it and the men who sailed in it. We had been through extreme dangers and it had brought us all together, forming us into a close knit crew, almost like a family. I knew I would miss it.

I did not know what to expect in the coming days and weeks and was rather anxious at what may lay ahead. However, I was with some of my shipmates and one of our medics, my friend Dougie Sears, was accompanying us to the hospital.

After a few minutes, I was able to ignore the sounds of war taking place outside the truck. Bombs, anti-aircraft and small arms fire and the awful sound the Ju87 Stuka dive-bombers made as they swooped down, the spats over their wheels wailing like demons as they attacked ground targets. I was able to disregard all of it. I was able to pretend that the freezing temperatures were of no concern to me.

However, I did allow the rumbling of the truck, as it bounced over ruts, potholes and rubble to have a relaxing effect upon me, and despite all the reasons not to, I somehow managed to fall asleep as the war raged on around me.

HELL AND HIGH WATER

Twenty-One

We arrived not long later at a building that looked like it had once been a school. Playground furniture lay scattered around the area, broken and rusted and covered in snow adding to the surreality of the situation I now found myself in. Childish scribblings adorned the inner walls as we entered through dilapidated double doors, mementoes of a happier time. A framed picture of Joseph Stalin hung broken and crooked on a wall facing us and below it, on a simple table, was a large bust of Lenin, boldly and confidently staring out at us as we shuffled past.

Next we found ourselves in a much larger room I took to have once been the assembly hall or school gymnasium. The windows had been boarded up with wooden planks, the glass long since shattered and destroyed. A rudimentary lighting system provided a dim light, the bulbs hanging loosely from cables that looped down from a cracked and damaged ceiling. Here too hung a large picture of Stalin, dominating the wall to our right, and various other Communist Party posters and murals filled the walls around us. Walls that showed obvious signs of battle damage, where the plaster had fallen away to reveal bare bricks in parts. These posters displayed pictures of tough looking men and even harder looking women, their determined faces staring out as they worked in the fields and factories of the Soviet Union, holding aloft scythes and sledgehammers. The writing made no sense to me.It was a language and an alphabet I had never seen before, but I could guess the message they were attempting to convey. Work hard for the state.

The room was filled to bursting point with beds and stretchers, each of them occupied, with both men and women with varying injuries. I was shocked to see a number of children, lying peacefully and uncomplaining in iron beds and cots in the far corner, their bandaged heads and limbs stained red with the blood of their wounds. Instantly I felt my own wound was trivial and unimportant in comparison. It reminded me that so far my own war had been somewhat shielded. The only casualties I had seen thus far had been adult combatants and the reality of the wider conflict was revealed to me in graphic detail as I noticed some of these children had lost arms and legs. Although I had been in Liverpool during the Blitz, I had never actually seen any of the casualties, the bombings always some distance from where I had been.

A number of nurses and doctors, dressed in olive green quilted coats and hats, moved from bed to bed and from stretcher to stretcher, doing their best with the limited medical supplies they had. I could see in an instant just how much these people needed the supplies from our convoys.

The stench of the place hit me. Sweat mixed with tobacco smoke and human waste filled my nostrils. I could see one or two of my comrades physically cringe as they looked around, holding their hands to their mouths and noses lest they breathe in the germs that no doubt flew around in the air. The looks on their faces gave me the impression they too were as appalled as I was at the suffering in this room.

There seemed little heating. A lot of those in the beds had greatcoats over their blankets and, as they breathed, we could see their breath form like fog in front of them.

A bomb exploded close to the building, shaking the floor and walls around us and causing plaster dust and flakes of curled paint to fall from the ceiling onto the patients below. Although one or two of us flinched, none of the doctors, nurses or patients seemed particularly bothered by it. I guessed it must be a common occurrence. The noise of battle could be clearly heard but nobody seemed overly concerned about what was happening outside the hospital.

At the opposite end of the room I noticed a man standing alone leaning against a wall. He wore a large, fur-lined overcoat over an olive green tunic, and breeches tucked into rather clean and new looking brown boots. Sitting upon his head was a large fur hat with a red star in the centre and flaps that hung loosely over his ears. I could make out, under his coat, a holstered pistol. He had a stern look upon his craggy face and gave me the impression he was somebody of importance, maybe someone to be feared.

'Political officer,' said Dougie Sears, who had come to stand next to me and noticed my gaze.

'Excuse me?' I replied.

'Probably a commissar,' he went on. 'They're political officers. The Soviets have people who go around doing nothing other than making sure everybody does as they're told. They make sure they're all being good communists.'

'What kind of a daft job is that?' I asked. 'How do you know?'

'I read a lot,' said Dougie. 'Maybe you should try it. Very educational, you know.'

My good hand moved absentmindedly towards the pocket where I had put Wally's copy of *Oliver Twist.* My gloved hand fingered it protectively.

'Maybe I will.'

Eventually, Russian porters carried our stretchers to a far corner where nurses hurriedly made room for us. The walking wounded were given a dirty blanket each and after a bit of to-ing and fro-ing, we managed to find some space and made ourselves as comfortable as we possibly could, which was not very comfortable at all. My shoulder was beginning to ache and the pain was making me feel light-headed again. I craved a cigarette.

With Dougie's help I sat down with my back against the wall a few yards from where the commissar stood observing us indifferently. The Russian then took a packet of cigarettes from his pocket, put one in his mouth and lit it from a book of matches. He casually blew out the smoke into the room to add to the awful stench.

Movement to my left caught my eye and when I turned my head I could see more people in an adjoining room. This was probably once a classroom where young children would have at one time been educated and maybe had some fun, but now it had taken on another more medical and sinister purpose. Soldiers and nurses moved around purposefully, one or two with masks over their faces. I could see some leaning over a trolley where a casualty lay, his feet dangling over the edge, moving in small jerking motions as if he was in a lot of pain. Above the din of the room I swear I could hear his groans.

After a while, with nothing to do and boredom taking over, I closed my eyes with the intention of getting some sleep but it did not come. For a while I just sat there trying to ignore my quite awful surroundings.

In the middle of the room the officer who had accompanied us from the *Virtuous,* Lieutenant Freeman, the ship's Electronic Warfare Officer who had been given the task of ensuring the wounded were treated well, spoke to a Russian doctor. He pointed to our group. I could not hear what he was saying but from the look on his face it appeared he was involved in an argument, his face reddening. He gesticulated wildly to make himself understood and to ensure he got his point across. Like the commissar, the doctor did not seem interested and I presumed he had other, more important, things to worry about other than dealing with a few wounded British sailors. I guessed he had enough on his hands and us turning up like this had only added to his woes.

The sailor sitting next to me, a stoker who had burns to the left side of his face and neck, and in obvious agony said, 'I hope they aren't thinking of leaving us here in this shithouse. We can't stay here. I'd sooner be back on the ship and take my chances with the Germans.'

He had a point. There looked to be nothing hygienic about the place. I feared those with open wounds may be vulnerable to picking up infections. This was more of a casualty gathering station than a hospital.

We stayed in the gymnasium for a few more hours. Some of us slept and others merely sat or lay there watching the room and generally feeling sorry for themselves. Eventually Lieutenant Freeman came over to speak to us. It looked as though he might finally have some good news.

'They've made room for us in one of the classrooms,' he told us. 'We'll be moving out of here in a few minutes so get yourselves ready. They're scraping together enough beds for us in there.'

I could see he was annoyed. He had had to argue for the best part of the day to get us into a ward where we could be better looked after when the beds had been available all along. He had probably expected that, as our allies, the Russians would have been more accommodating, that they would treat us with more respect. Myself, I thought maybe they were just looking after their own people and prioritising in that way, particularly when there were a lot of children among the casualties. I was, however, very relieved we did not have to stay in that huge room. It made me feel nauseous and we had thus far received no attention other than from our own medic.

An hour later we were led down a short corridor and through another door into a room where we could see nurses making up beds. The sheets did not look very clean and there were minimal blankets but at least it was away from that awful gymnasium. Again, pictures of Soviet leaders and propaganda posters filled the walls and the windows had been blocked out with wood. A huge blackboard took up most of the far wall, where faded chalk marks could still be seen.

We quickly settled onto the beds. Having a mattress beneath me for the first time in many months felt almost luxurious. I was used to a hammock and although I had found them fine, nothing could compare to a real bed that did not move or rock.

It was very cold when we first entered. However, once the door was closed and with so many people crammed inside, either still wearing cold weather gear or laying our greatcoats and leather jerkins over us, the temperature rose a few degrees to a more bearable level.

Once I was comfortable, Dougie Sears came over and gave me another shot of morphine. I closed my eyes and a few minutes later, as the drug took hold, I finally fell into the sleep my body had been for hours craving.

JOHN McKAY

Twenty-Two

When I awoke it was night-time. I could still hear the sound of bombs outside but they seemed further away and did not concern me too much. I felt a loose spring digging into the small of my back and tried to shift onto my side, but the pain from my shoulder was unbearable and I had to remain as I was. I turned my head and saw most of my fellow patients were asleep. I was pleasantly surprised to feel warmer than I had been in a long time and when I looked around the room I could see a couple of paraffin heaters glowing in the darkness. Lieutenant Freeman's complaints and haranguing had clearly paid off.

A few feet away, in the corner of the room, a small table had been set up, where, by the light of a small lamp, a Russian nurse was busy writing onto a document I could not see. At last it looked like they had got themselves organised.

The nurse seemed to sense somebody looking at her and she turned her head slightly and caught my eye. In the dim light she probably could not tell if my eyes were open but she smiled at me anyway.

She was like no other woman I had seen before. She was dressed in the olive green uniform of the Soviet army but wore a red cross armband on her left arm. Her hair had been placed in a bun but a few strands hung down where the band had loosened slightly. A fur hat was on the floor at her feet reminding me of a pet cat lying peacefully at its master's feet. She looked around thirty five years old but I guessed she was probably much younger, no doubt the hardships she had endured over the past few years making her features appear hard and stern. But when she smiled there was a softness about her that contrasted sharply with this serious countenance. Her hair was a light brown and, even though it was dark, the light from the lamp made her large green eyes shine like emeralds.

I guessed this lady had been stung for the nightshift and had been allocated our small group of unfortunates to take care of.

Suddenly the pain hit me again and I moaned. It felt like the bullet was still inside me. I moved my hand to my shoulder to rub it.

Instantly the nurse jumped from her chair and came striding over.

'Nyet, nyet,' she said. 'You leave… Leave.'

The shock of hearing her speak English made me stop what I was doing.

'You leave,' she repeated, shaking her head. 'No heal… You leave.'

'Where's Dougie?' I asked.

She looked at me blankly, not understanding what I was saying.

'Dougie… Dougie?' I repeated. Why I thought repeating something she did not understand would make her realise what I meant, I do not know.

'Sears is assisting in the main hall.'

I twisted around and saw Lieutenant Freeman standing on the other side of my bed.

'You'll have to make do with this young lady, Martin,' he went on. 'And if I were you, I'd do as she says.'

'Shit, sir,' I said. 'I'm in agony here. It really hurts.'

'I'm sure it does,' he replied sympathetically. 'But then you've been shot by a high calibre bullet, after all. I know you're in a lot of pain but try and keep the noise down if you can. Some of your mates have more serious wounds than you and we need to let them sleep. In fact, you need to get some sleep yourself.'

I instantly felt guilty. Here I was, moaning about my lot when there were much worse off people in the building than myself. I needed to get a grip.

'Just do as this young lady says and you'll be fine,' said Freeman before walking away, probably to his own bed and back to the sleep he needed as much as everyone else.

Once he had gone the nurse spoke again.

'I change bandage… Clean.'

She helped me sit up and after a lot of painful moving around, she managed to take off my many layers of clothing. I was now able to see her close up and could see she was in fact quite young, maybe in her mid twenties. Her round face had a small flat nose, which I found strangely attractive, and her mouth was large with full red lips.

She fetched a bowl of water and when she took off my dirty bandage and placed the wet sponge on my chest I flinched with the cold of it. She pulled away slightly before frowning at me before continuing.

This gave me chance to look at my wounded shoulder for the first time in a lucid state. Mister Greaves, the ship's surgeon, had done a good job in flushing it out and stitching it up. There was a large jagged scar where the muscle had been torn and I could see it would be some time before the sinews knitted together. I understood it would never be as strong as it once was. However, it did not appear infected and the stitches looked clean and neat. I was very grateful for this and understood that as long as it was kept clean then I should have nothing to worry about other than dealing with the pain I knew would eventually subside. I decided I would endure with the current discomfort, which was considerable, without any further complaint.

As the nurse wrapped the new bandage I tried to make small talk.

'How do you know English?' I asked.

'Shush,' she said, inclining her head to the right slightly to indicate the others in the room. 'Do not wake…'

I found this response slightly comical seeing there was still some considerable noise outside.

I tried again.

'What's your name? I'm George.'

'Hallo, George,' she replied. 'Now shush.'

'Come on,' I persisted.

She frowned and then stopped what she was doing to look at me.

'If I tell name, you shush?' she asked.

'Erm… Okay,' I responded.

'My name Nika,' she replied, then resumed wrapping the bandage.

'Hello, Nika.'

She gave me a stern look and ignored me as she continued to work. I thought that I may be starting to irritate her and so decided to keep quiet while she carried on. I really could have done with another painkiller but understood supplies were short and so did not say anything. After she had finished putting on the bandage she helped me to get my shirt and jumper back on. I lay down and she placed the blanket and coat over me.

Her work for now completed, she took the bowl and stood up. For a second she hesitated, as though she was about to say something.

And then she did a very odd thing.

Placing the bowl onto the floor she looked around the room almost conspiratorially and then, when she was sure nobody was watching, she leaned over and kissed me on the mouth. As she pulled away she smiled at me again.

Before I had chance to react, she picked up the bowl and walked away to empty it, as though this had been the most normal and natural thing in the world. When she returned to the room a minute later she sat back at the table and continued with the paperwork she had been doing earlier.

Although I tried to catch her attention again she either did not notice or was avoiding eye contact with me. If this was down to embarrassment at what she had just done I was not so sure. After watching her a while, I slowly drifted off to sleep.

HELL AND HIGH WATER

Twenty-Three

The food in that Murmansk hospital left a lot to be desired. We had not taken anything from the ship and so had to eat the same meagre rations they were dishing up for all the other patients. We got no special treatment. Tasteless thin cabbage soup and black bread seemed the staple diet and the lack of protein did nothing to assist our recovery.

Those in the ward who had the worst injuries, the burns victims and those with broken limbs, in my opinion, did not get the treatment they needed. One of the stokers who had had his leg shattered when the bomb exploded beneath decks was carted to the operating theatre the morning after we arrived. We could hear his screams as they cut off the damaged limb below the knee. Having such an operation done without anaesthetic must have been horrendous and I physically cringed when I heard him bellowing through the corridors.

The lack of hygiene added to the general unpleasantness of the place. If it was not for Dougie Sears assisting Nika then it would have been a lot worse. Lieutenant Freeman had returned to the *Virtuous* on the morning of the second day with a promise to come back for us once the ship was repaired and ready to join a convoy on the return leg to Iceland. When that would be, he had no idea. This felt a little like an abandonment and some of the lads thought this was where we would remain until the war was over; forgotten and left to rot.

Over the next few days Dougie and Nika were often called to help in the main hall, their skills required by the Russians who saw using Dougie's skills as payback for us being allowed to use their premises. More and more of his time was being spent there. When he did return to us in our side ward he looked both mentally and physically exhausted. I really wanted to help him but my left arm was useless and I was still racked with pain every time I tried to move it.

As time wore on, those who could not get out of bed unassisted would soil themselves, often having to lie in their filth for hours before Nika could get around to cleaning them. The lack of clean bed linen added to the general bad hygiene. The sheets would only get a cursory wipe down before they had to be used again. The stench in the room got as bad, if not worse, than what we had experienced in the main hall. It got to the point we all wished we were back at sea, in the cold of the Arctic weather. Anything seemed more preferable to this.

After two weeks many of us were at the end of our tether and Dougie was at breaking point. He looked like he had aged ten years in the short time we had spent there. Lieutenant Freeman had not returned and we had had no word from the ship as to what was going on and what was to happen to us.

However, the people I felt most sorry for were my injured comrades. Because I was mobile, I could get out of bed and keep myself in a general clean state, but some of those poor sods were getting worse by the

HELL AND HIGH WATER

day. The irony of coming to hospital to recover and actually ending up worse than when you arrived was not lost on me. I was becoming very frustrated that I could not help them in any way.

I was not surprised when, despite the best efforts of Dougie and Nika, the stoker who had had his leg amputated got an infection in his stump and had to go through a second operation, the overworked surgeons cutting more of his leg off, above the knee. He quickly developed a bad fever and with his bed soaked in his own faeces, urine and sweat, a couple of days later we discovered him dead in his bed.

This affected the lads tremendously and our morale dropped to the lowest point since we witnessed the sinking of the *Dreyfus*, which now seemed such a long time ago.

Every day we could hear the bombs and anti-aircraft fire coming from the docks and now and again they would drop on buildings around us causing our room to shake. One or two of the lads expressed to me later that they had wished one would have landed on us and put us all out of our misery. I could only agree with the sentiment.

One night, when all was quiet, when the bombs had finally stopped falling on the city, there seemed a strange kind of calm. I could see Dougie sitting on a chair near to the nurses' station, his legs outstretched and his chin on his chest, snoring loudly. For a second I managed a smile. Nika was sitting next to him with her head in her hands and when he let out a loud grunt she turned and smiled at him. As she turned her head back our eyes caught each others.

Since that first night, when she had kissed me unexpectedly, she had never done so again, even though we had been alone on many occasions when she had been cleaning my wound or administering painkillers. However, this night something passed between us and I knew she was thinking about that first night and the kiss, just as I was.

I decided to ignore the memory and lay down on my back, raising my good right hand behind my head to act as a pillow. The light was very low and I was sure there was nobody else awake.

After a few minutes I sensed movement next to me. When I turned to see who it was, Nika was getting under the blanket beside me. She had taken off her padded coat, which she had left over her chair, and had undone the top two buttons of her shirt.

At first I did not know how to react but when she put her finger to her lips, whispered 'Shush' and kissed my neck, I decided the best thing to do would be to go along with whatever she had in mind.

An hour later, when Nika had left me, my mind once again strayed back to Liverpool and the short shore leave I had taken when the *Virtuous* was being refitted in Belfast.

HELL AND HIGH WATER

Twenty-Four

Liverpool

The first thing I did when I got off the ferry at the Pier Head was to look for a bus to take me to Egerton Street. I was eager to get home to tell my family about my adventures in the navy thus far; about the trips to Malta and the excitement of being onboard a fighting ship. However, what I wanted most of all was to find Glenda and carry on from where we had left off a few months ago, when I had first left Liverpool for basic training.

It had been a long time since I had seen her. She had come to Lime Street station to see me catch the train to Birmingham where I was to change for the onward journey, but she had remained hidden in the shadows. My parents wanted to wave me off and with father being the way he was and thinking my relationship with her was over, she had followed behind and remained out of their sight whilst we said our goodbyes on the platform. I knew she was there having seen her two nights before when again I managed to sneak her into the printshop, having had a secret key cut. I know this was wrong and breaching a good man's trust, but it was the only way we could be alone one last time before my departure.

We had never seriously spoken about our future plans and whenever it was touched upon in conversation neither of us elaborated. Personally, I could not make her any promises. In fact I refrained from doing so because I really did not know what the future would hold for either of us. I was going off to war and who knew where that would lead? There was also the added problem of having a father who would be totally resistant to any relationship with a Catholic girl, no matter how nice she was, or how lapsed her religious practice.

When I stopped to think about it, I was not too sure what our relationship was all about. Was it just a physical thing, merely a fleeting convenience for the two of us? Was I somebody to help her get over whatever it was that had happened in Flint? For I was sure something significant had taken place in Wales that she would not reveal to me. Was I using her for the fun I was having and as something to give me a reason to come back? Were we both actually using each other for our own selfish ends? All these questions would run around my head whenever I relaxed and thought about it. But due to the times we were living in, I did not really seek out the answers to any of them. I was somewhat indifferent to it all, truth be told.

As the ferry had approached the mouth of the River Mersey, and the familiar buildings came into view, I had felt an enormous sense of pride in the city of my birth. The site of the birds atop the Liver Building, standing proud and defiant in the early afternoon sun, gave me a sense of hope for the future. From the ferry I could see cars, buses, and people, all going about their daily business. It was the normal hustle and bustle of a major city, just the same as before the Germans had started to attack us and I knew in that moment they could never beat us. They may drop their bombs and try to destroy our will to fight, to break our spirit, but this very act only made us more determined to resist them. An old man on the ferry had told me that although the bombs had stopped falling with the regularity of a few months ago, the Germans were still coming over now and again. However, it was not with the same frequency and they did not cause as much damage as they had done at the height of the Blitz. It seemed at last Britain was getting its act together.

The bus took me as far as Great Homer Street where I had to walk the rest of the way, my kitbag balanced over my shoulder. As I strolled through the streets men and women smiled, said 'hello' or tipped their hats at me. Groups of children stopped playing to watch me walk by, some of them shouting over and asking me silly questions about my attire. The Mediterranean sun had tanned my skin slightly and I was in full naval uniform, complete with bell-bottomed trousers, shiny boots and rounded hat. I realised I had a big smile upon my face as I sauntered along the streets of my childhood. The familiarity of the place made me feel secure and only now that I was walking them did I realise how much I had missed my home city and the people in it.

Eventually I arrived on Egerton Street and as I approached the small terraced house that was home I saw Hilary and little Francis sitting on the doorstep, my young brother making invisible drawings on the pavement with a stick he held in his hand. Hilary's twin, Dorothy, was playing hopscotch on the cobblestones in front of them, skipping happily in the sunshine.

Even though I was their brother they did not recognise me immediately.

'Hello, you lot,' I said, smiling at them. 'I hope you're all behaving yourselves.'

Hilary stared up at me blankly.

It took a few moments before she realised who she was looking at.

'George!' she shouted, jumping up and throwing her arms around me. I dropped my kitbag to the ground and picked her up. 'George. You're home! I didn't recognise you.'

'I am. I am,' I replied laughing with her as she kissed my face.

Dorothy came bounding over, her game of hopscotch instantly forgotten. She too joined in with greeting me. 'George, George!... Mam! Dad! George is home!' she shouted.

Francis looked up from his idle scratchings but did not seem to comprehend what was happening. But then, I supposed, he was still very young.

Eventually I put Hilary down and kissed her twin sister. I could see neighbours looking out of windows up and down the street and one or two came to their front doors and waved over. I returned their greetings enthusiastically.

I felt a tap on my shoulder and turned to see my father standing in the doorway. He was wearing trousers and a vest and was barefoot. He did not say anything but took me in an embrace which I returned just as strongly.

And then mother was there, wiping her hands on an old tea towel, tears filling her eyes.

'You didn't tell us you were coming. This is a wonderful surprise. You look so healthy and tanned. How long have you got?' she babbled all at once, her words falling over themselves as they left her mouth.

I moved to her and held her by the shoulders. I kissed her forehead and embraced her just as strongly as I had my father, chuckling all the while at her reaction to seeing me.

'A few days,' I replied. 'The ship's in Belfast to have some new equipment fitted and they've given us all some leave.'

'Wonderful, wonderful,' she replied. 'Come inside. Put your feet up and I'll make you a cup of tea.'

I followed her through to the sitting room and then father said, 'Sit in my chair… Go on.'

I turned around and looked at him.

This was the biggest honour he could have given me and as I sat down and pulled off my boots, I could not have been happier, my smile stretching from ear to ear.

For the remainder of that day I was made to feel special. Mother fussing over me as though I was King George himself, making sure I was all right, ensuring I had enough to eat, that my teacup was full and sorting out the washing in my kitbag. Father sat on the couch with my brothers and sisters listening to my tales of life in the navy and all the friends I had made and the characters I had met. I decided I would spend this first evening with my family and then go in search of my friends in the morning.

That night I slept like a log and in the morning when I awoke and made my way downstairs, I saw father had already left for work and mother was busy in the kitchen making breakfast for everyone. Times were hard and with rationing now determining a family's diet, we had to make do with 'Eggs in a Nest'. However, fried eggs and fried bread made with dripping did not really appeal to me and so I let my younger brother, Jimmy, have mine. He was dressed in his postman's uniform and hurriedly wolfed it down before heading off for his shift at the sorting office.

I decided to walk Dorothy and Hilary to school and then made my way over to Mister Johnson's printshop. I felt it only right that I paid my former employer a visit while I was home, as he had been very good to me when I was an apprentice.

When I entered the reception area I was surprised to see Billy Jones standing there, a clipboard in one hand and a cup of tea in the other.

'George!' he said, clearly shocked to see me. He put his cup and board down on a nearby table and came over to greet me.

Shaking me enthusiastically by the hand and clasping me a little too tightly on the shoulder with the other, he said, 'Bloody hell, George, it's so good to see you.'

I was very confused.

HELL AND HIGH WATER

'What are you doing here?' I asked. 'I thought you were in the army.'

Letting go of my hand, he replied. 'A long story, Georgie boy. A long story.'

As I was about to ask him to tell it to me, Mister Johnson appeared in the doorway.

'My goodness,' he said. 'Look at you. You look really well, George. Really well.'

They showed me through to the rest room and I spent half an hour with the two of them, telling them about my adventures aboard HMS *Virtuous*. Mister Johnson must have told me at least five times I would always have a position with him once the war was over if I wanted it. Although I knew he meant well, I could not see how he could make this offer not knowing what his business needs would be in the future.

After his initial excitement at seeing me, Billy seemed a little quiet, letting Mister Johnson do all the talking, only asking me the briefest of questions every now and again. This was unlike him as he was usually the heart and soul of any conversation and pretty much loved the sound of his own voice. I found this slightly strange.

Mister Johnson was called back to the shop floor to deal with a minor emergency and I took this as a cue to take my leave. As I stood up to go, again I asked Billy what had happened in regards to his time in the army.

'Crocked my knee on an assault course during training,' he told me. 'I jumped down from a bloody big wall and landed all awkwardly. My knee ballooned up like a… well… like a balloon. And not a small balloon either, George. Like one of them big bloody things over the docks. Seems I've done irreparable damage to it and so they medically discharged me. Mister Johnson was kind enough to give me my old job back. Bit of a bugger really.'

'I suppose, looking on the bright side,' I replied, 'Iris is probably grateful for it.'

'Hmm,' he replied frowning slightly. 'Come on, George. I'll see you out.'

I could not say I had noticed him limping in any way when we had met earlier. But now, as he walked me to the exit, there was a pronounced, if not exaggerated, awkwardness in his gait.

That night I went in search of Glenda.

It was seven thirty in the evening and there was drizzle in the air. I turned my collar up to stop the rain from running down my neck and boldly stepped up to the front door of the Shepherds' house. I could see lights on and hear movement inside.

Taking a breath, I rapped a couple of times on the door and waited. I could hear female voices inside, each telling the other to answer the door and after a minute or so the door opened. Ida Shepherd, Iris's mother, stood before me.

'Hello, George,' she said abruptly. 'What do you want?'

I was taken aback by this rather harsh greeting.

'I was wondering if I could have a word with Glenda…'

'Glenda's not in,' she interrupted. She was about to close the door in my face when I saw Iris in the hallway behind her. On seeing me she came over, stopping her mother from shutting the door.

'Can I have a word with George, please, mam?'

Before Ida had a chance to reply, Iris grabbed a coat from a stand to the left and stepped past her mother and out into the street beside me.

'Looks like I don't have much of a choice,' replied Ida. 'Don't be long.'

With that she shut the door, leaving us both standing in the rainy street.

'Come on, George. Walk with me.'

She grabbed my arm and led me purposefully away from the house, putting up the hood of her coat as she dragged me along.

'Iris,' I said. 'What the bloody hell is going on?'

She did not answer but kept on walking, pulling me along with her.

Eventually, when we got to the end of the street she stopped. Beneath the glow of a streetlamp she turned to me and pulled her hood down.

'I don't think my mam is too pleased with Glenda, to tell the truth,' she said. 'And, to be honest, I don't blame her.'

'What do you mean?' I asked. I could not understand how Glenda could upset anybody.

'She's often late home from work and never lets her know what she's up to,' she replied. 'To be honest, George, she never confides in me about anything… about work… about you… about anything. She just seems to be a lodger at the moment and it's starting to irritate us.'

I was shocked. Although Glenda was a little odd, I did not take her for the thoughtless type. If what Iris was telling me was correct, then she was being extremely selfish towards people who had been very kind to her.

'Has she written to you at all?' asked Iris.

'A bit. I've had the odd letter. But then it's difficult to get mail and that, in the navy,' I replied. 'We're away at sea so long. And I'm not exactly the best at keeping in touch with people myself. Let's face it Iris, Glenda and I aren't exactly official, are we?'

'I suppose not,' said Iris with a small frown. 'Although I think she thought you were for a time. If I can be honest with you, George…'

'Please be.'

'I think she was a little upset about you keeping her a secret from your mam and dad…'

'You know what he's like,' I interrupted. 'Although I think the world of him, he's a bloody pain in the arse at times.'

'I think it made her feel she was your dirty little secret,' replied Iris. 'And that's not a nice thing to feel, George. Maybe you should have either cut her loose or stood up to your father more.'

I was not used to receiving criticism in this way and although I wanted to defend myself no words came to me. As I stood there in the rain, with little Iris Shepherd looking up at me, I realised what she had said was totally correct. I had not done enough to make

HELL AND HIGH WATER

Glenda feel special and I deserved to be criticised for it. This was something I would have to rectify.

'Maybe you're right,' I eventually replied. 'Maybe I haven't treated her as well as I should.'

'To be honest, George,' went on Iris. 'I wouldn't put all your eggs in one basket where she's concerned.'

'What makes you say that?' I replied.

'Oh, nothing. It's just that she can be quite flighty. She doesn't take life too seriously when maybe sometimes she should.'

Suddenly there was movement to my right and when I turned to look I saw Glenda walking towards us. She wore a long green coat, a patterned scarf over her head and held an umbrella against the rain. At first she did not see us. When she did, she did not realise it was me.

'Hello, Glenda,' I said as she got closer. 'Nice to see you.'

The look on her face was a picture. First one of shock followed quickly by a nervous smile and then full blown excitement.

'George! Oh my God! When did you get home?... Are you back for good?' she blurted enthusiastically.

'Yesterday,' I replied. 'I've a few days shore leave. It's really good to see you, Glenda.'

Iris said, 'I'll leave you two to it,' and, without acknowledging her cousin, set off back to the house leaving the two of us alone.

'You should have written,' said Glenda immediately Iris had gone. 'You should have told me you were coming home.'

'I wanted to surprise you,' I said, smiling at her. 'However, it's a bit difficult to post a letter when you're on a ship and if I'd done it in Belfast, I'd have been home before it arrived.'

She giggled. 'Any excuse, George Martin. You'll tell me anything. What are your plans while you're home?'

'I haven't any really,' I replied. 'The ship's in dock for a week or so and they've let us come home for a bit. I was hoping to catch up with everyone and spend some time with you.'

'That's nice,' she replied somewhat sheepishly.

'When are you free?' I asked. 'I'm not doing anything this evening if you'd like to go out.'

'Erm… I'm sorry, George. I'm dead beat, if I'm being honest with you. I've had a really busy day and this is all a bit of a shock seeing you. If it's all right with you, can we do something tomorrow?'

'Of course,' I replied. 'Whatever you say.'

She reached up and kissed me on the cheek.

'I need to get out of this rain,' she said. 'I had a cold a couple of weeks ago and don't want to catch another.'

She took hold of my arm and we walked the very short distance to the Shepherds' front door. As she opened it she turned to me.

'Do you want to meet me after work tomorrow?' she asked. 'We could go for a coffee or something.'

'Erm… Yes,' I replied. 'That would be nice.'

She let herself in and offered a small smile before she closed the door behind her, leaving me standing alone in the rain.

HELL AND HIGH WATER

I took a deep breath and turned to walk back home. This interaction between us had disturbed me slightly. There was something about the nonchalant and almost indifferent way in which she had treated me that gave me concern. I know I was not one for writing but considering we had not seen each other for such a long time I half expected her to run into my arms and cover my face with kisses. However, this had not happened and after speaking to Iris I was not altogether too sure Glenda was pleased to see me at all.

The following afternoon, as arranged, I met Glenda outside the factory where she worked. As the workers filed out of the gates, she bounded over with a huge smile on her face and took my arm. I noticed a few of her colleagues watch on indifferently, but one or two raised their eyebrows or turned to talk to their friends. I had the impression we were their topic of conversation.

'Come on, George,' she said, in that accent I found so appealing. 'Let's get out of this place.'

We found a coffee shop nearby and ordered drinks and a plate of sandwiches.

'So, how have you been?' I asked.

'I've been fine,' she replied. 'Although your lack of correspondence has not been nice, George.'

'Like I said yesterday,' I replied. 'It's very difficult to post letters when you're in the middle of the Mediterranean Sea. And anyway, I'm not one for writing. I think I only sent one letter to my mam.'

'Well then, you should be ashamed of yourself,' she said, and I did not think she was joking.

Maybe she was right. Maybe I should have made more of an effort about keeping in touch with everyone. When in Gibraltar between the Malta convoys there had been plenty of time to write. I had been very lacking in this and so made a mental note to apologise to my mother when I got home.

'I cried my eyes out the day you left,' she said sadly. 'I went home from Lime Street and bawled like a baby over you, George Martin. I stood there, away from all your family as they waved you off. I watched them kiss you and hug you and I felt so alone, so rejected. It was as though you were ashamed of me.'

'My God!' I replied. 'That couldn't be further from the truth. I most certainly am not ashamed of you, Glenda. You know it's my father and the way he is…'

'Well I would have expected you to stand up to him if that was the case,' she said. I could see a tear start to form in her eye but she brushed it away quickly and took a breath. 'But you don't, do you, George? You're in the military now and you're supposed to be a man, but you're still scared of him. You're still a little boy really.'

I did not know how to respond. What she said was the truth and I could not argue with her.

I took a sip of tea and thought about how to answer her but she started speaking again, her confidence to tell me exactly what she thought growing strong.

'You were quite happy to take me to your workplace and do the things we did. Yes, you were quite happy to do that, George. You were quite happy to have your wicked way with me, but you couldn't take me seriously, could you? You made me feel like I was nothing more than your plaything…'

'Hang on a minute,' I interrupted. 'Don't go saying all that was down to me. From what I remember it was you who accosted me in that alleyway. It was you who came up with the idea to go to the printshop after hours. It was you who made the first move with all that stuff. Not that I'm complaining, but don't try and make out it was all my idea. That's not fair.'

'Maybe not,' she said after a while. 'Maybe it *was* me, but you could have stopped any time you wanted. But you didn't. Even when you knew you weren't going to become serious with me…'

'I had every intention of becoming serious with you,' I replied. 'In fact, I thought we *were* serious. I thought all that stuff made it serious.'

'Yet you still hid me from your parents. That's not being serious, George. That's being a coward. You may be on a warship and you may be going off fighting the Germans… but you're still a coward.'

We sat in silence for a few moments.

'So where do we go from here?' I asked, eventually. 'I didn't intend for you to feel like this, Glenda. I really didn't. I had no idea I was upsetting you so much.'

'How would you know when you couldn't even be bothered writing to me?'

I realised I would not get anywhere with her. She had made up her mind to chastise me and I did not have the energy to argue with her. The thing was, I agreed with virtually every word she had said.

JOHN McKAY

'If you give me a chance I'll put this right,' I said. 'I never wanted to make you feel this way. Frankly I'm ashamed that I have. It really wasn't my intention.'

She wrinkled her nose slightly but seemed to accept this answer. She sipped at her tea and picked up a sandwich and chewed on it thoughtfully.

'Okay, George,' she said after she swallowed a piece. 'You need to show me what you say is true. I've hung around for you while you've been away. And don't think I haven't had offers from other men, because I have. I've waited for you to decide what you want to do. You can't leave me hanging on like this.'

We finished our sandwiches without any further significant conversation in regards to our relationship. She asked me about life on board ship and was intrigued and excited when I told her of my new friends and about the dangers of the convoys. She thought my misdemeanour in Gibraltar was particularly funny. By the time we headed for home the mood between us had changed significantly.

She told me that, like the night before, she was quite tired and needed to get an early night. She promised to meet me the following evening at eight o'clock and that if she was feeling less fatigued, we would make more of a night of it. The twinkle in her eye as she said this reminded me of the nights we had spent in Mister Johnson's printshop, those nights after all the staff had left and I secretly sneaked her into the building. When I left her to walk the final few yards home the earlier awkward conversation that had taken place between us was almost forgotten and I had a renewed spring in my step as I headed for Egerton Street.

Twenty-Five

My shoulder was healing nicely. By the end of the fourth week I was starting to get more movement. As long as I could bear the pain, I was able to use my left hand to lift light objects. The muscles were knitting together well and I was told that, over time, I would probably gain full use of my arm again. Despite the harsh conditions, Dougie and Nika had done a remarkable job in keeping the wound clean and free of infection. As I was fairly mobile, I did not rely on them too much and tried to keep myself as clean as I possibly could. However, my shoulder was still very tender and I found it difficult to get comfortable at night. I would toss and turn on the rickety old iron bed, conscious of my restlessness keeping others awake.

The days had become monotonous and we found it difficult to keep ourselves occupied. Those of us who had been lucky enough to have wounds that were bearable tried to make life a little easier for those with more severe injuries, even if that just meant sitting with them to try to boost their morale. After a while we thought maybe we were getting on their nerves and were doing nothing to alleviate their suffering.

I took it upon myself to assist Dougie and Nika with basic hygiene in the ward. Some of the sheets the lads were lying on were filthy and I took them away to the laundry. This was basically another former classroom where old iron baths filled with cold water were laid out in rows. I had to scrub the dirty sheets with carbolic soap, the water turning brown and mucky as I did so. It was disgusting but necessary work. There was no running water and orderlies would have to go outside and bring in barrowloads of snow to melt and use for washing the sheets and bandages, and also to boil for drinking water. It was extremely difficult to get the sheets dry and they would hang for hours, stained and ragged, drip drying in a separate room. We did our best but I feared it was not good enough. The place was probably rife with germs.

I would go at the sheets until the pain in my shoulder became unbearable and I could not continue. I wore a scarf over my face as I worked, the stench from the soiled bed linen overpowering, and would often recoil as this awful miasma hit my nostrils causing me to heave and retch. Whenever his happened I would run from the room and go out into the freezing cold to get some fresh air before quickly returning to the sanctuary of the hospital due to the intolerable temperatures outside.

During these times outside the building I was able to take a closer look at the surroundings. The hospital was in the centre of a built up residential area. Bomb damaged blocks of flats surrounded us, dominating the landscape like broken and dejected behemoths. They gave us a degree of protection from enemy air attacks. But then the Germans were more interested in the port than wasting their bombs on targets away from the front line, although now and again a lone plane would drop their explosives on targets nearer to where we were housed.

In my immediate vicinity the snow covered everything and continued to fall incessantly. Soldiers and civilian workers passed along the roads with snow ploughs, trying desperately to keep them passable for the wagons. On one occasion I saw lorryloads of troops heading for the port, no doubt to relieve those protecting it from the Germans.

In the distance anti-aircraft fire pounded the skies. What looked like a murder of crows circled the far away port, swooping down to drop their payloads on the docked ships or port buildings. Now and again I saw enemy planes leaving the battle, smoke pouring from their engines and once I watched as a pilot baled out, his white parachute almost indistinct against the grey sky. I feared for what would happen when the Red Army soldiers got hold of him. This worry for the enemy airman quickly dissolved when I returned to the ward and saw the damage his bombs had caused to those on the ground and to my shipmates who lay in their disgusting beds. What happened to him happened to him. I would lose no sleep over it.

One evening as I was making an attempt at reading the copy of *Oliver Twist* Wally had given me, Dougie approached my bed.

'Hey, George,' he said. 'Are you up for a bit of work? We need someone to help us in the operating theatre and everyone's occupied. There's been a few Russian soldiers brought in. Looks like their truck took a hit from a Stuka. Some are in quite a bad way. We just need someone to do a bit of fetching and carrying and stuff. Nothing too strenuous.'

HELL AND HIGH WATER

I put the book down and stretched my arm out to my side to test its strength. The pain was diminishing with each passing day. Once content I would be able to cope, I climbed off the bed.

'Yes, Dougie,' I replied. 'Lead the way.'

I was not prepared for the sight that met me when I entered the operating room.

Lying on a trolley in the middle of the room was a young Russian soldier who had clearly been hit by a large piece of shrapnel. His right leg was broken just below the knee and it flopped loosely to his side. His bloodied trousers had been torn to reveal the sharp, white bones of his tibia and fibula, jutting jagged out of his clothing at an unnatural angle. Blood poured steadily from the open wound, dripping onto the tiled floor, adding to the dirty stains already there. He lay quietly, his hands covering his face. I was immediately taken by the lack of any moaning or screaming from him. I knew if I had been in his position, the air would have been filled with my cries.

A harassed looking surgeon was hacking at his clothing with some blunt looking scissors and getting annoyed when they did not cut as quickly or as cleanly as he wanted. A young nurse stood to his side, holding a tray of hastily scrubbed surgical instruments ready for his selection. Through the far door I could see into the main hall. A number of medics and orderlies were giving first aid to more injured soldiers. One was having his head bandaged, the nurse wrapping the cloth around his forehead and right eye. No sooner was it covered than a red stain appeared over his damaged socket.

'What do you want me to do?' I asked Dougie.

'You might need to help us hold this fella down,' he replied. 'They need to take the leg off and we've run out of anaesthetic. There's not even any vodka to get him drunk before we do it. If you don't think you're up for it, if you think your shoulder can't take it, then tell me now.'

I moved my shoulder around again and although the pain was quite severe, I thought it could not be half as bad as what the poor Russian lying uncomplaining on the trolley before me must be enduring.

'I'm fine, Dougie,' I replied. 'I'll be okay.'

'Right,' he said. He turned to the surgeon who had by now completed cutting off the trouser leg and nodded. The doctor nodded back and then spoke to his nurses.

Immediately they started to act. The doctor indicated for his assistants to prepare themselves and Dougie gave me a nudge. The surgeon held a saw in his hands and waited whilst Dougie positioned himself at the head of the trolley. He was ready to use his quite considerable strength to pin the patient down. I sat myself on the edge and took hold of his left leg as the doctor and another nurse positioned themselves at his right. Throughout all this, the soldier lay still, his hands covering his face, not uttering a sound.

And then the doctor got to work.

I went straight back to bed and lay down. Just like the young Russian soldier had done, I put my hands over my face. However, unlike him, I sobbed.

I cried like a baby.

HELL AND HIGH WATER

We were never too sure at what point he died as he had been so quiet throughout the procedure. All the time he had been in the hospital he had not uttered a word. He had just taken it with a sort of quiet acceptance. The doctor was unsure of why he died. Whether he had already lost too much blood by the time he had arrived or whether it was down to the shock of having his leg amputated without any anaesthetic whatsoever. He could not be sure. It may have been a mixture of the two.

The doctor had quickly had us remove the body from the surgery, his concentration immediately turning to the next patient. As we carried the young lad out into the back yard for later collection and burial, I thought about how life had become so cheap and the individual so insignificant. It upset me to know that should I die here, I too would be dumped unceremoniously onto that growing pile of frozen corpses. I was not sure if I could handle that.

And so I wept. Selfishly.

I wept for myself and the hell I found myself in.

JOHN McKAY

Twenty-Six

Liverpool

I decided to tell father everything. I felt I owed it to Glenda.

After leaving her that evening, with thoughts of what she had said running around my head, I knew she was right. I had not treated her well at all. In fact, I had treated her abysmally and I felt I should do something to right that wrong.

I was in no way ashamed of her, as she thought I was. In fact it was quite the opposite. Whenever I walked along with her holding onto my arm I felt proud. I felt ten feet tall. She was a beautiful young woman and she had decided she wanted to be with me. So why on earth had I allowed her to feel this insecurity?

As I had walked home I decided that no matter how much it upset my father, I would tell him all about her and I was not going to give her up due to an old prejudice the rest of the city had long since banished to history.

As soon as I entered the house I found the whole family in the front room, listening to the BBC news on the radio. From what I could hear, the war was not going very well. But the war was the last thing on my mind at that moment.

'I need to speak to you,' I said.

They all turned to look at me, apart from an irritated Jimmy who told me to shush.

'What is it, son?' asked my mother, looking up from her knitting.

'I need to speak to you, Dad.'

He was sitting in his usual spot by the fire, his work clothes on. I knew he was on the night shift and would soon be leaving for for the docks.

'Yes,' he replied, tapping his pipe on the chair arm. 'What is it, lad?'

'I don't think I've been quite honest with you,' I replied, my nerves starting to kick in.

'What do you mean?'

Everyone had stopped listening to the radio and all their attention was focused on me.

'That girl I was seeing a few months ago. Glenda…'

'The Shepherd girl? The Catholic?'

'Yes, her.'

'What about her?' he asked.

From the corner of my eye I could see mother starting to look nervous. She pretended to carry on knitting as though this was a perfectly normal conversation but I could tell from the rhythm of her needles she was anticipating the bombshell I was about to drop.

'You've been seeing her, haven't you?' he asked, almost too calmly.

'I never really stopped,' I replied. The truth of what I was saying made me instantly feel good about the whole situation. I did not feel fearful for his reply. I did not really care if he was upset by it. I was seeing Glenda Bradshaw and I was serious about her. She was a Catholic but that held absolutely no importance in the whole scheme of things. It simply did not matter.

'I didn't think so,' he replied.

'I'm sorry?'

I was confused. Where was the ire? Why didn't he blow his top and threaten to kill me?

'I said, "I didn't think so",' he repeated.

I was lost for words. I had prepared for a huge argument. For him to come at me all guns blazing.

'Can you all please leave the room,' he said to the others. 'All of you. Upstairs. I need to speak to George, man to man… and someone switch off that bloody radio.'

They knew not to argue with him. There was now a distinct atmosphere in the room but it was not coming from my father, who seemed far too relaxed about the whole thing.

Billy walked over and turned off the radio. He turned to his siblings. 'Come on, you lot. You heard Dad. Upstairs, now.'

He took his sisters by the hand and left the room. Mother put down her knitting and stood up. She stooped down to pick Francis from the floor and carried him to the kitchen, closing the door behind her. This left my father and I alone.

'Sit down, son,' he said, indicating the chair opposite. 'I haven't got long because I have to go to work in a few minutes.'

'I don't understand, Dad,' I said. 'I thought you'd go mad.'

He sighed and ran his left hand through his thinning grey hair.

'When you've seen what I've seen down at those docks, George, some things just aren't that important anymore. If they ever were. This war, and the last one come to that, should have made me realise a lot sooner what's important in life. Worrying and getting worked up over trivial things sap your energy. They drain you. And for no good reason.

'Look… You knew what I thought about Catholics and that was important to me. When you first started seeing this Glenda girl, I took it as a slight against me personally. But now I realise that's not the case. You can't help who you fall for. Who you fall in love with. What I should have done was to be happy for you. If you're happy then I'm happy. That's all I want for any of my kids. It's as simple as that. Some parents want their children to be doctors, solicitors, accountants and all that bollocks. All I want is for mine to be happy. And if it means you fall in love with a Catholic, then so be it. You'll get no objection from me.'

I could not understand this change in attitude from him.

'I still don't understand, Dad. All our lives you've had this hatred for them. Something I never understood if I'm being totally honest with you, by the way. Why this sudden change?'

'I don't think it's a sudden change,' he replied softly. 'It's probably been a slow realisation that my attitude has become somewhat redundant. Outdated even. This is a time when people need to come together. We've a common enemy. We're at war again, against a familiar foe and they need to be stopped once and for all. Arguing and squabbling amongst ourselves isn't going to help anything.

'While you were away we had a number of bombing raids. On one occasion some of my fellas didn't make it to the shelter on time. Charlie Collins… Do you remember him?… Well he died, George. He was killed in the bombing. And a couple of others were badly injured too. It made me think long and hard about everything. You know I'm not a complicated man and I like a quiet life, but after seeing this, I think things sort of fell into place for me. Hatred breeds hatred and that's all negative. It drains you. It's tiring. It eats you up and can eventually kill you. So to cut to the point, George. If you want to see this girl, don't let me hold you back.'

I could not believe what I was hearing. For a brief moment I felt choked. I felt a tear start to form in my eye but forced it back. I did not want my father to think I was still a child.

Eventually he continued, moving the subject away from his somewhat epiphany moment.

'So. What's she like?' he asked.

'She's lovely,' I replied. 'She's also very frustrating and sometimes quite annoying.'

He smiled. 'All women are. Take my word for it.'

'I'm finding that out for myself,' I replied.

'So what are your feelings towards her? Do you love her?'

'I'm not sure,' I replied honestly. 'I'm not sure of what my feelings are.'

HELL AND HIGH WATER

'Put it this way. Does this girl make you catch your breath when you look at her? Does she knot your stomach and make you choke whenever you think of her? Whenever you're not with her, are you desperate to see her?'

'Sometimes I feel like that,' I replied.

'Take your mother back there,' he went on. 'She may not look much to you but she does to me. And she does that to me every day. Every morning when I wake up I look at her and I thank God and Jesus that she chose to be with me. And every evening too. Every time. And when I have a break at work I take her picture out of my wallet and stare at it for a few minutes. When you find somebody who does that to you... Well, then you know you've found the right person. When you do find her, then hang on to her, George. If this Glenda's the one, I don't know. Only you know that. But don't settle for anything less. Life's too short.'

To say I was shocked at this change in my father's attitude would be an understatement. I was flabbergasted at this transformation in him.

He rose from the chair. I stood up to face him.

'Time for me to head off, George,' he said. 'I may not tell you enough, but I'm fiercely proud of you and what you're doing. We all are. You should hear your sisters talking about you to their friends. They're so proud.'

And then he embraced me and I hugged him back. He went to the kitchen to say goodbye to mother and to give Francis a kiss and then he put on his coat and left.

That night, as I lay in bed, I thought about what he had said to me. All those things about what love felt like to him and how he had spoken of his adoration for his wife. My mother. What he had said sounded like something you would read in a romantic novel, and not at all like real life.

No matter how much I tried, I could not summon for Glenda the same strength of feeling as he had described. As I drifted off to sleep I wondered why that was so.

Twenty-Seven

Midway through the fifth week, Lieutenant Freeman returned.

It was a Wednesday morning and when he walked into the ward we did not immediately recognise him as he had grown a beard, which suited him, I thought.

'The *Virtuous* will be ready to sail on Friday,' he announced to the room. 'The captain has told me to pass on that all those fit enough will be brought back onboard tomorrow evening. Those who are not will have to be left to get a berth on another ship when they're able to do so. A convoy is returning to Iceland and we're providing escort duties. The majority of the repairs have been carried out but once in Iceland there'll be a few more to be done before we can head back to Scotland. Those not able to make this trip may pick us up again in Iceland.'

He stayed long enough to speak to each of us and triage who was to leave and who would remain in the care of the Russians. I was lucky enough to be selected to travel. Dougie Sears volunteered to stay behind with the most severely wounded until they could be repatriated. My already high opinion of him was increased even further.

Although many of my shipmates would have to remain in Murmansk, I was very happy to be leaving. The thought of returning to the familiarity of HMS *Virtuous,* and eventually home, made me smile for the first time in a long while.

Wally greeted me with a huge smile. I have to admit it was really good to see him after so long.

'Welcome home,' he said simply.

Home? Was HMS *Virtuous* now my home?

Eight of us had been collected that evening by Lieutenant Freeman as planned. He had arrived in a truck he had borrowed from our Red Army allies. However, they had not given him a driver and so he had driven it himself. When he had arrived at the hospital he looked harassed and stressed.

'All those selected, get your gear and get in the truck right away,' he had said after we had all gathered in the ward. 'The *Virtuous* is in dock now but we need to get a move on. The convoy is leaving in the morning.'

I said my goodbyes to Dougie Sears who remained with the most seriously wounded, just as he said he would.

When we had gathered our gear and were ready to move out I looked over to Nika. She sat at her table watching us line up. I tried to catch her eye but she seemed unconcerned as to what was happening. I had to stifle a smile at this indifference towards me. She had visited me in my bed almost every night for the past two weeks. But now, as I was about to leave and would probably never see her again, she was totally uninterested. As we filed out of the room, she turned her attention back to her paperwork and left us to it, as though all this was perfectly normal. In my heart of hearts I think I wanted her to at least be a little upset I was leaving, but I understood that what we had had was little more than two people offering each other some moments of comfort in a world gone mad. A few stolen minutes each day where we could forget about the mayhem and death taking place outside and rejoice in the fact that not everything in the world has to be bad. I knew I would never forget Nika and the time we had spent together. However, I was under no illusion that by the time I had left the building she had probably already forgotten my name.

My attention turned back to Wally.

'It's really good to see you again, George?' he said, taking my right hand in his. My left arm had again been placed in a sling and he motioned as if to pat my shoulder but quickly stopped himself.

We were gathered outside the sickbay to be assessed by Mister Greaves, the ship's doctor. I stood in line with the other walking wounded waiting to be seen.

Wally had come straight to the sickbay when he heard we were back onboard.

'And it's good to see you, too,' I replied. 'What mischief have you been up to while we've been away?'

'To be honest, we've been bored shitless,' he replied. 'Stuck at a place called Rosta for the last few weeks while the shipwrights have been patching the old dear up. We got a bit of shore leave but there's nothing to see here. It's just ice and snow. What I'd give again for another Gibraltar run.'

'I know what you mean,' I smiled.

'We had the odd air attack and that,' he continued. 'But they mainly concentrated on the port itself, so they weren't as often as we thought they'd be. How were things for you lot?'

'I'll tell you all about it later,' I replied. Mister Greaves was beckoning me to come through.

I was asked to remove the sling and he took a look at my wound. He was happy with how it was healing and when I showed him that some movement was returning he looked especially pleased, telling me it was my strong young body that was the reason for such a remarkable recovery.

'I have to admit, Martin,' he said. 'I thought you were a goner when I first saw you lying there. Thought you'd had it. Now look at you. You'll be fit for service in no time at all. In the meantime get some more rest if you can and I'll see you again in the morning.'

These words from the ship's doctor left me feeling the most positive I had felt for a long time. I was going to be fine and would probably make a full recovery. I understood that I could quite easily be dead and this sense of meeting Death and repelling him made me feel invincible.

Early the following morning, under the cover of darkness, the ship set sail. Wally had assisted me into my hammock which I was pleased to see was in the same state I had left it, all my things and personal items not having been touched. It had taken some pushing and shoving, and quite a lot of pain, but eventually I had settled and fallen asleep almost immediately.

For the first time in a long while I slept well and when I awoke I discovered we had been travelling for a few hours. I looked out of the porthole and saw the weather was no better than it had been on our voyage

HELL AND HIGH WATER

in to Russia. The sea was very choppy and sleet and snow poured from the dark clouds above us. Once again, as the *Virtuous* headed out towards the mouth of the Kola Inlet and past Polyarny, (where we had originally been bound for), moving out to the wider waters of the Barents Sea, the feeling of unease I had felt so often on the journey in returned.

We understood U-boat wolf-packs were patrolling in the open sea, waiting for us to show our faces. Lookouts were posted at all the high points on the ship and the E.W.O. operators had their eyes glued to their ASDIC screens, looking for those electronic pings that would show us where they were.

It was now mid morning. I headed to the radio room to find my old friends and was surprised to see Petty Officer Singer sitting in the chair I used to occupy, my good friend Walter Honeyman sitting beside him.

'Hello, P.O.,' I said upon seeing him.

'Good morning, laddie,' he greeted me, a huge grin on his face. 'Glad to see you up and about.'

'I don't understand,' I replied.

Walter looked over. 'The Petty Officer's been helping out here, while you've been incapacitated.'

'That's true,' replied Singer. 'After all, I'm a signaller too, you know. And a damn better one than either of you two laddies.'

I perched myself on the edge of the desk next to Wally.

'I know I'm classed as unfit for duty, P.O.,' I said. 'But let's face it, radio work is hardly digging trenches, is it? I'm more than happy to come back to work if I can be let off the more physical stuff in between. I've got to see the M.O. this morning and can ask if it's okay, if you want.'

'Hmm,' he responded, rubbing his chin in thought. 'If you're sure. I'll see what Mister Guthrie has to say about it. If it's all right with him and you get clearance from Mister Greaves, then I don't see why not.'

'Yes,' chipped in Wally enthusiastically. 'I can make sure he doesn't overexert himself.'

'You trying to get rid of me, laddie?' asked Singer, turning to face him. 'You not like working so closely with me? Do my superior skills make you feel inadequate? Is that it? And you'd better say yes to that, by the way.'

'That's exactly it,' replied Wally, laughing. 'You make me feel redundant, P.O.'

'Okay, seriously,' continued Singer. 'Go to the sickbay now and if Mister Greaves is happy to release you then get straight back here and take over. I've a thousand things to do and all this flaming Morse code is getting on my bloody nerves.'

I did not have much trouble getting the medical officer to allow me to carry out light duties and so I returned to the radio room some minutes later and relieved Singer. The smile on his face and the awkward way he attempted to pat my back told me he was pleased with the situation and was glad to go back to his usual duties.

It seemed like life was getting back to normal.

Over the next few hours I managed to catch up with all my mates who had remained on the ship whilst it was undergoing repairs. Ralph Reid had a new second, a shy young lad from the galley named Greg Cooper who was a familiar face to us, having served us our meals for the last year or so. Harry Benson and Jack Holland, our two counterparts on the opposite shift, were very pleased to see I was alive and well. They wanted me to tell them all about the time I had spent in the hospital. I did not go into too much detail, particularly about what had happened with Nika, and tried not to make it sound as bad as it actually was. I did not want them to worry about the lads we had left behind.

Johnny Spencer, who worked on the bridge, made a point of coming to see me, as did the ASDIC operator, John Steadman whom I had formed a small friendship with before being wounded. Dave Higson, the big killick from the galley whose brother had been on the *Lancastria*, also popped his head around the door during the afternoon shift, bringing us both a cup of kye. He sat on the edge of my desk, biting his nails as we chatted about what we would do once we got home and could take some well earned shore leave.

With all my mates making such an effort to make me feel at home again, I was starting to feel positive about the situation.

And we were finally headed for home.

Twenty-Eight

The days were starting to get longer and during the first afternoon after leaving the Kola Inlet, I once again found myself on watch. The repairs to the ship had included a servicing of the heating system and for the first time in a long while, ice had not formed on the inside bulkheads. We no longer had to sit in full cold weather gear as we carried out our duties. However, we made sure our jerkins, balaclavas and gloves were close to hand, having dumped them untidily in the corner when we had relieved Jack and Harry.

Before going on duty I had looked through the mess deck portholes at the other ships of the returning convoy. They were positioned some distance away to our port side so I determined we were patrolling at the convoy's extreme northernmost position. I thought I could see land in the distance and one of the lads who squinted his eyes along with me suggested it may be Bear Island, but we were not really too sure. We were probably too far away and this may have been a mirage or a large iceberg.

The sea outside was not as choppy as it had been earlier in the day but there was still some movement in the ship as it rolled with the waves. It had not taken me long to get my sea legs back after spending so much time ashore and I was content with how I was feeling generally. My shoulder was still giving me pain, which was quite severe at times, but I did not complain. Some of my crew mates would not be returning from this trip and so I considered myself fortunate I was still in one piece. I felt moaning about my lot would not go down well with the others and it did not seem right anyway.

We had done about an hour on watch when we felt a sudden lurch to port. Clearly the ship was changing course and when the whooping sound of action stations blasted through the speakers, we knew that once again we were going into battle.

I was getting rather sick of it. The constant threat of attack from the depths, the surface and the air gave us no respite at all. Although it had been some time since I had been through this kind of thing it made me tired nonetheless. I was constantly exhausted but felt I had to do my bit. I had to carry on just like the rest of the lads. Nobody complained, but I could tell from their solemn faces they were feeling it as badly as I was. The only time I had ever felt safe on this voyage was when I had been holed up in Murmansk.

We could hear the familiar sounds of the Bofors and Oerlikons as they blasted away at the attacking aircraft outside. Above the sound of the guns and action stations klaxon, we could make out the boom of the heavy guns from the destroyers and the whooshing of enemy bombs as they exploded on the surface not too far away.

'I've a bad feeling about this, George,' said Wally. 'Those bombs sound very close to me. It might be an idea to get your gear on.'

I looked at the jumble of clothing in the corner of the room and sighed. He might have a point. It was better to be safe than sorry. After what had happened on the journey in, it was probably best to take Wally's advice just in case we needed to go outside.

As Wally assisted me into my jerkin, Petty Officer Singer appeared in the doorway. He too was dressed in his cold weather gear, his balaclava pulled back onto his head, ready to be brought down over his face.

'Get yourselves sorted, laddies,' he said. 'There's loads of the buggers up there. And it might be wise to get a life jacket on too.'

'That bad, P.O.?' I asked.

He frowned at me and walked away.

Eventually I was dressed in all my cold weather clothing and sat back in my seat taking a breath. It was still a struggle to dress myself and the hurried way in which I had just got my gear on made the pain in my shoulder hard to bear again.

Having spent the last couple of minutes assisting me, Wally now picked up his own things put on.

Suddenly I was thrown from my chair with a ferocity I had never experienced before and I immediately knew the *Virtuous* had been hit.

It felt as though the whole ship was lifted from the ocean and then slammed back down onto the water. My head was thrown against the side of the bulkhead. For a few seconds I was dazed, not comprehending where I was. No sooner did my senses return when I was again thrown across the room and then out into the walkway where Petty Officer Singer had been standing only a few seconds before. For some insane moment I felt myself rolling up the bulkhead, as though the laws of gravity had deserted the ship. I realised, to my horror, that the ship was listing violently to port and I could hear explosions throughout the superstructure. Lights flickered and sparked as the electrics short circuited.

I looked down the walkway. Sailors lay motionless further along the passageway towards the stern. A fire was beginning to take hold, the smoke moving over the casualties and coming my way.

Again the ship lurched and I was thrown back into the radio room. This time I was more prepared and held out my arms as I crashed towards the opposite bulkhead. However, the force of the ship's movement was too strong and I again crashed my head against the steel wall, instantly feeling the warm trickle of blood running down the side of my face.

'George! George!' shouted Wally.

I turned to look at my friend. He was curled up under the desk. He had obviously fallen into it during the initial blast. With the follow up explosions and the rolling of the ship he was now jammed underneath at a very odd angle. He sounded terrified.

'Come on, Wally!' I shouted. 'We have to get out. This is bad.'

Above the noise I could hear the frantic screams of my comrades outside. The desperation in their voices told me the one thing I dreaded was taking place. The ship was severely hit, maybe mortally. The lights continued to flicker in the radio room for a few more seconds and then went out.

'The ship's going down!' I yelled above the din. 'Come on, Wally. We need to get out or we'll go down with it.'

'I'm stuck, George,' he screamed back in darkness. 'Get yourself out, pal. Just leave me here.'

I somehow managed to get back to my feet and struggled over to him, wobbling along as the ship listed from side to side. The pain in my shoulder and head was starting to hamper my movements. I gritted my teeth. I knelt down and took hold of his legs. I prayed the adrenalin would numb the pain and allow me the strength I needed to help my friend.

'Just go, George,' he repeated, as an immense grinding noise filled our ears. It was clear the ship was breaking apart. I understood if we were both to survive then I needed to get Wally out of his tangle as quickly as I could. There was no way I was going to do as he was asking and leave him to die.

After some pushing and shoving I managed to free his left leg which was twisted behind his back. Once it had been released he was able to crawl out. Luckily, it was not injured and he was fine.

'Come on, Wally. Let's get on deck.'

Grabbing hold of each other for support we went out into the smoke filled walkway. Covering our mouths and noses with our hands, we moved as quickly as we could away from the fire. After stumbling along for a minute or so, we eventually found the ladder that led to the next deck and to where we could possibly get outside and find a lifeboat.

It was then I realised Wally was still without his warm clothes. He only had on a jumper and would

HELL AND HIGH WATER

freeze within no time if he did not get a decent coat and gloves on.

'Shit, Wally. You'll freeze out there.'

'Let's just get out first,' he replied. 'We can worry about that when we're off the ship.'

Eventually we made it outside and onto the deck. I could see the ship was in a really bad way and did not have much longer before it went under. The whole of the bridge was engulfed in flames and the forward 3 inch heavy gun was smashed and twisted, the metal bent at funny angles. Oddly, I could still see the bloodstain from young Howard's hand where the heat had melted away the ice. It seemed surreal, an oddly comical thing to notice in this complete mayhem.

Above us, German planes swooped down to attack other ships around us. I could see smoke billowing from two merchant vessels further to our port side. It appeared the planes were now leaving us alone, their job clearly done, and they were dropping the remainder of their bombs amongst the other ships. Spreading out the destruction.

'Get those lifeboats in the water,' I heard someone shout from behind me and when I turned I saw it was Lieutenant Mitchell, the ship's Executive Officer. 'We haven't got long,' he yelled.

The flames from the bridge and the middle of the ship were taking hold. Those who had made it above decks had now given up trying to fight the fires. It was obviously a battle they could not win. The ship was lost. I quickly realised this was now all about self preservation. It had become every man for himself.

JOHN McKAY

The *Virtuous* was listing further to port. Shipmates clung desperately to the superstructure, hanging on with all the strength they could summon to stop themselves falling overboard into the icy waters. Wally and I grabbed the side of the door to the forecastle mess deck as the ship again lurched to the side, before it settled back to a more level bearing.

By now my shoulder had become numb. I could not feel much pain but the use of my left arm was becoming very limited and I struggled to hang on. Wally could see I had problems.

'Just hang on, fella,' he said. 'Hang on, George. We'll get out of this, trust me.'

'But what about you?' I replied. 'You'll freeze to death out here.'

'The rescue ship will pick us up,' he said calmly. 'They'll be with us in no time. Stop worrying.'

Behind us Lieutenant Mitchell and a small group of matelots he had gathered were working the rigging on one of the lifeboats. After much pushing, shoving and shouting, they managed to free it. It hung over the side and, with another huge effort, they managed to lower it into the water. Further along I could see other groups doing the same with the other boats. It disturbed me to see their numbers were so few.

'Into it, boys,' yelled Mitchell, once it was in the water.

They did not need telling twice and one by one they lowered themselves or jumped into the boat as it bobbed almost indifferently in the water. I was happy to see my friend Ralph Reid climbing aboard and his young second, Greg Cooper, jump into it with him.

HELL AND HIGH WATER

Petty Officer Singer was also amongst them. When he saw us standing close by he shouted over.

'Come on, you two,' he yelled. 'Get yourselves in before she goes down. Save yourselves, laddies.'

Behind me I heard the groaning of metal as it twisted and buckled, the ship grasping desperately, yet hopelessly, to life. This noise made our minds up for us and we rushed forward in their direction, clinging to each other as we moved, careful not to lose our footing and be thrown overboard.

Suddenly I spotted a body to the right of the group. An officer lying face down, his corpse lolling with the motion of the ship. What caused me to pause was the fact he was wearing a warm looking overcoat.

'Wally, get his coat,' I shouted, pointing to where the poor, unfortunate man lay.

'What?' he shouted back, not understanding what I meant.

'His coat,' I yelled again, above the noise and pandemonium all around us. 'Get his coat!'

Realising what I was talking about, we both moved over to the body. When we turned it over, we saw it was Midshipman Guthrie. Half of his head had been staved in by a piece of metal, turning his features into a horrible caricature of himself. He had once been a handsome looking man but now death had turned him ugly.

Swallowing back the vomit that had risen in my throat, I grabbed Wally's arm.

'Come on. Get it off him. You need it more than he does.'

JOHN McKAY

Despite the disorder and confusion taking place all around us and the predicament we were in, I paused for a brief moment. Although this man had not exactly been my favourite person, to see him in this state was upsetting. In my head I said a quick prayer for his soul. It was the least he deserved.

Suddenly the ship lurched to the side causing me to slip to my knees. We could see the seawater was rising against the side and starting to wash over onto the deck. We had to move fast. There could not be much longer left. My mind was taken back to the *Dreyfus* and the speed in which it had gone down and I feared if we did not move quickly then we would be subject to the same fate. The image of the young sailor sliding off the upturned lifeboat filled my mind. The thought of the same thing happening to us spurred me to hurry up.

Putting all thoughts of mourning to one side, I grabbed Guthrie's corpse. Twisting him to the side, Wally was able to get his arms out of the sleeves and we soon had the greatcoat off him. Somehow it did not feel right, manhandling him in such a disrespectful manner, but I knew that without a proper coat Wally would struggle in the coming hours if we managed to make it off the ship alive. We had no choice but to do what we were doing. As heartless as it was, I had the attitude that Guthrie no longer needed it. As his body fell back to the deck the blood from the gory head wound mingled with the icy water that was beginning to lap at our ankles. Again I was filled with a huge sadness for the young officer.

HELL AND HIGH WATER

As we turned away I could see in the developing dusk that the lifeboat to my left was now in the water. In it were the sailors who had been with Lieutenant Mitchell. They were frantically grappling with the oars, pushing them against the side of the sinking ship, desperate to get as far away as possible before it sank and dragged them down with it.

'Come on you two,' I heard one of them shout. 'Hurry up. The ship's going down.'

'Come on, laddies,' yelled Singer, who was sitting next to Lieutenant Mitchell. 'Get in. Get yourselves over here.'

I looked around. The ship was sinking lower in the water and fires were now burning throughout the twisted and mangled superstructure. Thick black smoke rose high into the greyness of the early evening sky.

I suddenly became overcome with an immense feeling of sadness. It was like watching the passing of a family member as they declined and withered away, succumbing to an incurable disease. This ship had been my home for so long and I realised I had come to love it. I had come to love the shape of it; I loved the sounds it made as it ploughed through the water and the rhythm of its motion that I had fallen asleep to each night in my hammock. But most of all I had come to love the life it provided and the camaraderie of my shipmates who had made it such a pleasure to sail in, despite all the hardships we had gone through. These very hardships had brought us all together, forming us into a brotherhood that could not be experienced anywhere else.

JOHN McKAY

And now it was dying before my eyes. Taking with it many of those brothers I had come to love as much as my siblings.

'Come on, George,' I heard Wally shout.

He was standing at the gunwale which was now dipping into the sea, the lifeboat only a few feet away. He reached out to me. I could see Singer urging the others to bring the boat up tight against the ship to prevent Wally from falling into the water. It was then I realised we were probably the last two to leave the ship, the deck now empty except for us. I could see two more lifeboats moving further away from the *Virtuous* and understood that I needed to get a move on if we were going to survive. Pushing all melancholy thoughts from my mind I moved forward.

'Let me help you, George,' yelled Wally.

I did not have the strength in my arm to get to the lifeboat unaided.

I leaned across the gap between the ship's hull and the lifeboat, reaching out towards Singer and Mitchell who held out their arms to receive me. Wally held onto my jerkin to prevent me from falling into the sea. I threw Guthrie's coat into the boat and prepared to jump across. As I was about to make my move the ship suddenly lurched to starboard, the deck rising up sharply as it did so. Fearing the ship would rise too high, Wally pushed me with all the strength he could summon.

I fell forward, landing on top of the two men who were trying to assist me, all three of us falling into an untidy heap. My head struck the planking at the bottom of the boat with a resounding thud. They quickly

HELL AND HIGH WATER

righted me and I was soon sitting upright, next to Ralph Reid. He looked in a bad way, his face caked in blood and soot. This was the third time I had received a strong blow to the head in the last five minutes. I was starting to feel dizzy and nauseous.

'Jesus, George,' said Ralph, with no hint of irony. 'You look like shit.'

'Where's Wally?' I said, looking frantically for my friend. I could not see him. The sudden rolling of the ship had taken him from our view.

And then another explosion tore through the ship and I saw Wally once more. This time he was flying through the air over and above us, caught in the concussion of the blast. He splashed into the water twenty yards from the lifeboat.

'Quickly, lads,' yelled Mitchell. 'Get those oars in. Let's move.'

'We have to save Wally,' I screamed. 'We have to save him.'

By now I was worse than useless. My arm had given up the ghost altogether and I could not move it at all. My head pounded to a point that it was affecting my hearing and the noise of the ship's death throes and the frantic shouts of the crew as they tried to get to my friend all combined to form a shrilling cacophony. If Hell had a sound then this was surely it.

I looked out to where we had seen Wally enter the water and was pleased to see him a few yards away, desperately trying to stay afloat.

'Get him out of the water!' shouted Mitchell. 'Grab him boys. Get him into the boat!'

The lifeboat rolled to the right as men moved to grab my friend. Being totally exhausted I felt the only way I could assist would be to move to the left, to help balance the boat and prevent it from overturning. I did not have the strength to do anything more.

'Come on, laddies,' I heard Singer shouting. 'Get him out of that bloody water. He'll freeze to death.'

And then he was onboard. They had managed to haul him from the sea and he now lay on the floor of the lifeboat, shivering madly.

'For Christ's sake,' said Mitchell on seeing the lack of weather protection Wally was wearing. 'Get some bloody clothing on the lad.'

I then remembered Mister Guthrie's greatcoat was in the boat and was mostly dry.

'Here,' I shouted, grabbing it with my good arm. 'Get this on him quickly.'

'Keep moving, boys,' shouted Mitchell. 'Row for your lives. Get us away from the ship.'

There was activity all around me as the oarsmen rowed frantically to get away from the stricken ship. Although I was frozen to the core, I could still feel the heat from the fires that burned aboard the dying HMS *Virtuous* only a few yards from us.

I looked back to the ship and knew there would be numerous matelots still inside who had no chance of getting out, if they were actually still alive. It not only felt like I was abandoning the ship but I was also abandoning those men who were still in there. Those who would go down to the bottom of the sea, their bodies confined there for eternity. I was not sure if it was the cold that made me shiver or the thought of so many lives lost, many of whom were my friends.

I tried to fight back the tears. I did not want them to freeze to my cheeks.

And then a final explosion lit the evening sky as the flames reached the ship's magazine and it exploded in a gut wrenching roar, before turning onto its side and sinking below the water line. There was a loud hiss as the flames hit the cold water, steam rising into the air. As the ship went down, we felt a surge under the lifeboat and it rose and fell in the swell. Instinctively we hung on to the sides, terrified of capsizing. After a few scary wobbles it settled and we knew we were not going to end up in the water.

I was shocked at how quickly the *Virtuous* went under. Although I had seen the *Dreyfus* sink just as quickly, it still amazed me that such a huge vessel could be taken by the sea so fast. It was as though the ocean was proving a point. I had the power to do what it wanted and if men were to carry out acts of violence upon it, then it would simply wipe them away, erase them from its surface forever.

I again felt an immense sadness. I tried to fight this feeling of depression. I needed to concentrate on keeping alive. I knew the time for mourning my shipmates would come soon enough, but right now I needed all my wits about me if I was to survive.

From the light of the explosion I saw three more lifeboats further away. Two looked full to capacity and the other, like our own, contained only a handful of survivors. I noticed many icebergs to the north, clearly silhouetted by the light of the flames. I twisted around and could vaguely make out the shadows of other ships, but they looked far away now. It was clear others in the convoy had also taken direct hits from the German planes, smoke from their superstructures rising high into the sky.

'Where's the rescue ship?' I heard someone say.

'It'll be here,' replied Mitchell. 'They'll be with us shortly. We'll just have to be patient.'

The skies were now clear of aircraft and a strange calm had settled which was in sharp contrast to the pandemonium of only a few minutes ago. The sea around us had a peacefulness about it that belied the extreme violence that had only just taken place upon it. It was like the sinking of the *Dreyfus* all over again, but this time it directly involved us. This was a contrast I found hard to accept. This difference between tranquility and turmoil I found hard to cope with.

We could not be sure how many had survived. I had seen the three lifeboats in the water when the ship had gone down but could not be certain how many people were aboard each one. I was unsure if any had been launched from the starboard side of the ship. When I looked around for them, I could only see one more to the south. It seemed to be drifting further away from us despite our efforts rowing in its direction. I hoped the others had not capsized or gone down when the ship had succumbed to its injuries.

There were nine of us in the boat. Ralph Reid was on one of the oars and I was pleased to see Johnny Spencer, the rating who worked on the bridge with Lieutenant Mitchell, handling the other. Together

HELL AND HIGH WATER

they worked in a slow rhythm. It was clear that, like the rest of us, they were exhausted.

Mitchell sat facing us. He had quickly taken charge and I was eternally grateful to the man for waiting for Wally and I to get on board before moving off, despite the danger of the ship pulling them under with it. I do not think he realised how brave he had been.

Besides the two rowers and Lieutenant Mitchell, Greg Cooper, the galley cook and Ralph's new second, sat shivering on the bench in front of me. Next to him were Jack Holland and Harry Benson, our opposite numbers in the radio room. They also looked worse for wear. Jack had a huge bump the size of an egg on his forehead and he held his right arm tightly against his body. Harry on the other hand looked remarkably well considering the trauma we had all just been through.

To my left sat Petty Officer Singer. By the look in his eyes he was distraught. He sat quite still, not speaking. Occasionally he shook his head from side to side as he stared vacantly at the area of water where the *Virtuous* had just gone down. I thought it best not to engage him just yet and let him deal with his grief privately.

My biggest worry was for Wally. There was absolutely nothing we could do for those men who had perished with the ship, but there was a lot we could do for him. He sat on the floor of the boat, his knees tucked up to his chest, shivering uncontrollably in his soaked clothing. If we did not assist him in some way very soon then he would freeze to death. It was bad enough for the rest of us, but to be drenched in ice cold water with no way of drying out could only result in one fatal outcome.

'The coat,' I reminded those near to me. In the hurry to get away from the sinking ship, they had not been able to get it over him. 'Get the coat on Wally. He'll die otherwise.'

I felt useless. There was nothing I could do to help as Jack and Harry took hold of my friend and grabbed the greatcoat.

'You need to get some of that wet gear off him,' said Singer, breaking from his momentary trance. 'Check the locker at the stern. There should be blankets and more life vests. If you take off his jumper and shirt and wrap him in whatever you can then he may stand a chance.'

Mister Mitchell was also getting busy at the opposite end of the boat. He had opened the bow locker and taken out a hawser line.

'We need to strap ourselves in, gentlemen,' he shouted. 'We've no idea how long we're going to be out here for. Who knows how the weather may turn.'

The lifeboat was beginning to bob more roughly in the water. I had a sense that bad weather was on the way, the air around us becoming more disturbed. I looked out to sea and saw the waves rising and falling to the north and knew it was only a matter of time before another storm hit us. I turned my head to the south and in the fading light was dismayed to see no lights from any of the ships. I fully understood they could not put on their navigation lights for fear of a wolf-pack spotting them and delivering to them the same fate as had befallen us. It did not give me any

HELL AND HIGH WATER

confidence to believe the rescue ship was out there looking for us.

I looked over to Lieutenant Mitchell. It was clear he too was as troubled as I was.

Harry had opened the stern locker and was pulling out blankets and spare life vests which he handed to Jack and Singer. At first, they could not get Wally to move his arms from his legs. He was in no fit state to understand what it was they were asking of him, his senses still not fully responsive. He clung on tightly, trying to generate as much warmth as he could. However, after some coaxing, and Singer using brute force, he eventually relaxed enough for them to assist him. They put on two vests and wrapped his torso in a blanket before putting on the greatcoat. They gave him two more blankets to wrap himself in.

After a few minutes we were all sitting forlornly huddled together in two small groups, using each others' body heat to keep as warm as we could.

However, Lieutenant Mitchell would not let us rest for long.

'We need to get this hood sorted, lads,' he shouted. He kept looking to the north and when I followed his gaze I could see what was troubling him. The waves were getting ever stronger and it would not be long before they were upon us. He was right, we needed to put up the weatherproof protection as soon as possible. The trouble was, we were all so utterly tired.

However, we all knew to sit and do nothing was an invitation for Death to come and join us. Although sitting doing nothing felt like a good idea and seemed the easiest option, none of us wanted to die just yet.

Working as quickly as we could, we managed to get the canvas hood into position and after fifteen minutes of grunting, swearing and cursing the day we were born, we managed to get it into place. We huddled beneath it and waited to see where fate would take us.

Mitchell was loathe to fire a flare just yet. We could only find four on board and he did not want to waste them. He was also convinced a rescue ship would be on its way to us as this was convoy procedure. They would surely know the position and co-ordinates of where the *Virtuous* went down. It was only a matter of time, in his opinion, and we just had to persevere with it all.

This optimism was not felt by me. The *Virtuous* had been sailing at the northernmost edge of the convoy and if the tide and currents were against us then we could drift anywhere, even further north. Surely the convoy would be steaming on relentlessly westward. I did not claim to know all the tactics of naval warfare, but to me, this made sense. Surface ships could outrun a submerged U-boat and so the safest option would surely be to carry on and put as much distance as possible between themselves and any stalking German submarines. After all, one of the anti-submarine ships, the *Virtuous* itself, had been sunk, leaving them more open to U-boat attack.

I feared with each passing minute the distance between the convoy and ourselves was getting greater. Although I did not want to say anything for fear of panicking my fellow survivors I could tell by the silence and the looks on their faces that they too shared those fears. From their anguished looks they were as pessimistic as I was.

As the night wore on it got even colder. Huddled together in a tight group, we tried to stay awake. We knew to fall asleep could be fatal. We were scared of drifting into a slumber from which we might never awake, our bodies giving in to the freezing temperatures. We found drinking water in one of the lockers but it was frozen solid, and some tinned rations which after opening with our fumbling, frozen gloved hands, found them just as frozen as the water. As there were so few of us we knew the lifeboat would have enough rations for us to last some considerable time had we been sailing in sunnier waters.

After a long while I chanced a look from under the canvas canopy. There was nothing to see other than pitch darkness. At first my eyes did not accustom to the blackness and I could not make out where the sea finished and the sky began. It was a moonless night and the stars were covered by a heavy cloud. I had no way of knowing which way was north or south and I could not see anything to give me any indication of where we might be. Slowly, as my eyes adapted, I could make out huge icebergs. They looked closer than earlier, the white of the surf splashing heavily against their bases.

The lifeboat bobbed roughly in the growing swell. We were under no illusion that we could overturn at any point. We knew there was nothing we would be able to do to prevent it and so sat grouped tightly together with a growing understanding and acceptance that whatever happened, happened. Our lives were now in the hands of the sea and God.

Mitchell was starting to get worried.

'The rescue ship should have been here by now,' he said, through chattering teeth. 'Can you see anything, Martin?'

'No, sir,' I replied. 'Nothing.'

I heard a groan in front of me and realised it was Wally.

I placed my hand on his shoulder. Even though I was wearing a thick mitten I could sense the coldness of his body. It emanated through. I knew if he did not get warmth very soon, then he may not last the night.

'Mister Mitchell,' I said. 'Can we light a fire or something? Wally is freezing here.'

No sooner had the words left my mouth than I realised my remark had been quite ridiculous. But we had to do something if he was going to make it.

'Don't be stupid,' he replied. 'And burn the boat? We're all cold, Martin. We're all cold.'

'What about the lockers?' I asked. 'Isn't there anything else we could use to generate some heat?'

After a minute or so, Mitchell replied.

'All of you. Check the lockers nearest to you.' The strained way in which he spoke told me he was struggling with the increasing cold. 'See what you can find. It doesn't look like a rescue ship is about to pick us up anytime soon.'

Slowly we moved. I leaned towards the locker under the bench in front of me. When I managed to get it open I found another fresh water tank which looked

HELL AND HIGH WATER

frozen solid and a few boxes of hard tack biscuits. There was nothing that could help us.

Searching in the almost pitch dark was near impossible.

'I think there's a paraffin lamp here,' said Johnny Spencer, fumbling around in a locker to his right. 'This might be of some use.'

Suddenly there was light at the bow as Mitchell struck a match. He used the side of the canvas cover and his hand to shield it from the weather and, in the dim glow it gave, we could just make out each others faces.

We all looked the same. We resembled monsters from a Boris Karloff horror movie. All of us tired and drained. Our faces were full of soot, bruises and blood. And there was something missing from our eyes. At first I could not understand what it was and then with a sudden shock it dawned on me.

It was hope.

We looked like we were dead already.

'Come on,' said Mitchell. 'Get it lit. Let's see if it helps.'

The lamp was passed to him but the match burned out before he could light it. After more fumbling he managed to strike another and eventually he got a light to the lamp. Turning the valve at the side, the flame started to grow and soon enough we were bathed in light. He placed the lamp in the middle of the group and we all huddled around it.

It was pointless. Although it gave off light, it was too small to provide any kind of heat. After an hour or so of frustration he removed it and placed it at the bow of the lifeboat to give anyone searching for us a better chance of spotting us.

The wind was beginning to pick up and we could hear rain as it hit the canvas cover above our heads. We checked and re-checked the lines to make sure it would not blow off but, as the storm slowly started to gain momentum, we knew if we remained out here for much longer without being picked up there was little chance of survival. Occasionally a wave would lift us high and then suddenly drop us down so hard that our stomachs hurt and we bashed into each other.

I kidded myself that the lack of conversation between us was due to trying to conserve our energy. The reality of it was we all knew our situation was becoming desperate and we were leaving each other to our own private thoughts.

I was getting increasingly worried about Wally. I was scared should he fall asleep, he would not wake up.

'Wally,' I said.

He did not respond.

'Wally,' I repeated.

'Yes, George,' he replied.

'I was just checking you were all right.'

'Apart from being stranded in the middle of the Arctic Ocean and freezing my bollocks off, I'm just fine, mate,' he replied.

There was not a hint of sarcasm in his voice. Despite the enormity of his situation, he was still trying to cheer me up. He was the most selfless man I had ever met in my life.

'Okay,' I said. 'Just checking.'

HELL AND HIGH WATER

'Have you still got that book I gave you?' he asked after a while. 'Or did it go down with the ship.'

'Yes,' I replied, patting my coat. 'It's here in my pocket.'

'Read us some of it,' he said weakly. 'It might cheer us up.'

'It's too dark,' I replied. 'Sorry, pal.'

'Then you'll just have to tell us another story, George,' he said after a while.

'I don't know any stories.'

'Yes you do,' he replied. 'Tell me the story about you and that Glenda girl.'

'That's not a very good one,' I replied.

'Yes it is,' he said. 'I know you don't think so but, trust me, it made me laugh.'

'It's no laughing matter,' I replied.

'Yes, laddie,' chipped in Singer. 'Tell us all about you and this Glenda girl.'

'Do I have to?' I replied.

'Yes you do, Martin,' said Lieutenant Mitchell suddenly. 'Consider it an order.'

'Very well,' I said reluctantly.

And as the storm began to get more fierce around our little boat, throwing us around indiscriminately and causing us to knock into each other regularly; and as the temperature continued to drop below that which was in any way bearable, I told them of how Billy Jones had persuaded me into going to the function at the Catholic church hall where I had first met her. I told them about our dalliance in the alleyway during the air raid and all that followed after.

I missed out nothing. My father's initial opposition to the relationship. How I volunteered to stay behind to lock up the printshop for Mister Johnson. The many times Glenda and I had met there after work. The way she hid herself at Lime Street station when I set off for the navy.

I told them everything. I missed nothing out.

And as the storm built steadily around us, growing more fierce with each passing minute, they sat in silence as I related to them all of what had happened after I returned to Liverpool on shore leave. They let me talk, not interrupting at any point. I was not sure if this was because my storytelling skills were good, or whether they did not have the energy to tell me to shut up.

Twenty-Nine

Liverpool

I spent the following day with my parents and accompanied them when they visited my father's older sister, Margaret. She lived on the other side of the city with Stan, her much older husband.

Uncle Stan was a funny old bloke. Thin and scrawny with a bald patch that stretched to the back of his head, his pate full of freckles and blemishes. I had always been a little apprehensive of him. Throughout my life he had never said two words to me, preferring to sit in his chair all day in front of the fireplace. He would sit there, reading the paper Aunt Margaret would fetch for him each morning from the shop on the corner of their street. He was not prepared to pay the little extra it would have cost to have it delivered and so Margaret had to get up an hour before he did each morning to collect it and prepare his breakfast.

They had not been blessed with children. Apparently Margaret could not have them and, due to this, she would spoil us whenever we went around to visit, giving us fruit and bestowing us with as many kisses as she could manage. However, Stan would simply sit there pulling faces at us, making his irritation at us being in his company quite obvious. He was not the most hospitable of men and I was always glad to leave when the time came to go home.

JOHN McKAY

I felt sorry for Margaret. She was a lovely woman who would do anything for anyone and how she had got herself lumbered with such a miserable old sod as Stan was beyond me. I believed the real reason for them being childless was simply because Stan hated children and had denied her the opportunity of being a mother out of pure selfishness. He was not my favourite person. Apparently, as a young man, he had been a kinder and more lively fellow. However, he had given in to a gambling habit that had caused problems in his marriage. He had left them stony broke on more than one occasion. He had now curbed the habit, but the ending of his vice had also led to the ending of his personality it seemed.

It was very odd then, that on this particular visit he was the life and soul of the group.

He asked me all about life on the *Virtuous* and gave his opinion on the current state of the country and the way the war was being run. I was shocked to discover he was very well informed and his opinions on politics and other things were not only based on sound knowledge, but very persuasive when he argued them out.

I was also surprised to learn that he too had once been a naval man.

'Six years I did,' he said, scratching his leg. 'Six years, man and boy. It was before I came to Liverpool. Sailed all around the world I did, all around it. And it's bloody big, you know, the world. We could be on the ocean for weeks without seeing land or another ship. I used to have a friend, you know. Fred Biggs he was called. Me and him were inseparable we

HELL AND HIGH WATER

were. Me and Freddy. Loved that fella, I did. Then one day he disappeared, vanished into thin air. Never saw him again.'

'What do you mean, disappeared?' I asked, intrigued.

'All very odd, all very odd,' he replied, lost in the memory. He scratched the inside of his ear with his forefinger and looked at the tip when he pulled it out. Oblivious to how disgusting this was, he wiped his finger on the chair arm.

He went on. 'One minute he was there and the next nobody could find him. Bloody mystery it was, you know.'

'So what do you think happened to him?' I asked.

'Oh, we know full well what happened to him,' he replied. 'We presumed he'd fallen overboard because nobody could find him, you see. We were in the middle of the ocean so he couldn't have deserted or anything like that. Not that he was the type to desert. Freddy Biggs was no deserter. However, what Freddy Biggs was, was a drunk and a thief.'

'How so?' I asked, humouring him.

'Well, the night before he disappeared three bottles of rum were taken from the galley. How he carried them with only two hands is beyond me, 'cos Freddy was only a little fella, you know. Anyway after much searching of the ship, we found two of the bottles empty in one of the lifeboats. This whaler hung out slightly over the ship and the tarp was unhooked on the far side. The captain reckoned he probably got himself inside and drunk himself into a stupor. Probably disorientated himself and got out the wrong side of the boat when he'd finished.'

Stan made a whooshing sound and motioned with his hand towards the floor.

'Woo… Splash!' he said. 'Straight into the briny. Gone forever. Poor old Freddy Biggs. I loved that fella, you know.'

I did not know whether to laugh or to offer my condolences. I was not totally sure he had made the whole silly story up but, after meeting some of the characters I had, there was a possibility his tale was genuine.

'What was wrong with Stan?' asked my father when we got home later that afternoon. 'Never heard the daft old sod talk so much.'

'No idea,' replied mother. 'Maybe he's making up for lost time.'

It was getting late in the afternoon and I was looking forward to seeing Glenda again. As the day wore on, I was getting more excited and realised my feelings for her were still strong. I decided to go to my room for a lie down before the youngsters got home from school.

I walked into the bedroom and decided I needed a change of clothes if I was to take her out. I wanted to make more of an effort with her after the conversation we had had the previous day. I did not want her to feel I was letting her down in any way. I knew I had a lot of making up to do.

As I opened the top drawer of the chest of drawers at the side of my bed, I heard something rattle. Moving some clean underwear to the side, I saw a key.

HELL AND HIGH WATER

I smiled to myself. This was the key to the back door of Mister Johnson's building. The one I had secretly had cut some months ago in order to conduct our illicit liaisons.

I suddenly had an idea. Grabbing a pencil and a piece of paper from the table at the side of Jimmy's bed, I hurriedly wrote a note.

It was half past five when I knocked on the Shepherds' front door.

It was opened by Iris's brother Richard, my old childhood friend. Like my father, Richard worked on the docks and was exempt from military service.

'Hello, George,' he said. He looked tired, as though he had just got out of bed.

'Hey, Richard,' I replied. 'Is your Iris in yet?'

'No,' he replied. 'What do you want with our Iris? I thought it was Glenda you were keen on.'

'It is…' I was slightly flummoxed. I had not expected him to answer the door.

'What is it you want, George?' he said irritatedly. 'I'm on nights later and I've only just got out of bed.'

'Oh, right. Sorry,' I replied. 'Can you give this to Glenda when she gets in?'

I held out an envelope.

'What is it?'

'It's a message,' I replied.

'Why don't you just wait for her to get home and tell her yourself? I'm not a bloody postman. Or your messenger boy.'

Now it was my turn to get annoyed.

'There's no need to be like that,' I said sternly. 'Can you just give her the bloody letter or not? I'm not asking you to do anything difficult, am I? It's not like I'm asking you to do algebra, is it?'

'All right, all right. Keep your hair on,' he said, taking the letter from me. 'No need to get all shirty.'

'Can you make sure she gets it?'

'Yes, yes. Now bugger off will you, I've got things to do.'

And with that he shut the door in my face.

I walked slowly in the direction of the printshop. I did not want to arrive too early in case there were still people in the building. The place usually closed at six o'clock at the latest and I did not want to get there and risk being seen.

When I arrived, the gates were shut. This was a good sign as Mister Johnson only ever closed the gates when everyone had left for the day. He would leave them wide open during the working day for deliveries, and so I was confident there was nobody inside. However, to be on the safe side, I waited around the corner out of sight for another twenty minutes before I was completely sure the place was empty.

I walked around to the rear of the building to the door where I used to let Glenda in. After checking nobody was watching me, I put the key in the lock and turned it.

The door opened to a stock room filled from floor to ceiling with shelves containing rolls of paper for the machines. Scores of metal cans containing black ink were piled to my right and it was through this narrow passage that I slowly walked after carefully shutting the door behind me. I did not lock it. I would do that once Glenda was in the building just like I had done many times before.

I knew what I was doing was technically illegal but then, I thought, what the hell. Life was for living after all. If I got caught I was sure I would be able to think of some excuse as to why I was there. I could say I was looking for Billy and the door had been left unlocked. I was confident I would be able to talk my way out of it.

Even though I knew it to be empty, I still treaded carefully, not wanting to take any chances. Slowly I made my way to the restroom and as I got closer I could hear voices. My heart started beating very quickly, to a point where I could almost hear it. I had thought everybody had left and the shock of me getting it so wrong stunned me for a moment.

I thought if I turned around and walked back out, then no-one would know I had ever been there and all would be well. I would be able to meet Glenda outside and stop her from going in.

But then something compelled me to stay. I do not know what it was but there was something inside my head telling me to continue. To move cautiously and see who it was that was still in the building when it was supposed to be closed.

Slowly I edged forward until I was outside the door to the restroom.

There were two people inside and it suddenly became very clear who they were. I recognised both of their voices. A man and a woman. And they were not having a normal conversation. They were not exactly discussing the weather or what they were going to have for their tea that night. It was the conversation of two people engaged in a certain act.

As I stood outside the room, my ear pressed to the door, I did not know whether to laugh or cry. I had no idea which emotion to feel. Should I be angry? Should I be sad? Heartbroken, even? Or should I just leave them to it and make my way home? As I stood there contemplating what to do I was overcome with a huge feeling of disappointment, which quickly turned to rage.

It became clear now. The way Glenda had not seemed overly pleased to see me when I first arrived home. The way Iris had tried to give me a warning about her cousin. It was all becoming obvious.

Taking a breath I opened the door.

'Hello, you two,' I said.

Both naked, they fell off the couch and onto the floor, the shock of my sudden entrance into their private world total and complete. Had I not been so furious, so utterly mad and at the same time devastated, then maybe I might have laughed at the sight before me. Frantically, Billy jumped for his trousers which lay in a heap on the floor near to the sink. Glenda grabbed the blanket they had been lying on and wrapped it around her body.

'George...' she said, almost apologetically.

I closed the door behind me and leaned against it, raising my hand to stop her from talking.

HELL AND HIGH WATER

'George... mate...' said Billy as he put his foot into his trouser leg before stumbling and falling back to the floor.

'Shut up, Billy,' I said. 'Don't say a word.'

'How the hell did you get in here?' he said, ignoring me.

'I said, shut up,' I repeated. 'Are you deaf?'

'He has a key,' said Glenda, answering his question. She had not made any attempt as yet to clothe herself.

'Yes, Billy boy, I have a key,' I said.

'What are you doing here?' asked Glenda. 'We were supposed to be meeting at eight o'clock.'

I burst into laughter. She said this as though it was the most normal thing in the world and I should maybe walk out and go and wait for my appointment with her.

'I know we were,' I said. 'But I was hoping to meet you here first. I even took a note around to Iris's house. I gave it to Richard.'

'What did it say?' she asked.

I don't know if she was stalling for time to think up some suitable excuse as to why she was here, engaged in a carnal act with my one time best friend, or whether she was genuinely this stupid.

'Does Iris know about this?' I asked, turning to Billy.

'Of course she doesn't bloody well know about this,' he replied. 'Iris and I haven't been seeing eye to eye for some time now.'

'Oh,' I said nodding my head in mock understanding. 'That might be because she probably suspects you're having it off with her bloody cousin.'

'There's no need for that kind of talk, George Martin,' said Glenda.

'Don't give me bloody "George Martin", Glenda Bradshaw,' I said sarcastically. 'Whatever you say isn't going to help.'

'George, let's all go for a drink and discuss this like adults,' said Billy, who had now managed to put his trousers on.

'What happened, Glenda?' I asked, ignoring him. 'What did I do to you to make you hate me?'

'I don't hate you,' she replied. 'I just missed you, George. I told you yesterday how you made me feel. You let me down. You really did.'

'I was going to make it up to you,' I replied. 'I really was, Glenda.'

'You never wrote. You hid me away from your family like a dirty little secret. I cried over you hundreds of times, George.' She started to weep, using the edge of the blanket to wipe away her tears. 'I never stopped crying for months. And when I never heard from you, I thought you'd found somebody else. Or that you didn't care about me at all. You were just using me.'

'I was never just using you,' I replied. 'That was never what it was for me.'

I looked over to where Billy now stood, leaning against the sink. He was buttoning up his shirt, content to leave us to our conversation.

'That bastard is using you,' I replied. 'Not me…'

'Steady on, George,' said Billy, clearly affronted by the remark.

'Oh, shut up, Billy,' I said. 'If anyone's being used around here then it's me. Whatever it was you were

HELL AND HIGH WATER

running away from in Wales, then you just used me to help you get over it. I see it clearly now.'

'I wasn't running away from anything,' she said, lowering her head. However, I did not believe her. I knew she was lying.

'To be honest,' I replied. 'I've always had my doubts about you, Glenda. There's always been that little something you weren't telling me. I'm convinced of it. There's something about you that doesn't ring true. Whatever it is… well, you know what?… I'm not really sure if I care any more. I'm not really sure I'm actually curious enough to want to know what it is. I give up with you.'

She was crying now, holding the blanket to her chest.

And then I felt something towards her I had never felt before.

Pity. That was it. I pitied her.

'So what are you going to do?' asked Billy.

'What? Right now?' I could tell he was scared in case I attacked him, or reported them both to Mister Johnson. He would lose his job but then I would be made to look a fool too. I also had a key to a building that I should never have had. I did not really have any kind of moral advantage.

'I'm going to spend another day with my family and then I'm going back to Belfast,' I decided. 'Don't worry. Your little secret is safe with me. If this is what you both want then I'll leave you to it.'

'I have needs,' sobbed Glenda. 'I can't help myself. And you were gone away so long. You abandoned me.'

I looked at her again and this time I felt nothing.

'How's your leg?' I asked Billy.

'My leg?' he replied, bewildered at the question.

'Yes, the reason you left the army, remember. Or so you told me.'

'It plays up a bit now and again. Why are you asking about my leg?'

It took me four strides to reach him. Before he could react, I kicked him as hard as I could in his left leg. I could not remember if this was the one he said he had injured but I really did not care as long as I hurt him. He fell heavily to the floor with a shriek and once there he curled up in a ball.

He was clearly expecting me to continue the assault but I did not. Instead I left him there, whimpering like a child. As far as I was concerned Billy and Glenda could have each other. I did not care anymore. Billy had once been my friend, but friends don't commit this kind of betrayal, so now that friendship was over for good. When I considered everything, I was not really too bothered that this particular association had come to an end. I had a new group of mates on HMS *Virtuous* and every one of them was worth ten of the useless idiot who lay cowering on the floor in front of me.

I was not a violent man. I had kicked him because I felt I had to punish him in some way and a kick would have to do. It was quite childish but it was the only thing I could think of at the time.

I turned to the door and opened it. I was tempted to look back but, like Glenda had done so many times to me in the past when walking through doors, I did not

HELL AND HIGH WATER

turn my head. I just left them there. Billy Jones cowering on the floor clasping his bruised shin and Glenda Bradshaw bawling her eyes out at how shitty her meaningless life had become.

Thirty

As the night wore on the weather became increasingly worse. The wind howled through gaps in the canvas rigging, bringing with it snow and sleet, soaking us all as we desperately struggled to retain as much warmth as we could. It was clear to us now that a rescue ship was not coming.

Some had started to give up. Ice formed on our balaclavas and no sooner did we brush it away than it was back again, sticking and freezing to the wool. There was a very real danger none of us would survive the night. We grouped together as close as we could to share body heat, Wally sandwiched between myself and Singer. He had remained quiet throughout the telling of my sorry tale and when I had finished he had not said a word. The others had asked me a few questions which I answered as best I could. What had happened after I left Billy and Glenda at the printshop; whether I had seen her again before I left; what my parents had thought about the whole thing. I was just glad the story had given them something else to think about other than our impending death.

Wally's shivering vibrated against both me and Singer. I was somewhat heartened by this. If he was shivering then he was still alive. But it was clear he could not last much longer. Being blown into the water had done for him. The soaking was surely something he would not be able to recover from, no matter how much we tried to help him.

HELL AND HIGH WATER

He had selflessly assisted me into the lifeboat, meaning he was still on deck when the explosion occurred. Had he left me to it then he would not be in such a bad state as he was now. I owed it to him to try as hard as I could to keep him alive.

I was scared that if he succumbed to sleep we would lose him. I needed to keep him alert.

'How are you feeling, Wally?' I asked. It was now very hard to speak. My jaw had locked and I was forcing the words out through tightly clamped lips.

It was a while before he replied.

'Not good, George... not good,' he replied just as slowly. 'I'm not sure I can hang on... this might be it for me.'

'Don't go saying that... there's still hope yet.'

'Is there?' He did not sound convinced. 'Maybe for you, George... But Wally here has had it.'

I could not let him give up.

'Come on, pal,' I said. 'Think about what's waiting for you when we get out of all this. Think of all the good stuff you're still yet to do... the people who love you.'

'And who would they be, George?' he replied after a long pause. 'There's no-one for me back home... The Royal Navy is all I have.'

I was disheartened to hear this. Although I knew Wally had lived a sad life and had not had much of a childhood, I never gave much thought to his emotional well-being. This was a fault in myself, not in him. I felt ashamed.

'So are you going to forgive her, do you think?' he said suddenly. 'Glenda… Are you going to forgive her?'

'Forgive her for what?' I replied. 'We weren't exactly courting really. Thinking back we were just two people having fun. I don't think there's anything to forgive.'

'Do you think you loved her?' he asked, his voice getting quieter with each question.

'I'm not exactly sure what love is. Not in that sense anyway. You know, somebody outside of your family and that. If you could define the word for me then maybe I could answer that question.' I was trying to keep his mind active. I was really scared he would drift away and I would lose him.

'How would I know, George… you know my story.'

I thought for a few moments. 'I don't think what I had with Glenda was love exactly.'

'Well maybe not,' he replied weakly. 'But you felt something. Something I've never felt. And you've had it in other forms too, from your parents, from your brother and sisters. You are capable of it, George, you are capable of it. I sometimes think I'm not, because I've never known it. I've never received it and I've never had anyone to give it to… So I'm not sure if I'm able… But I understand what it is because I've seen it in others.'

'That's so sad, Wally,' I replied. 'But there's time yet. There's plenty of time for you to find someone. Jesus, man! You're still very young.'

'Maybe,' he shrugged. 'Maybe…'

HELL AND HIGH WATER

'What is it anyway?' I asked pensively. 'Love? Is it really so important to have it? Can you not have a fulfilling life without it?'

This remark seemed to stir him. He shifted slightly before responding. I was happy this conversation was keeping him focused on something other than his dire predicament.

'Now, I'm by no means a religious or spiritual man. But I do understand something,' he said, his voice laboured and drawn. He was struggling. Each word was an almighty effort yet he seemed determined to speak. He needed to say what he was about to say.

'I understand that love is the one thing, the only emotion people live their lives by. It dictates which paths they take... who they wish to spend their time with... where they live... who they are, even. It defines them. So therefore their whole existence is dictated by it. All their choices are made because of it. If you have never loved then you have never really lived. The thing is, we're all born capable of it, although this capability has been lost in me.'

He paused to gather his strength before continuing. 'Those who choose to ignore it, well, to me, they're empty, vacuous even. If they choose to reject love then they're not really human. There's no point to life if there's no love in it. Everything else is peripheral. Do you think all this around us is the true meaning of life? All this death and suffering? No, my friend, the reason for living and the true meaning of life, is love. It's that simple.'

And as the waves crashed into and over us, throwing our lifeboat around as though it did not exist, we contemplated Wally's words as we each awaited death in our own way.

HELL AND HIGH WATER

Thirty-One

Eventually the storm subsided. I had drifted off into a disturbed and restless sleep and dreamt of home. When I awoke I was at first confused as to where I was, thinking I was back in my room in Liverpool. When I realised I was still stuck in the middle of the Barents Sea, freezing to death, my heart sank to its lowest point since the *Virtuous* was lost.

I was horrified to have allowed myself to give in to sleep and shook myself fully awake, patting the ice off my body. I knew I would have to be careful. I could not allow it to happen again, for it could be fatal.

I chanced a look out of the canvas awning and could see the sun slowly rising on the eastern horizon, casting its rays across the water. How far we had drifted we had no way of knowing but icebergs could be seen even closer than they were the previous day, the white foam of water at their bases clearly visible to me. I feared we had drifted further away from the convoy which would be many miles away by now. I doubted anyone thought we were still alive. They would have assumed we had perished with others.

By the little light that was available, I looked around the boat. We were all in a very bad way. Each of us had a thin layer of ice covering our clothing where the snow and sleet had frozen to our stiff and tired bodies. Lieutenant Mitchell was moving his arms around in a windmill motion in an attempt at getting some circulation back into them. Wally appeared to be sleeping, as was Singer who sat clamped to him, his arms enfolding his body, protecting him. At first I feared they had passed away while I was asleep. I quickly checked their mouths and was pleased to see their breath exhaling through the wool of their balaclavas.

I shook them with my good arm and was relieved to see them react, pushing me away irritably.

After a couple of minutes I decided to do the same thing as Lieutenant Mitchell and try and get some circulation back into my body. I tried moving each shoulder in turn, but my damaged left shoulder would not respond to what my brain was telling it to do. My arm hung uselessly by my side. In frustration I bashed at it with my right hand, thumping it hard, trying to get some movement from it.

'Can somebody help me with the boy?' I heard Mitchell say, interrupting my attempts at getting warm.

Everybody stirred at his words, raising their heads to look at him.

Mitchell was at the bow, at the point where the awning had fallen short, leaving the front open to the elements. Part of the rope holding it down had come away from the hooks and the canvas was flapping slowly in the now quite gentle wind. Curled up against the side of the boat, to Mitchell's left, was young Greg Cooper. However, Greg had not stirred like the rest of us. He looked to be sleeping.

'He's dead,' said Mitchell matter-of-factly. 'We can't have him in here with us.'

HELL AND HIGH WATER

There was no response from any of us. As well as our bodies being numb, our senses and emotions seemed the same.

'What are you suggesting?' asked Singer eventually. He had let go of Wally to see what the fuss was about. 'That we throw the poor boy overboard?'

'That's exactly what I'm suggesting,' replied Mitchell. 'We can't have him in here. We need to let him go.'

Jack Holland moved forward and looked at the corpse.

'We've lost him,' he confirmed. 'The poor lad's had it.'

I could hear Ralph Reid begin to moan. I looked at my gunner friend and could see in his eyes the grief he was feeling. He was despondent at the loss of his friend. He had come to like the young lad and had taken him under his wing. He was clearly heartbroken.

'There's nothing we can do for him now,' said Mitchell. With the help of Jack, they managed to shuffle Greg's corpse to the side of the lifeboat. With what looked like a huge effort, they edged his frozen body over the side and out into the sea. We all watched silently as the boy slowly floated away from the boat. After a few seconds he peacefully sank beneath the surface.

'Bloody hell,' I shouted over. 'You should have taken some of his clothes. We could have used them for the rest of us.'

'Too late now,' said Mitchell with a frown. I could see he was upset at his own lack of thought regarding this.

'For Christ's sake,' shouted Ralph. 'You didn't even say a prayer for him.'

'Well, what's done is done,' replied Mitchell softly. His eyes showed he was upset with himself for this lack of thought. He sat back down and turned his head from us, looking hopefully out to sea.

Wally had not stopped shivering and was in danger of suffering the same fate as young Greg. There was not much more we could do for him. I looked around at the others in our little dejected group. It was clear to me that their only concern was for their own survival. Nobody, other than myself, Mitchell and Singer, was giving Wally any attention at all. But then I could hardly blame them. We were all slowly freezing to death. All of us suffering our own private hell.

The morning settled. This calmness of the sea belied its murderous capabilities. The contrast of the morning weather as opposed to the storm we had ridden out overnight was huge. It was one extreme to the other. The sea could be rough and violent and then, very soon after, it could be equally tranquil and serene.

After a couple of hours of daylight Mitchell ordered us to take down the awning. Johnny Spencer expressed his concern with this. He did not appear happy at all, arguing the bad weather could return at any point. I believed Mitchell thought keeping us active and focused would possibly prevent us from losing our will to live. It would stop us from freezing.

HELL AND HIGH WATER

Exercising our weakened limbs may put some warmth back into them. He said we may benefit from the sun's rays that had now risen into a virtually clear blue sky, the odd white cloud to the south the only blemish to be seen upon it.

Once this was done we assessed our situation. We could not see any land, only the nearby icebergs. When we scanned the horizon we became disheartened as there were still no ships to be seen. We checked the rations again and managed to eat a few of the hard tack biscuits. They slowly thawed out in our mouths but the frozen food made the our tongues numb and our lips crack further, causing us great pain.

The drinking water was frozen solid. Mitchell ordered us to tie a rope to a couple of jerrycans and hang them over the side. He thought maybe the seawater was warmer than the air above it and it might melt some of the ice inside. I was not too sure if this was true.

I noticed Ralph licking at the ice that had formed on his clothing. When I tried this myself, I felt my tongue stick to the fabric. I had to wait a few seconds for the heat of my mouth to melt it enough in order to pull it free. I decided that no matter how thirsty I got, I would not be doing that again.

Wally was fading fast. The calmer weather did little to bring up the temperature in the lifeboat. We did not have a thermometer, but we did not need one to know it was clearly still well below freezing. No matter how hard I rubbed his arms and pressed myself against him, he would not warm up. How he had survived the night at all was a miracle.

Another couple of hours passed and then we noticed a disturbance in the water underneath the boat. Gentle at first and then suddenly becoming more violent. I could not understand what was happening as the boat bobbed roughly on the water, knocking us off the benches and onto the wooden floor.

'Oh, Jesus,' I heard Singer say. 'Look out, laddies. Stay calm… Don't panic.'

Turning my head to the left I could see something rising from the surface. At first I could not comprehend what it was, thinking it was some kind of sea monster ascending from the depths to haul us down. Like the Kraken of Norse mythology that was once believed to dwell in these waters, attacking ships, wrapping its grotesque tentacles around their hulls and dragging them beneath the waves. But that was a fiction I had read about in books as a child. What was happening now, right before my eyes, however, was very real.

As it rose higher, to my horror, it became apparent what it was. A radio antenna, snorkel and periscope, each pointing towards the sky, rose slowly before us, followed by the rest of the conning tower. Emblazoned across the superstructure were the letters *U-403* confirming that this was in fact an enemy submarine and not some fictional sea monster. A few seconds later the rest of the boat emerged, settling on the surface some twenty five yards away from us.

I had never seen a submarine before, other than in pictures and photographs. It was a lot smaller than I expected, only around two hundred feet in length. Narrow, cylindrical and grey, it had one deck gun and other smaller artillery on the conning tower, probably for anti-aircraft use when surfaced. I could not take in that such a small craft could cause so much damage to a fleet, striking fear into the crews of the largest of surface ships.

In that moment I wondered what it would be like to live in one of those things. Cramped up in such a confined space for weeks on end with other men. Living, working and sleeping together with hardly any means to remaining hygienic. It was a strange thought to have in such a situation as this. However, I believed the conditions on board the *U-403* would be a lot more bearable than the frozen hell we had been made to endure for the past eighteen hours or so.

'Don't panic, gentlemen,' said Lieutenant Mitchell. 'Stay perfectly calm.'

We watched as the hatch at the top of the conning tower was thrown open, falling back onto the steel structure with a metallic clang.

We waited in nervous anticipation for someone to show themselves and, sure enough, after only a few more seconds, a head appeared. It was a sailor dressed in a thick winter coat wearing a scarf around his face and a battered peaked cap upon his head. Clearly shivering, he clambered outside onto the conning tower and then reached back as another person, beyond our view, handed up a weapon. I recognised it as a Mauser 98, the standard issue rifle for German forces, which the enemy officer shouldered as he waited for his comrade to join him.

After a few moments there were three of them on the tower, one of whom took hold of the anti-aircraft gun and levelled the weapon at us.

'Stay calm, boys,' whispered Lieutenant Mitchell. 'Don't do anything that might make them want to fire that thing.'

Wally stirred.

'What's happening, George,' he said, looking up to me.

'Germans,' I whispered. 'There's a U-boat.'

He turned his head to look a them, the blanket he had around his shoulders falling away. He moved uneasily but became more alert than I had seen him for hours.

Jack and Harry began to wring their hands. I was not sure if this was due to the cold or out of fear of the German manning the anti-aircraft gun.

Four more German submariners exited the hatch and one of them carried a length of rope that was coiled over his shoulder. Once on deck he threw it over, indicating for us to tie it to the boat. Johnny Spencer took hold of it and attached it to one of the hooks at the bow. Once secured, the Germans began to haul us over until the lifeboat was touching the side of the submarine, just to the right of the conning tower.

Suddenly the German officer in the middle of the three moved the scarf from his face and spoke.

'Which one of you two officers is in charge?' he asked in perfect English.

Mitchell looked bewildered. He was the only officer in the lifeboat. Then he glanced in the direction the

German officer was looking and noticed Wally was still wearing Mister Guthrie's overcoat.

'I am,' he called back. 'To whom am I addressing?'

'That is of no matter,' replied the German. 'You will come aboard this vessel immediately.'

'I'll do no such thing,' countered Mitchell, stoically. 'Unless you intend to take us all as prisoners of war.'

'Alas, we do not have the room,' said the German. 'However, I will take one officer as prisoner. Can you confirm from which ship you were sailing?'

'We're survivors of HMS *Virtuous*,' replied Mitchell. 'But that's all you'll get from any of us. The Geneva Convention states we're to give you our names, ranks and serial numbers. Nothing more.'

'I am well aware of the Geneva Convention and what it states,' said the German officer half smiling. 'And whilst you are aboard this vessel, it will be complied with fully. Now, will you kindly step aboard.'

'As I've just told you. I will do no such thing. The safety of my men is my only concern.'

As this exchange was taking place, I watched the other Germans. Although the anti-aircraft weapon was pointing at us, they did not look as though they wanted to open fire. The sailors on the deck all stood watching, clearly not understanding the words being spoken. None of them looked menacing in any way.

I had a thought. I knew if Wally was to stay with us for much longer, without getting picked up, then he would not survive.

'Wally,' I whispered. 'There may be a way out of this for you.'

Singer, who had overheard this, put his hand on my shoulder.

'Steady, laddie,' he said. He knew what I was about to suggest, but looked apprehensive.

'Come on P.O.,' I whispered to him. 'It's his only chance. If he stays with us then he won't make it. This is his one chance of survival… What do you say, Wally?'

'I'm just so cold, George… So cold.'

'Mister Mitchell,' I called.

Slightly irritated that I had interrupted his conversation with the U-boat commander, Mitchell turned to me.

'What is it, Martin?'

'It's Wally, sir,' I replied. 'What about Wally?'

Mitchell looked at my friend and then back to me before he realised what I was suggesting. He turned back to the German.

'You seem a man of integrity,' he said. 'I have a very sick man on this boat. Would you consider taking him on board as your prisoner? Can you assure me he'll be well looked after and treated properly if you do?'

The German looked over to Wally.

'Ach, so be it,' he said with a dismissive wave of the hand. 'I suppose any officer will do. Bring him onboard.'

With that he barked some orders to his men and turned away before Mitchell could inform him Wally was not actually a commissioned officer, but an ordinary seaman. He disappeared down the hatch and back into the submarine.

HELL AND HIGH WATER

Personally, I thought Wally's chances as a prisoner were a hundred times better than if he stayed with us, where he would surely freeze to death in a few hours time.

I stood up and took hold of his left arm with my right. My own left arm still hung loosely at my side, completely useless. Singer took hold of his right and together we brought him to the side of the lifeboat as two German sailors leaned over and pulled him onto the deck of the U-boat.

'Don't worry about me,' he said weakly as he looked back at me. 'Take care of yourself, George. I'll be okay… don't you go worrying.'

As the sailors manhandled him to the conning tower I had mixed emotions. I did not know if I was saving him or introducing him to another hell. This was something that would haunt me for years to come.

'He's right, laddie,' said Singer. 'You may have just saved his life.'

The Germans motioned for us to release the rope. Once we had thrown it over, they coiled it up, one of them placing it over his shoulder. As they walked to the ladder at the conning tower one of them stopped and threw something to us. Singer caught it. We were pleased to see it was a large bottle of fresh water.

It took a while for them to get Wally up the ladder, him being so weak, but eventually he made it. As he was about to go through the hatch, he turned to us and waved. I could see from his hunched figure that he was distraught at what had happened to us all. He may now have a chance of making it through the war but, for the rest of us, still stranded in the freezing wilderness, our fates were less certain. Whether we lived or died was now at the discretion of the weather and the gods.

As I raised my hand to wave back, I felt something dig into my armpit and realised it was Wally's copy of *Oliver Twist*. I had promised I would read it and return it to him but now, with him leaving like this, I would not be able to do that.

'Your book, Wally.' I tried to shout. But the words only came out as a whisper and he did not hear me. 'Your book.'

And with that, Walter Honeyman disappeared into the *U-403* and I never saw him again.

HELL AND HIGH WATER

Thirty-Two

You can learn a lot about people, and human nature, when you are marooned in a lifeboat with them in the middle of the Arctic Ocean.

The day wore on. The weather was not as extreme as we had experienced overnight and although the lack of wind was welcome, it did nothing to increase the temperature. We ate more hard tack and managed to drink some of the water the German submariner had thrown to us. The bottle was passed around until it was all gone, each of us taking our fair share.

Lieutenant Mitchell told us that, as yet, he was not looking to ration anything. There was still enough provisions for a few days and he remained optimistic we would picked up sooner or later.

However, by early evening without sighting any ships, he decided to let off one of the flares. By this time we did not care if our rescuers, if they ever came, were to be friend or foe. We just needed to be picked up and warmed up. If this meant spending the rest of the war in a camp in Germany then so be it.

Taking the Very pistol from the locker, he fumbled as he loaded it. Pointing it skyward he fired. We watched as it arced high into the air before exploding, releasing its bright light and coloured smoke into the atmosphere.

I was not confident of it being spotted. He had done this out of a sense of "doing something", more to keep our spirits up than a belief anyone other than ourselves would see it. As he sat down, placing the pistol back into the locker, I contemplated the man.

Before being stuck in the lifeboat with him I had only ever spoken to him once. That was on the bridge when I had taken the signal to the captain when the tubing system had failed. I had never given much thought to him following that day but now, as I watched him sitting thoughtfully at the far end of the boat, I was able to consider him.

He was not much older than I was, maybe mid to late twenties. He was by no means a handsome man but he exuded an authority that automatically generated respect. He had taken control of things during the sinking of the *Virtuous*, ensuring as many of us as possible could get off the ship, even waiting for a dangerously long time for Wally and I to disembark. He had done this without any thought for his own personal safety. Had he ordered the others to row away to protect themselves then I would already be dead. Wally too. For this I would be eternally grateful to him.

The way he had not been fazed when the German U-boat had surfaced and the enemy sailors had pointed the anti-aircraft gun at us also added to my growing admiration for him. He would not be forced into doing anything and had refused to board the submarine, risking a backlash that thankfully never came. He also knew, as well as I did, that the only way to save Wally was to let the Germans take him. We just hoped when they discovered he was not an officer they would not be too hard on him. It was a chance

HELL AND HIGH WATER

both Mitchell and I were prepared to take. The man could quite easily have abandoned us and taken his chances with them but he had not, sacrificing a chance of his own survival out of duty to the rest of us.

My thoughts then turned to Petty Officer Singer who sat on the bench beside me.

I was starting to worry about him. He had always been fair towards me and had treated me in an almost fatherly way. He was a bit of a joker and had made my stay on the *Virtuous* both bearable and enjoyable. He was normally the life and soul of any gathering and had an optimism and outlook that was infectious.

But now, as he sat next to me hardly speaking a word, I feared he had already given up. He was clearly finding it difficult to cope. I placed my hand on his shoulder but he did not react. I thought at first he had not felt it, his body being so numb, but after a few seconds he turned to me and offered me a small smile. His eyes, however, remained devoid of any emotion.

Further up the boat Harry and Jack sat together, pressed up against each other like two lovers. The two were inseparable both on board the *Virtuous* and now as they were marooned in the lifeboat. I was worried how the other would react should one of them succumb to the elements like poor your Greg had done a few hours earlier. I feared if one of them died then the other would follow shortly after. These two men had become close friends with many people and now that they had time to think about the sinking of the ship I could see they had already started the mourning process. I, on the other hand, chose not to think about it.

JOHN McKAY

I knew the enormity of what had happened would hit me later but right now I had to concentrate on remaining alive.

Sitting on the bench in front of them was Johnny Spencer, the young rating who had worked on the bridge with the captain and the other officers, plotting navigation and doing whatever it was that he did. He looked a little more positive than the rest of us and was keeping as busy as he possibly could. He had handed out the food to us and sorted out the distribution of the drinking water. I think he wanted to remain active to keep his heart beating and his blood pumping. It was clear he was not going to give up any time soon.

Curled up on the bottom of the boat, to his side, was my friend Ralph Reid. He had not spoken a word all day other than to shout his dismay at the unceremonious dumping of Greg Cooper's body into the sea. He had not bothered to concern himself when the U-boat had surfaced and taken Wally away. It looked as if he did not care anymore. Although he was my friend, I felt there was nothing I could do for him. He was too far gone. I doubted he would listen to me should I make any attempt to converse with him and so I left him to his own thoughts.

I now felt no pain at all in my arm and shoulder. In fact I could not feel them at all. I tried to move them but the instruction from my brain to that area of my body was going ignored and it hung limply to my side. I used my right hand to pull the arm into my jerkin and sat with it tucked in, leaning into it and against Singer to retain as much heat as possible.

HELL AND HIGH WATER

After a while, dark clouds appeared above us and as the evening drew in the temperature took an even bigger drop.

'Come on, lads,' said Mitchell. 'We need to get the awning back on.'

At first nobody moved, all of us too weak, expecting someone else to do it.

'Come on,' he repeated. 'Don't give up, boys. Someone will be here for us soon.'

After a few more moments we began to stir. Jack and Harry reluctantly moved forward and Johnny Spencer stood up, taking hold of the canvas hood with Mitchell. Eventually Singer started to assist them. I offered whatever support I could, which was not much due to having only one serviceable arm. Ralph did not move. He did not even look at them as they tried to get the weather protection in place.

We could feel the wind beginning to pick up and the awning started to flap in our hands. It was becoming very difficult to get it in place whilst Johnny tried to fix it to the boat.

Suddenly a huge gust hit, forcing the awning on top of us. I tumbled to the floor, Singer falling on top of me.

'Jesus Christ!' yelled Johnny. 'We've got to get this on before the weather hits us. Why we took the bloody thing down in the first place is beyond me.'

Snow was starting to fall again. Slowly at first but, as the wind whipped up, it came down more heavily, mixed in with rain and sleet. It was now nearly impossible to get the awning rigged and we were becoming desperate. It was clear by the look in Lieutenant

Mitchell's eyes that he was regretting having had us remove it earlier in the day. I knew Johnny had been right. It had proved to be a stupid idea.

The sea was getting more and more choppy and standing up against the side of the lifeboat was becoming dangerous. Jack was gripping the canvas with all his strength as he tried to pull it against the side. Then another sudden gust yanked it from his grip and it flapped away out to sea. Harry and Mitchell, who had been holding the other end, could not hang on and it was also ripped from their hands.

We watched helplessly as the awning was blown away from the boat, rolling and crashing against the waves until it was eventually beyond our sight.

'For Christ's sake,' said Singer as he slumped back down into the boat. 'We've had it now.'

'Nonsense,' said Mitchell, himself sitting back down. 'It isn't over until it's over... Now hang onto those blankets and wrap as many around you as you can. If we all huddle ourselves into the middle of the boat then we can ride this out. Don't give up.'

This was the most desperate we had been. The snow now poured from the sky and the sea began to rise and fall taking our little boat up its watery mountains to then smash it down into its deepest valleys. I could see the waves rising forty, fifty feet over us and was scared out of my wits. Frightened beyond any nightmare I had ever had as a child. But then a child could never dream up a hell like this.

I clamped my eyes shut as the sea did its damnedest to drag us down. How we remained afloat without capsizing was nothing short of a miracle.

HELL AND HIGH WATER

We could feel the spray from the crashing waves hitting us and freezing on our clothing and any exposed skin. I was aware that our body cores would be dropping well below what was sustainable for much longer and knew that should the storm not abate soon, then we would not survive.

But the storm did not abate. It rolled and crashed around us throughout that long, hellish night. Smashing us like rag dolls against the sides, lockers and benches of the lifeboat, covering us with freezing water at every turn. The snow and sleet soaked us to the skin and as the night wore on I could feel myself slipping away.

Deep into the night I feared I was the only one left alive. I heard no noise from any of the others but then the roar of the sea may have drowned out any whimpering or words they may have spoken. In fact, at one point, I was not sure if I was actually dead myself.

According to many religions of the world and to the thirteenth Century Italian poet, Dante Alighieri, Hell is a hot fiery place in the bowels of the earth where the souls of the damned burn for eternity in pits of brimstone and sulphur. My own belief is somewhat the opposite. Hell, to me, can be found at the earth's surface, on the unforgiving oceans of the far north. Where storms such as this, and ice, U-boats and dive-bombers all combine to create a somewhat different version of the abode of the damned. This was my own personal vision of Hell and throughout that night I not only witnessed it, I lived it.

And in the darkness, as I lay there shivering in the lifeboat, my life slowly ebbing from me, I swear I saw

JOHN McKAY

Death himself coming to greet me, gliding over the surface, his ice cold scythe ready to strike.

Again the morning broke to a calm that was in sharp contrast to what we had just experienced. The sea was once more flat, but the temperature remained dangerously low. Although the sun had started to rise, nobody moved. If we had all made it through the night then God was clearly looking out for us.

Eventually I felt movement near to me and when I looked I saw Lieutenant Mitchell wearily pull away from our congealed mass of humanity and move towards the bow. I watched as he looked out to sea. I was amazed he still held out hope we would be picked up. After last night, I could not understand how he could remain so positive.

Slowly we all started to separate ourselves, shaking off the snow and brushing away the ice that covered us.

Mitchell turned to us. Then his eyes moved to the area in front of the front bench.

'Bloody hell,' was all he said.

I followed his gaze and then saw what he was looking at.

Ralph Reid had separated himself from our huddled group during the night and had lay down alone, away from the rest of us. He was covered in snow and ice and, when Mitchell bent down to brush it away from his face, it was clear he was dead. His eyes were wide open and had lost their colour. His skin was as blue as the sea around us. I could not understand why he was not wearing a balaclava or any face protection. I

HELL AND HIGH WATER

could only assume he had taken it off himself during the night. In the end, maybe he had wished for death. He must have been in a desperate state to have done it. His mind must have gone completely, not able to endure this hell another minute.

I did not know how to feel. Again, much like when Greg Cooper had died the previous day in much the same way I merely felt a kind of numbness. I felt no emotion. Maybe it was because we were still going through this trauma and death may yet be waiting to pay a visit to us all. Or maybe it was because I was as cold in my heart as the air that blew around me. I was not sure. This indifference to the death of my good friend scared me.

'Come on,' said Mitchell. 'We need to get him over the side.'

'Are you going to say a few words this time?' asked Harry. 'Do you think…?'

And then he turned his head to look out to sea, either forgetting what he was about to say or thinking better of it.

'Right,' said Mitchell, after a short pause. 'Come on, boys. Let's shift him.'

Johnny Spencer crawled over to where Ralph lay and, together with Lieutenant Mitchell, bent down to take hold of the corpse. After much grunting and groaning they both eventually stopped. Ralph's body had not moved an inch.

'Shit,' said Johnny. 'He's frozen stiff. He's stuck to the bottom.'

'Well you can't just leave him there like that,' said Jack.

'I think we may have to,' replied Mitchell. 'He can't be budged. He's frozen solid. If we try to break him free we could damage the boat.'

Reluctantly, Mitchell and Johnny sat back down.

And, as the lifeboat bobbed along aimlessly in the Arctic waters, we sat quietly, the frozen corpse of Ralph Reid staring grotesquely at us from the far end of the boat.

The day wore on much like the previous. We had now lost three of our party, two to death and one to the Germans. My thoughts wandered to my friend Wally and to what he may be experiencing. I hoped he had warmed up and been given something hot to eat. The thought of hot food filled my brain and I started to salivate. What I would have given for a hot cup of kye and a plate of tram smash!

We huddled together again, all six of us pressing tightly against each other. We could do nothing else but wait. Our conversation had seized up completely. Nobody spoke for hours. I could sense Lieutenant Mitchell had lost faith we would ever be found. We were all so utterly exhausted. We needed sleep but to sleep meant to die. However, at that moment, the thought of death did not seem too bad a proposition.

And then Petty Officer Singer spoke.

'So what do you think of life in the navy?' I was not sure if he was addressing anyone in particular. When nobody answered, I replied.

'It's a bit shit, really.'

He started to laugh. Despite everything he was laughing.

HELL AND HIGH WATER

'Aww come on, laddie,' he replied. 'What's there not to like? What other job could you do where you get to see the world like this?'

We remained silent for a while longer.

'It is all shit,' said Harry suddenly. 'You were right... it's shit... all of it.'

We remained silent. If Harry needed to get it off his chest then we were not going to interrupt him. None of us had the strength.

'All those people back home,' he went on. 'All those people... friends, family, everyone... What do you think they're doing right now? Are they in the pub having fun? Are they at work? Are they sitting around the fire completely oblivious to all this? Do you think they even know we're stuck out here in this godforsaken place? Do they know if we're alive or dead? Do they even care? Do you think that when you last saw them and said goodbye they thought it could be the very last time you would ever clap eyes on each other? You were right, George... it is shit. It's all shit.'

Without warning he stood up and stepped to the side. None of us moved, remaining in our positions huddled together on the bottom of the boat, unaware of what he was about to do.

With a final look back at the five of us he placed his right foot on the edge of the boat and, with one last effort, launched himself over the side and into the sea, leaving the boat rocking behind him as we all instinctively lurched forward to try to stop him.

'Harry!' shouted Jack. 'Harry, you fool!'

But it was too late. By the time we had steadied the boat and looked out to where he had jumped, he was nowhere to be seen. Only a few bubbles on the surface indicated the point where he had entered. There was nothing to be done. He was gone.

Jack fell back onto the floor and began to sob quietly. Harry had been his best friend and he had given up. In the end he had seen death as a better option to more of the hell we were enduring.

But I was determined not to let that happen to me. Even though I was at the lowest point in my life, I decided that despite how easy it would be, I would not let despair consume me in the same way it had Harry and Ralph. I would not let that happen.

I was determined to survive.

HELL AND HIGH WATER

Thirty-Three

Another long night was drawing in. It still amazed me how short the days were this far north, daylight lasting only a few hours. With the darkness came the drop in the already extreme temperature. The remaining five of us sat huddled together, still waiting for the ship we now believed would never come. All our strength had left us and it took a huge effort to even eat a hard tack biscuit. Our lips had swelled to twice their normal size and to swallow the pathetic food had become too painful. Our eyebrows and eyelashes had all fallen out and this made blinking very painful. I found it easier to just close my eyes but when I did this I got scared they would freeze shut and I would never be able to open them again. And we still feared sleeping and the death that would surely accompany it.

I felt a light upon my face and when I opened my eyes I saw the most wondrous thing I had ever seen in my life. Playing out above us, the aurora borealis jumped and danced to a tune only it could hear, its green lights shimmering across the night sky in an ethereal ballet. It showed me not all in the world was bad, that nature was both ugly and beautiful in equal measure. I was reminded of hearing the whales sing and how I had been humbled by the beauty of it all. All it needed was for them to make an appearance and I would be convinced I had died and this was my heaven.

JOHN McKAY

I could not take my eyes from the sky. The greens then mixed with other colours; purples, blues and reds, criss-crossing the sky in a beautiful extravaganza. It was as though the angels were putting on a light show just for us. A bit of relief from the suffering. Something to take our minds away from what had happened and what was yet to come. They seemed to be telling us to forget all that for a short while. To put it to the back of our minds and to just enjoy this private and exclusive display.

The light show went on for a long while until it finally subsided, fading to nothing, leaving the sky as black as coal, its darkness broken only by the speckled, distant stars. Stars that spread for millions of miles all around the planet. I started to think about what was beyond our own earth. Were there other planets out there just like ours? Were there other civilisations that thought fighting each other and destroying the world in which they lived was a good idea?

I felt Singer move to my side. He was getting restless. I worried he would go the same way as the others. He was struggling to keep himself alive and had thrown his rations into the sea in frustration when he had struggled to swallow anything earlier. He was very weak.

'Hey, P.O.,' I said encouragingly. 'Won't be long now. Take my word for it.'

'Won't be long until what?' he replied. 'Until we're all dead, eh, laddie?'

'No,' I said. 'Until a ship comes our way.'

'Aye, whatever you say.' He was not convinced. How could he be?

HELL AND HIGH WATER

'You know what?' he said after a while. 'I've been thinking. How would you like to go, George? How would you like to die? If you had the choice.'

'In a warm bed when I'm a hundred years old,' I replied. 'Certainly not out here.'

'I'm not sure what the best way is,' he said thoughtfully. 'I'm not sure how I want it to happen. You see I always thought there's only two ways to go; quickly or slowly. And neither of them are good. But I'm not so sure anymore. I think there's another way.'

Glad that he was speaking, even if his talk was as depressing as this. I encouraged him to continue.

'How do you mean?' I asked.

'Well look at young Harry earlier,' he went on. 'He's been freezing to death over the last couple of days. He was going slowly, wasn't he? Death was not coming quickly enough for him. Then suddenly… Boom!… and he's gone. We were expecting him to go eventually. But it all happened so quickly in the end.'

'Who knows what was going on in his mind,' I replied.

'Oh, come on. I think we can all guess, can't we?

I could not argue with him. I had been having the same thoughts as Harry before he decided to jump into the ocean. I had even considered doing the same thing myself on more than one occasion. It would at least put an end to it all.

'You see, laddie, I've often thought about how I'd prefer to pass. I've seen death in many forms and none of them have been easy. It's never easy. There's no easy way for any of us who are left behind.

JOHN McKAY

Whether they linger for a while and you can say your goodbyes or whether they just drop dead all of a sudden. Neither way is a good way. If they linger, you can at least say farewell to them, tell them all the things you wanted to. But then you have to watch them deteriorate before your eyes until they're not the person they once were... The person you wish to remember.

'If they go quickly you don't have that chance to say the things you wanted to say. You don't get to say sorry for the times you hurt them or disappointed them... But then you don't have to watch them suffer...No... No way is a good way.'

I gave some thought to what he said and, as the skies darkened above us, I succumbed to a deep and dreamless sleep.

I could not tell what was happening. I was being shaken awake forcefully. I did not know where I was or what was going on. The only thing I knew was I was cold beyond endurance. I also knew that I was not dead.

'No, sir,' I heard somebody say. A voice I recognised but could not remember to whom it belonged. 'He's still alive. Come on, laddie... Wake up, wake up!'

I put my frozen right hand to my face and rubbed my eyes. The pain was unbearable and when I opened them, I could not see properly, everything a blur.

I could sense activity around me, almost frantic. Voices shouting. The boat rocking.

'Come on, come on,' I heard someone say. Then, with a sense of despondency, I remembered where I was and who I was with.

'Bloody hell, come on!' It was Lieutenant Mitchell and he was fumbling with something. It was still dark but the sun was starting to show the tip of its head on the distant horizon, giving a little light to see by.

'Hurry up, hurry up,' pleaded Johnny Spencer.

'I am hurrying,' snapped Mitchell. 'Stop rushing me.'

Finally my full vision returned and I could see what was happening.

Outlined against the southern horizon was a ship, its lights shining brightly in the early morning dawn. Beyond it I could just make out another, sailing close behind. They were not heading towards us, more parallel. There was no way they could see us.

'Okay, okay, I'm ready,' said Mitchell.

I watched calmly as he fired the flare into the sky, it bursting high in the altitude, lighting up the sea around us. No sooner had he fired it than he was loading another. He waited for a minute and then fired again.

'We only have one round left, sir,' said Johnny.

'Okay,' acknowledged Mitchell. 'This is our only chance. They have to see us.'

'Are they ours?' asked Jack.

'I can't tell,' replied Mitchell. 'But, to be honest, I don't really care.'

We could now only wait to see if they had spotted us. There was no guarantee that even if they had they would come to our aid, but you had to expect that they would. It was the correct thing to do. It was the humane thing to do.

The miracle we had been waiting for then happened.

We could see the ship at the front changing course, turning to head in our direction.

Could this be it? Could this really be happening?

I closed my eyes again and held them tight. Was I dreaming? Was this all some kind of hallucination brought on by my weakened mind? Was it an illusion sent by an evil force to toy with our already disturbed and weakened brains? When I opened them again would the ship not be there and this had all been a dream? Was this another evil trick my frozen mind was playing on me? A mirage teasing my sanity?

I finally opened my eyes and understood this was all very real. The ship was closer now, it's outline getting larger against the horizon. Mitchell fumbled again and fired the last flare to guide the ship towards us, as Johnny Spencer and Jack Holland stood up, waving their arms frantically, adrenalin now giving them the strength they had lacked for hours.

I could not believe it. This was real. We were going to be rescued.

The ship got ever closer and blew its horn, an acknowledgement we had been seen. As it got nearer we could see activity on the deck.

'Is it one of ours?' asked Jack.

'I don't think so,' replied Mitchell. 'I think it's Russian. A destroyer, by the looks of it.'

A few minutes later the ship was virtually upon us. Mitchell ordered two of our party to grab the oars and row towards it as rope ladders were lowered over its starboard side. Eventually, after a few minutes of effort, the lifeboat was up against it, near the stern where the deck was lower.

It quickly became apparent that transferring ourselves to the destroyer would be tough going. We were all totally drained and lacked any kind of strength. What made matters doubly worse for me, was that my left arm was of no use at all.

The lifeboat rose and fell on the swell, banging against the hull. We could not tie it to the side as the movement would certainly capsize us. It would be a major irony to get this close to safety only for it all to be pulled away from us at the very last moment.

'Okay,' said Mitchell, once again taking command of the situation. 'Let's move, fellas.'

Jack Holland was the first to go forward. He was desperate to get off the lifeboat. As it lifted in the water he lunged for the rope ladder, his eagerness to get to safety spurring him on. He clung on to the rung with a fierce determination, hanging for a few moments as the lifeboat drifted away from him, leaving him suspended at the side of the ship. At first I thought he was not strong enough and would fall from the ladder but eventually he summoned up the energy and slowly made it up the ladder where Soviet sailors grabbed hold of him and pulled him on board.

'Okay,' said Mitchell, looking at me. 'Martin, it's your turn next… Do you think you can manage it?'

I was not sure. The thought of hurling myself across the gap between the lifeboat and the Russian destroyer frightened the living daylights out of me.

'I don't know,' I replied, honestly. 'I'm not sure I have the strength. But I've got to try.'

I stood up and made my way to Mitchell's side.

'Be careful,' he said. 'Go when you feel it's right.'

He stood behind me, holding onto my waist, but the thickness of his gloves and the clothes I was wearing, together with the life vest, made it impossible for him to grip me strongly.

The boat bobbed up and down a few more times. I saw an opportunity. With all the strength I could muster I launched myself forward. I grabbed at the rope ladder with my good right hand, willing my left to react.

But it did not.

For that brief moment of realisation that I could not hang on and was going to fall, something odd happened. Memories of my childhood, my family and my friends came jumping into my head all at once. I could see clearly the faces of those I loved, those who had meant anything to me at all. My mother, my father, all of my siblings and my dear friend Wally. Even Glenda Bradshaw and her cousin Iris Shepherd jumped into my head.

And then I felt a new, ineffable horror as I hit the surface and quickly sank beneath it. I closed my eyes as tightly as I could lest they froze in the sockets, which I was sure they would. For some incomprehensible reason, I immediately felt a kind of reluctant resignation that I was going to die and decided not to fight it. I let myself sink. I am not sure if I had given myself up to die but knew to resist it would be pointless. Futile even. I decided to let God decide if I should live.

I felt myself going deeper, but was not sure if this was real. All I knew was that my body was already becoming numb. I could sense my soul begin to leave my body and allowed Death to collect it, for I could not fight him any longer. I did not have the strength.

Suddenly I felt myself rise up. It was as though I was being dragged upwards towards the surface and the sounds that were so distant and muted only moments before now became clearer to my frozen ears.

I hit the surface and found I was floating. I realised I had minutes, if not seconds to live, before my body core froze and I would drift into a sleep from which I would never awake. But to sleep would be to find a peace. A peace that at that moment I found completely appealing.

I heard voices around me and my head struck roughly against something solid. I was not sure what it was but before I could think about it I was being dragged by many hands and felt myself being lifted, as though weightless, hauled unceremoniously back into the lifeboat. I could hear voices around me, familiar yet at the same time strange, as they asked each other if I was gone.

I could feel frantic hands mauling over my body and then something being tied tightly around my chest. After a few moments I felt a strange lifting sensation. I could feel myself swinging and banging against something hard, and then more hands over me, picking me up and carrying me.

JOHN McKAY

I heard a steel door open and close and for a brief second, before consciousness totally left me, I felt a warmth I had not experienced in over three days. The sleep I had been fighting finally won its battle, and everything went black.

HELL AND HIGH WATER

Thirty-Four

Five months later - Liverpool

The ship that had rescued us from the frozen hell of the Barents Sea was the Soviet Gnevny class destroyer, *Gremyashchy*. They had taken us back to Murmansk and transferred us to another homeward bound British ship, the aptly named HMS *Liverpool*. It left Murmansk in the second week in April to escort a returning convoy. After another eventful journey, which saw the loss of four more merchant ships, we arrived in Iceland eleven days later.

Along with the other survivors from the lifeboat I was kept in the sickbay throughout the journey. All of us suffered from extreme hypothermia and other injuries received during the sinking of the *Virtuous,* and the almost three days lost at sea that followed. I was pleased to hear the three other lifeboats I had seen escape during the sinking had all been picked up the same night. In total there had been seventy five survivors. The remaining crew had all perished, including the captain, Lieutenant Commander Harrison. I was extremely sad to hear this news and fell into a heavy depression for a short while after. I also felt guilty I had somehow managed to survive everything, and others, more important and better people than I, had lost their lives.

I was pleased to see that Dougie Sears, who had remained in Murmansk to tend to the wounded from the inbound trip, was also on the *Liverpool*. I spoke to him daily about what had happened. Dougie was an inspiration to me. With his help, and that of my saviours, Lieutenant Mitchell, Petty Officer Singer, and Johnny Spencer, who had hauled me from the sea when I had fallen overboard, getting me safely aboard the *Gremyashchy*, I was soon thinking more positively about my survival.

We stayed in Iceland only a few days before heading to the naval base at Scapa Flow. The trip from Iceland to Scotland was a lot less tumultuous than the outbound journey, the voyage being relatively smooth and attack free. Before long we were back in Britain.

On my return, I was sent to a convalescent centre outside Manchester to recuperate from my ordeal. After a lengthy stay I made a full recovery. I was concerned I would lose my arm, it being numb for so long, but the doctors and medical staff who looked after me were nothing short of miracle workers. Although very stiff at times, it did heal to a point where I could sometimes forget I had ever been shot.

The Admiralty held an inquest into the sinking of the *Virtuous*. I was asked to provide a statement on what had happened to me. I was not able to supply any significant information as to what had caused the ship to sink and so was not required to make the journey to London to give evidence in person.

I discovered the ship had been destroyed by a concerted attack by German Heinkel He-111 bombers which had scored three direct hits. The first had been

HELL AND HIGH WATER

very close to the bridge killing almost everyone inside, including the captain. Lieutenant Mitchell and Johnny Spencer had been lucky to be on the opposite side to where the bomb exploded and were shielded somewhat by the others. Upon seeing the devastation, it was clear to Mitchell the ship was lost. With two more hits, one blasting a huge hole in the starboard side, and the fires that quickly spread, Mitchell had given the order to abandon ship to anyone who could hear him above the noise and the mayhem that had ensued.

The rest I knew, and the vision of the ship going down in the same manner as the *Dreyfus* would come to haunt my dreams for years to come.

After being declared fit for light duties I was told to report to Portsmouth the next week to await a new posting. In the meantime I was given leave and was able to spend some time with my family. After what I had been through, this was something I would make sure I made the most of.

I arrived home on a cold and damp day in mid September. When my mother saw me she broke down in tears. I learned there had been some initial confusion following the sinking. They were told the *Virtuous* had gone down with all hands; that there had been no survivors. She had broken her heart and mourned me like any mother would who found out their boy had been lost at sea. When I walked through the front door she hugged me and clung to me to the point of pain. My father had to unhook her arms from me. He also had tears in his eyes when he greeted me.

JOHN McKAY

I did not tell them too much about what happened. I could not put either them or myself through it. It was clear my mother did not want me to go back to the navy. She suggested I desert and hide somewhere until the war was over. Although I was very much tempted I knew this was a very bad idea and would only lead to more hardship and pain.

I decided to avoid Glenda. I did not want to see her after what had happened on my last trip home and was sure she would not want to see me. That chapter of my life was closed, in the same way as my time on the *Virtuous* was. As far as I was concerned, I could not go back to either. Those two parts of my life had been despatched to places where they could never be recovered.

The funny thing was I had not thought about Glenda for some time. It was only upon returning to Liverpool that she had again come into my head. It was like when you see familiar places or hear certain tunes and it reminds you of someone or something that once happened, pulling memories to the surface of your mind you had hidden. The familiarity of the Liverpool streets had done that to me. I thought about her and contemplated how I felt and realised the very fact it had taken my return home to think of her again meant I was now indifferent to the girl. I did not really care about her at all. She meant nothing to me.

On the morning of the second day, which happened to be a Saturday, there was a knock at the front door. I was sitting in the living room with my mother, reading a newspaper. My father was at work and my younger siblings were outside playing in the street with their friends. Jimmy was somewhere in the city with his new girlfriend, a sweet young thing called Grace, whom I had met the previous evening.

My mother went to answer the door.

'George, it's for you,' she shouted back to me.

I did not want to see anyone. I was not in the mood for my old friends or anyone else for that matter. I looked down the hallway and could see it was Iris Shepherd. I put down the newspaper and walked over.

'If you go out, make sure you're back for your tea,' said mother as she passed me. 'I'm doing a stew tonight and I want us all to sit down together.'

'Hello, Iris,' I said, when I reached the door. 'What drags you over here?'

'Hello, George,' she replied. 'I'm glad to see you're okay. I heard you've had something of an ordeal.'

'You could say that. Is there anything you wanted?'

She looked a little taken aback by my abruptness. The truth was I did not want to see anyone who reminded me of Glenda. I felt I had grown out of them all and was not bothered about renewing old friendships.

'I was wondering if you would like to go for a walk. But if you're not feeling up to it…'

I thought for a moment and then decided that a bit of fresh air might do me good.

'I'll just get my coat,' I said, and turned back into the hallway.

A few minutes later we found ourselves heading towards the city centre.

'So how have you been, George?' she asked eventually. 'We were all so worried when we heard your ship had been sunk. It was an awful time. Especially for your mam. She was distraught.'

'I've been better,' I replied. 'If it's all right with you, Iris, I don't want to talk about it really. It's something I'm dealing with in my own way.'

'Yes, of course. Of course… Do you want to go and get a cup of tea or something?'

'Not particularly,' I responded. 'What is it you want, Iris? I'm sorry for not being good company and appearing a bit rude, but what is it that you really want from me?'

'I thought it was time you knew certain things…' she replied.

'Listen,' I interrupted, stopping in my tracks. She stopped too and looked at me sadly. 'If this is about Glenda then I'm not really interested. I don't know if she told you about what happened before I left for Russia but it's not something I want to dwell on.'

'Oh, she told me, all right,' replied Iris. 'I know exactly what happened. And with that bloody fool, Billy Jones too. I've no idea what she was thinking.'

'Well it was up to them, I suppose,' I replied nonchalantly. 'If they want each other then that's fine.'

'A lot's happened while you've been away,' she went on. 'A lot. Billy was sacked, you know. That Johnson fella fired him. He kept turning up late for work all the time and then one evening Johnson had to go back to work because he'd left some paperwork in his office. He caught Billy in the building with a girl. And it wasn't Glenda, before you ask. Apparently he sacked him on the spot. I hear he's working on the docks now.'

HELL AND HIGH WATER

'I really couldn't care less,' I replied. It was the truth. Billy Jones was a part of my past and I did not care at all what the man was up to.

We continued to walk and remained silent for a while.

'Aren't you interested in Glenda?' said Iris after a while.

'Not really.'

'I think you should know something,' she said. 'I know you probably hate her guts but I think you should know about her.'

It was clear this was the reason she had asked to walk out with me. I decided to humour her.

'Okay, Iris. If you want to tell me about Glenda and what she's up to then go ahead. I can't promise I'll be the slightest bit interested though.'

'She was a disturbed girl,' she said, which I thought a bit of a strong an adjective to use. 'I know you always wondered why she came to Liverpool from Wales, didn't you?'

I did not reply, preferring to let her tell her story. To get it over with.

She took a breath.

'Well… The reason she left Wales was because of her baby.'

'Her what?'

'Her baby, George. They made her give it up…'

I was confused. 'You're not making much sense, Iris.'

'She had a baby in Flint,' she continued. She seemed to be getting angry. 'She met a boy when she was seventeen and he used her for what he could get. A bit like yourself and that idiot Billy Jones.'

'Oh, hang on a minute,' I protested. 'I hope you're not suggesting that I took advantage of her. What happened between… well a lot of it was down to her.'

'Did you not think it strange?' asked Iris, ignoring my attempts to justify myself. 'Did you not think it odd she gave herself to you so willingly?'

'I thought…'

'What? That you were irresistible to her? That you're irresistible to us girls? Trust me, George Martin, don't flatter yourself. You're nothing special.'

I did not know what to say, so said nothing.

'It's clear now she was craving someone to love her. That boy in Wales was awful to her and denied the baby was his. His mother and father backed him and her own parents disowned her. They made her have the baby in secret and then give it up for adoption. They couldn't have the scandal of it upon them.'

'I… I didn't know,' I stammered.

'Of course you didn't know. How would you? It's not something she was likely to brag about, was it? And then they kicked her out. Threw out their own daughter. Can you believe that? She had nowhere to go until my mam took pity on her and said she could come and stay with us. Give her a new start. And, of course, she jumped at the chance.'

'I'm at a loss,' I replied. 'I knew there was something about her that wasn't quite right.'

'I know. She used to tell me she was worried about how you'd react if you knew.'

'But Billy… What was all that about?'

HELL AND HIGH WATER

'Oh, I don't know,' she replied thoughtfully. 'I don't know what she was thinking. When you made her hide from your family when you were leaving for the navy. That upset her a lot. A lot, George. When she never heard from you when you went to sea, she thought you were just like that boy in Wales. You'd had your fun and now you were moving on to something new. And I don't think she could cope without having anyone in her life to love her. I think she thought giving herself so freely would make men desire and love her. She was very mixed up.'

'You keep saying "was". What do you mean?'

'In the end she felt nobody really cared about her, George,' replied Iris. She was crying now. 'Her own parents hated her. My mam and dad got fed up with her and Billy Jones was using her for what he could get. And when you told her you'd given up on her, well, she went downhill from there. I think she even stopped caring about herself.'

'So where is she now?' I asked. I was starting to worry. I was not liking what Iris was telling me.

'She's gone, George. One day we got home and she'd packed her things and left. We've no idea where she is. It was a few days after we heard your ship had gone down and you were probably dead. She became so quiet and depressed. She hardly spoke to anyone. And then one day she was gone. We've no idea if she's alive or dead.'

'Maybe she's gone back to Flint,' I said.

'No. We checked with her mam and dad, but they told us they hadn't seen her. They didn't care either.

Me and our Richard went to Wales to see them. They wouldn't even let us in the house.'

Eventually we turned around to walk back home. We did not speak much more, each of us mulling over the conversation that had just taken place. I supposed it all fell into place. The strange way Glenda had been with me. When I thought about it I felt I should have worked all this out way before things had got out of hand.

Was I to blame for any of it? Of course I was. I never truly got to know her. She had never trusted me enough with her truth and that upset me a little. Because Iris was right. In the end I had been using her and I knew I would be ashamed of that for as long as I lived.

When we reached the end of Egerton Street, Iris said, 'Please don't let this get to you, George. I'm sure you have enough on your mind as it is. You weren't to know, not really. There's no denying you could have handled it a lot better, but then so could most of us. None of us are blameless.'

'That's as maybe,' I replied. 'But I'm sure it won't stop me feeling terrible about the whole thing.'

She smiled a small sad smile.

Then I saw something in her eyes. I could not be certain but it looked like an expression of sympathy towards me. Or was it compassion? Although she had admonished me quite severely, and not without good reason, she had clearly taken into account the trauma I had been through and probably held back on other things she wanted to say. She had not been too scathing although I had clearly deserved it. I realised at that moment that Iris Shepherd was quite a lovely person. But then she always had been, ever since we were children. This empathy had always been within her.

She leaned up towards me and kissed me lightly on the cheek.

'Take care of yourself, George,' she said softly. 'Whatever happens, make sure you come home safely. I don't think any of us could go through losing you again.'

With that she turned and walked away.

As I watched her move along the street back to her house, I had a sudden feeling of warmth towards the girl that I had never experienced before.

I stood and watched her until she closed the door behind her, leaving me standing outside.

Alone again.

Thirty-Five

Polyarny, Russia - 22nd May 1945

I stood on the deck of HMS *Obdurate*, a cigarette in my hand, and looked out into the bay. The weather had eased slightly allowing me to take off my glove whilst I lit it, but it was still bitterly cold. I needed to get away from the claustrophobia of being stuck inside with nothing to do other than listen to the whinges of my shipmates who all wanted to be at home. Having escorted a small convoy here, codenamed *JW67*, we were now waiting for them to unload their cargoes before we escorted them on the return leg back to Iceland.

The trip over had been a sharp contrast to the last time I had been on these waters, nearly three years ago. There had been no air attacks, the German Norwegian bases long since evacuated, but the threat from U-boat attack had still been ever present, despite the fact the war in Europe had officially been over for two weeks. The weather had been remarkably kind to us. Only one quite violent storm, but nothing as compared to the voyage I made on HMS *Virtuous*, which seemed so long ago now.

However, the cold had been the same. Temperatures well below freezing making it impossible to stay out on deck for too long. Having to go out on hawser lines and smash ice from the bulkheads, decks and guns had exhausted us all. When my younger shipmates

HELL AND HIGH WATER

found out I had been stranded in this weather, and worse, for almost three days a few years ago, they thought I had made the story up. How could anyone survive it, they had asked. Many did not, was my reply. I still could not talk about it to any great length. I felt uncomfortable every time somebody mentioned it.

The war was won. We had received word the Red Army was now inside Berlin and Hitler was dead. It was only a matter of time before we would be stood down, our duty done. It could not come quickly enough for us. This was to be the final Arctic convoy.

The surrender of Germany meant for the navy, not an easing up, but greatly increased activity. Ports needed to be opened; mines needed to be cleared; supplies needed to be brought to military personnel still in theatre and to displaced civilians who had suffered many hardships over the past six years. The Norwegian merchant ships which had travelled with us carried supplies for the newly liberated areas of polar Norway.

There was also the job of rounding up German units, chief among them the submarine arm of the Kriegsmarine.

Because of the unpredictability of the crews of the U-boats still at sea, among whom numerous Nazis could be counted, it was decided to continue the convoy system even though the war was over. The technical advances made in the design of the later marques of the U-boats had constituted a very real threat up to the last day of the war. Although U-boat construction sites had been bombed regularly they had still managed to manufacture a significant amount of submarines, many of which were still at sea. Our captain had warned that their crews would now have only one object in mind: the disruption of the final Allied effort, of which the most accessible targets were those off the Norwegian and polar coasts, namely us.

Admiral Dönitz had made a broadcast a few days before the war ended, ordering all Kriegsmarine ships and U-boats to cease hostilities and return to their bases. We could never be sure this message had got through to all ships or if it would be ignored by those still believing in the Nazi ideology and wanting to cause as much mayhem as possible. We had been on constant alert for the whole trip. Thankfully we had not come under any attack.

It had been in this atmosphere of instability and uncertainty that our convoy of twenty-six merchantman under the flags of Norway, Great Britain and the U.S.A. had set sail. They were escorted by vessels of the Fourth Escort Group including, my own ship, HMS *Obdurate*. We were also joined by ships of the Canadian Ninth Escort Group.

I was unsure of what I would do when it was all over, when peace returned to this damaged and ravaged world. I considered staying in the Royal Navy and making a career of it, but in the end I decided I would return home and do something different. I had made up my mind that I had had enough of the sea.

I blew out smoke and shivered, stamping my feet against the frozen deck. The sun was shining down but it had no effect on the low temperature. I looked

HELL AND HIGH WATER

to the sky, remembering the last time I had been in this region. I thought of the hospital in Murmansk, the city that was just around the headland out of my vision. I thought about Nika and wondered if she was still there, sitting at her table where I had left her. I pondered if she ever thought of me and the brief time we had spent together. Was she even still alive?

The last time I had been here the air had been full of German dive-bombers and Russian anti-aircraft shells. The current quiet and calmness contrasted sharply with that previous experience. Although I knew it was unlikely we would come under air attack again, I was still nervous whenever I looked to the skies.

I thought back over the last three years and to what had happened to me since I had been rescued from the icy waters of the Barents Sea. Due to my damaged arm I was not considered fit for active service and so spent eighteen months on shore duties. Eventually I was assigned to a motor torpedo boat, patrolling the English Channel and had taken part in the Normandy landings in June, 1944. After the invasion I stayed in the Channel, escorting supply and troopships to and from France.

Four months ago I was posted to the *Obdurate* and was disappointed to hear we would be sailing for Russia. It brought back too many bad memories for me. It was a place I hoped never to visit again. But when the navy tells you that you are going to Russia, then it's to Russia you go.

During this time I had been promoted to able seaman and then again to leading hand. I had surprised myself how well I had got on. Promotion was not something I had sought but I was happy to take the extra pay and the little bit of respect being a killick had brought me.

Drawing the last of my cigarette, I threw the butt over the gunwale and watched it drop into the water. A gull swooped down, maybe thinking it was food I was discarding, but on realising its mistake it corrected its flight and glided up and away. I stayed on deck for a few more moments before turning away and heading back to the door that led to the inner decks, glad of the warmth being inside would bring.

The following day we set sail for home, joining the merchant ships as they exited the Kola Inlet. I heard later that a lot of the cargo they had unloaded lay untouched on the dockside and some of the lads who had gone ashore had not received a very warm welcome from our Soviet allies. I had experienced this lack of hospitality at the same dockside three years ago and was not surprised. However, I had also experienced the warmth of some individual Russians and so could not discriminate against them all.

As we left the sanctuary of the inlet and sailed along the top coast of Norway we were told to remain vigilant. The guns were manned in shifts for twenty-four hours a day and spotters assisted those in the E.W.O. room manning the ASDIC screens. There was a palpable nervousness felt throughout the ship as we made the slow journey back to the Clyde.

On the fourth day, whilst I was on lookout duties on the starboard deck, I felt the ship slow. I watched as

HELL AND HIGH WATER

the destroyer's QF four inch guns turned in unison and pointed out to sea. I could see other escort ships ahead and behind us doing the same.

A few hundred yards away, I watched as the conning tower of a German U-boat rose from the icy depths. For a few moments I was transfixed, expecting at any time a torpedo to come hurtling towards us.

But it did not happen. Instead, to the left and right of the submarine, more conning towers appeared, until there were five U-boats all in line.

All the guns of the ship that were able had trained their sights upon them. I held my breath, expecting them to open up at any moment. However, the U-boats offered no threat and turned to sail alongside us, this being their surrender.

But we still could not trust them. After all, they were Nazis, and rumours and stories were filtering through about death camps in Poland and Germany, where they had been systematically murdering Jews. We found this hard to believe but as we became more and more aware of stories of this nature, they became hard to ignore. Therefore, as we watched them alongside us, I for one would not have hesitated to fire upon them should they give me cause to, war over or not.

I looked at the conning towers and tried to read the numbers on their sides but could not make them out. I was looking for the *U-403*, the submarine that had taken my good friend, Walter Honeyman, prisoner. I wondered what had become of him. Had he survived? The dreadful state he was in when he went into the submarine had not given me much hope he would make it, but I truly hoped he had. He was a good lad, someone who had had a hard life and had still smiled through it all. He kept me sane and alive during that voyage. I would be eternally grateful to him for keeping my spirits high when I was at the lowest point in my life. If anyone deserved some happiness it was surely him.

The designated mustering point for U-boats operating in the Western North Atlantic, North and Barents Seas was Loch Eriboll on the Scottish mainland, south of the Orkneys. A special reception of escorts drawn from the Western Approaches awaited them there. And so, as our convoy set course for the Clyde, the U-boats eventually broke off from us and headed in that direction.

On the 30th May 1945, with all our navigation lights burning, the convoy entered the Clyde and finally my war was over.

The church of St Luke's stands on the corner of Berry Street and Leece Street, just outside the city centre of Liverpool, not far from the Anglican Cathedral. The church was bombed during the Blitz in May, 1941, an incendiary causing a large fire, leaving only a roofless ruin. The building stands as a reminder to the city of the dark days it lived through during that time.

It was August 1945 and I had recently been demobbed. Mister Johnson had been kind enough to keep his word and had a job waiting for me when I arrived home. I had taken him up on his generous offer and was trying to settle into being a civilian once again. It was not proving as difficult as I thought it would be and I was enjoying a time of peace without the constant fear of someone trying to kill me.

I stood before the bomb damaged church, the sun beating down upon me. I did not know if I liked it. A building so badly damaged they had not bothered to try to repair it. I was not sure if the whole thing should just be brought down.

I took the cap from my head and wiped the sweat from my brow before replacing it. Iris Shepherd stood to my side.

'So what do you think?' she asked.

'About the church? I'm not sure really,' I replied. 'Maybe they should just demolish it and rebuild it again. Or maybe put a remembrance garden in its place. I'm not really sure, to be honest.'

'Oh, I think they should leave it as it is,' she replied. 'A reminder for future generations.'

'Maybe,' I replied. 'But it does look a bloody mess, don't you think?'

'Come on,' she said. 'We've a lot to do yet. A lot to organise.'

'Are you sure about this?' I asked. 'Are you totally certain? You know... after all that's happened.'

'Of course, I'm sure,' she replied.

She took hold of my hand and we walked away, back towards the city centre where we had arranged to meet my brother, Jimmy, and his girlfriend Grace. He was due to finish work in half an hour. We were meeting them for a few drinks and a bite to eat as we made arrangements for our wedding which was planned for the following Saturday.

JOHN McKAY

As we walked along I looked at Iris. She had a resemblance to her cousin. Not quite as beautiful, but certainly very pretty. It was odd to think I was marrying little Iris Shepherd, the young Catholic girl who used to sit on the stone step in front of her house as I played football on the cobblestones with her older brother.

Thinking about Glenda I felt a tinge of sadness. We had discovered that after she had vanished from Liverpool she had joined the WRAF and been stationed at an airfield just outside London. She had been killed in a V2 rocket attack in March, the missile landing on a hotel one evening where she had been having dinner with a young pilot.

When I found out I wept like a baby.

As we sauntered along Renshaw Street in the direction of Lime Street Station, I felt Iris squeeze my hand slightly. She looked into my eyes and smiled at me. She knew I had demons that would probably stay with me forever, but she was prepared to take me despite them. I loved her for that. It was one of the many reasons why I loved her.

A gull swooped down in front of me causing me to stop sharply. It had spotted a piece of bread, part of an unwanted sandwich someone had carelessly discarded to the side of the pavement. It took hold of a piece of crust in its beak and tore it from the rest of the sandwich. And then it seemed to stop for a brief moment, as if to observe me, its eyes fixed upon mine. It was as though the bird recognised me but could not quite place from where or when.

HELL AND HIGH WATER

And then it moved its head slightly, as if shaking away the memory, and took off into the air, looking for somewhere safe to consume its snack.

THE END

Author's Note

The historians among you will have noticed a slight 'chronological error' in the novel.

For literary reasons, I have taken the liberty of adjusting the timeline of the introduction of the Hedgehog mortar into active service.

Prototypes of the weapon were tested in 1941 but it did not come into operational use in the Royal Navy until 1942. I hope this does not detract too much from your enjoyment of the story

In total there were seventy-eight Arctic convoys during World War Two. The first, Operation Dervish, sailed only a few weeks after Germany invaded Russia, the last departing just after the war had ended. The Arctic Convoys provided approximately twenty percent of all hardware used on the Russian Front and made a significant contribution to the Victory in Europe.

This book is a homage to all who sailed on them.

HELL AND HIGH WATER

Acknowledgements

My first thank you is to my friend and former high school English teacher, Joyce Holden, for introducing me to the story of the Arctic Convoys and giving me the idea to write this book. Along with her husband, John, she has always been supportive of my writing endeavours and took a look at the early manuscript. Your support and encouragement have been invaluable.

The second thank you is shared between two men equally, veterans of the Arctic Convoys, Bill Halliwell and Jim Fairhurst, both who have since sadly "crossed the bar". Immensely humble, like many veterans of the Second World War, their stories and source material contributed immensely to the writing of this book. Bill was a telegraphist on the frigate HMS *Bazely* and sailed on the final Arctic Convoy in May, 1945. Jim sailed on the destroyer, HMS *Tartar*, which endured many trips to Russia, including the horrendous journey of PQ13, and the most heavily attacked of them all, PQ18.

A huge debt of gratitude goes to Oliver Webb-Carter of the on-line history magazine, Aspects of History, which held the unpublished historical novel competition for which this book won. Many thanks to him and all the panel for rating the book so highly.

A massive thank you also to Richard Foreman and all at Sharpe Books for their support and advice. It's great to be on board.

JOHN McKAY

I would also like to give a huge thank you to my family for all their support, chiefly my wife, Dawn, and my daughters, Jessica and Sophie. I love you all dearly.

Finally I would like to thank the author and historian Damien Lewis, for all his advice, encouragement and more importantly, friendship. To have this support from such a brilliant writer at the top of his game is immensely humbling. Thank you, my friend, I will be eternally grateful.

Some of the books that have assisted me with the writing of the novel include:

Forgotten Sacrifice, The Arctic Convoys of World War II by Michael G. Walling

Voices from the Arctic Convoys by Peter C. Brown

The Road to Russia: Arctic Convoys 1942-1945 by Bernard Edwards

Ordeal Below Zero, The Heroic Story of the Arctic Convoys in World War II by Georges Blond

The Kola Run - Ian Campbell & Donald MacIntyre

Also worth a look is the website of the Russian Arctic Convoy Museum based at Loch Ewe, Achnasheen. The museum itself is also worth a visit for anyone interested in the convoys. Website: https://racmp.co.uk/

Equally, the Western Approaches Museum in Liverpool is also well worth a visit. This is the location from where the Atlantic Convoys, and the early stages of the Arctic Convoys, were co-ordinated. In February 2022 a permanent exhibition to the Arctic Convoys was completed in the museum and I was both honoured and privileged to have played a minor part

HELL AND HIGH WATER

in its production. Website: https://liverpool-warmuseum.co.uk/

Printed in Great Britain
by Amazon